"You ___ ___,
Lady Elizabeth,"
Jordan Sneered.

"Ignoring for just the moment your complete inability to even attempt such a trip, what on earth makes you believe you could find the lost city of the Mande, much less the idol itself?"

With just the merest hint of smugness, the proper young Englishwoman played what she considered to be her trump card. "Because I have a map."

Her self-assurance was severely dented when he threw back his head and roared with laughter.

Odious man! *She wanted nothing more to do with him. But fate and her wayward heart were to decree otherwise.*

Books by Maura Seger

Defiant Love
Empire of the Heart
Flame on the Sun
Forbidden Love
Rebellious Love

Published by POCKET BOOKS

Most Pocket Books are available at special quantity discounts for bulk purchases for sales promotions, premiums or fund raising. Special books or book excerpts can also be created to fit specific needs.

For details write the office of the Vice President of Special Markets, Pocket Books, 1230 Avenue of the Americas, New York, New York 10020.

Maura Seger

Empire of the Heart

PUBLISHED BY POCKET BOOKS NEW YORK

This novel is a work of historical fiction. Names, characters, places and incidents relating to non-historical figures are either the product of the author's imagination or are used fictitiously. Any resemblance of such non-historical incidents, places or figures to actual events or locales or persons, living or dead, is entirely coincidental.

Another *Original* publication of POCKET BOOKS

POCKET BOOKS, a division of Simon & Schuster, Inc.
1230 Avenue of the Americas, New York, N.Y. 10020

ISBN: 0-671-49396-5

First Pocket Books printing January, 1984

10 9 8 7 6 5 4 3 2 1

Empire of the Heart

Chapter One

BENEATH THE BROAD-BRIMMED HAT SHADING HIS eyes, Jordan Nash squinted. The sun hanging over the churchyard was very hot. Soon the rainy season would come and the Gold Coast would once again bloom with the full verdant strength of tropical Africa. But for the moment, everything was withered and sere.

The small group of people of which he was a part shifted restlessly. A low, almost soundless sigh of mingled impatience and resignation rose from among them. Jordan repressed a sardonic grin. They were undoubtedly as eager as he for the sad event to be over and done with.

He suspected that he was not the only one who had come to the funeral more out of curiosity than respect, and that vaguely troubled him. Even though he had known Sir Alfred Derrick only by reputation, he thought it a shame for any man to die so far from home, surrounded by strangers.

Well, not entirely surrounded. There was the matter of his daughter. Piercing blue eyes shifted slightly, to the pale figure standing beside the open grave.

Elizabeth Derrick was holding up rather well. But then he would have expected her to do nothing less. The briefest glimpse was enough to tell him she was a full-fledged member of that rarefied breed, the upper-class Englishwoman.

His gaze softened as he mentally corrected that last observation. More girl than woman. He judged her to be in her early twenties, with the innocence that comes only from a rigidly circumscribed existence.

Her body, hidden by a voluminous shoulder cape and ankle-length serge skirt that made him feel hot just looking at it, was impossible to discern. An ugly straw bonnet covered her head, allowing only a few wisps of golden-brown hair to frame the pale oval of her face.

Except for overly large green eyes, her features were unremarkable. He had the vague impression that under different circumstances they might be pleasing, but despite the fact that he was looking at her directly, he couldn't be sure.

Her self-effacement was so complete that even standing perfectly still she seemed to fade out of focus and become no more than a blurred, indistinct image. Piqued by her elusiveness, Jordan found himself wondering how she would appear without all that cumbersome concealment.

What a thing to be thinking about. Had he been away from what passed for civilization so long that he had lost touch with the simplest proprieties?

Sighing, he pulled a red bandana from the pocket of his khaki trousers and wiped the sweat from his forehead.

It was getting hotter by the moment; the leaden heat of Africa filled with the drone of insects and the dry smell of the savannah shoving up against the doorstep of the colonial town. Smoldering incense could not quite disguise the stench of death.

Yesterday, Sir Alfred Derrick had appeared in the best of health, as he sat on the patio of the Accra Club sipping ginger beer and being fanned by a silent, expressionless native while he regaled his fellow Britishers with the plans for his expedition upriver into the heart of Ashante country.

Jordan had observed him quietly from the bar, struck as much by the man's unbridled cocksureness as by his almost stunning ignorance.

Sir Alfred might be a brilliant historian, but he knew absolutely nothing about life in the bush. He had spent his days writing pretentious tomes and dreaming of one great sortie into the wilderness. This was to be it.

Moments later, as Jordan had lit a cheroot and stared pensively out at the flat blue curve of the Bay of Benin framed by gently waving palm fronds and dotted by fishing canoes, a sound from behind caught his attention. He turned in time to see Sir Alfred grasp his throat, make a low choking gurgle, and crumple to the rattan-covered floor.

The colony's physician, summoned from his snooker game, had ruled the cause of death to be a heart seizure brought on by too much excitement and exertion. The Anglican priest, roused from a nap in the pastorage, went off to inform Lady Elizabeth, while preparations for the customarily hasty burial were begun.

The few other Englishwomen in the British colonial capital had done what they could to ease the shock of bereavement. But since the Derricks had arrived only a few days before, there was great reluctance to intrude on the grief of someone who seemed destined to remain a stranger.

The pallbearers were approaching with the coffin, preceded by a white-robed Anglican priest. Jordan pulled off his hat and surreptitiously stretched to relieve the kink between his shoulders. He wasn't used to standing still so long.

Thick black hair glistened in the sun. He hadn't gotten it cut in a while. It curled at the nape of his neck, just below the collar of his unbleached cotton shirt.

Thirty-two years of exposure to all sorts of weather had turned the white skin inherited from his Irish forebears to burnished gold. He was tall and large-boned, with none of the physical softness his acquaintances back in Boston evinced.

His body was honed to a peak of strength and agility in keeping with his rigorous, often dangerous life. Powerful muscles defined the broad sweep of his arms, shoulders, and chest.

His waist and hips were narrow, his abdomen flat. Long, sinewy legs were planted slightly apart, in the stance of a man who is as comfortable at sea as he is on land.

In defiance of Victorian fashion, he was clean-shaven. The strong, hard lines of his jaw and the unexpectedly sensual curve of his mouth could be clearly seen.

He shifted slightly, the tension of his big body communicating both compassion and unease. He was watchful of both himself and the event unfolding before him, as though uncertain about his ability to do the right thing.

Elizabeth Derrick looked away hastily.

She had been watching him for some time from beneath the concealing rim of her bonnet and was appalled by her lack of concentration.

How could she allow herself to be distracted at such a moment? And by a man, no less. The only man who had ever mattered to her was her father and now he was . . .

4

Her thoughts broke off. She could not yet cope with the reality of his death. It didn't seem possible that the larger-than-life figure who had dominated her world was suddenly gone.

She could still hear his booming voice declaiming his theories, interests, projects, all with the supreme self-assurance that characterized everything he did.

His "handmaiden," he had called her, ever since her mother's death fourteen years before when she was ten. Her father had wasted no time filling the vacancy left by his doting wife. The daughter he had previously ignored was swiftly transformed into a devoted audience for his grand ideas. After all, what higher purpose could she have in life than to minister to an illustrious man?

Elizabeth suppressed a grimace. She supposed she would have to find out. One thing was sure: she was not going back to the great gloomy house outside London and the great gloomy horde of relatives, who would undoubtedly be in a rush to marry her off.

In twenty-four years, she had learned much—more than her father could have suspected, since he never took the effort to discover to what degree, if any, his audience was benefiting from his erudition. She meant to put that learning to use without delay.

A hand touched her arm, startling her. She looked up into the gentle gray eyes of Nan Wentworth, the middle-aged wife of one of the colonial administrators who had come to her as soon as she learned of Sir Alfred's death and offered her help in such kindly terms that it could not be refused.

"My dear," the motherly woman said softly, "you must come away now. It is over."

Glancing back at the grave, Elizabeth realized she was right. During her reverie, the prayers had been completed. The service was done.

Two beefy-faced men waited to shovel the dusty dirt

in on top of the coffin. The broiling heat made it difficult for them to hide their impatience.

She nodded dumbly. Torn from the protection of her thoughts, she could only stand quietly while the small group of men and women filed past her, each offering a few murmured words of condolence before hurrying on to the shade of their carriages.

Jordan Nash was the last to stop before her. Unlike most of the others, he took her hand in his and held it gently. Through the thin cotton glove she wore, his grip was reassuringly firm. She was struck by his great height, which made her feel unaccustomedly small, and by the sense of quiet strength he exuded.

"Please accept my sympathy for your loss," he said quietly, in cultured tones that surprised her. Her impression of a rough-edged adventurer wavered. There was more to him.

Curiosity about what might be concealed behind those piercing blue eyes drove her to meet his gaze. He was looking at her intently, in a way that made her flush.

"Thank you," she murmured, feeling painfully inane and awkward. The frown that marred the smooth line of his broad forehead beneath stray locks of ebony hair made it clear that something about her troubled him.

Jordan abruptly remembered he was still holding her hand and let it go. He was baffled by the effect she had on him.

Elizabeth Derrick did not come anywhere close to his usual taste in women. Strictly speaking, she was plain. Yet he found himself unable to look away from her.

She appeared so fragile and vulnerable, yet he sensed great strength in her. The seeming contradiction baffled him. For the first time in his life, a woman

6

other than his mother and sisters aroused both his protective instincts and his admiration.

Nan took it upon herself to end the uneasy encounter. Gently but implacably, she said, "We must be going now, Elizabeth." Beside her, Mr. Wentworth nodded.

Jordan knew they were right, but he found he could not simply walk away. Instead, he heard himself saying, "Allow me to escort you to your carriage."

Elizabeth hesitated barely an instant before inclining her head. She took the arm he offered, leaving Nan to follow with her husband.

As they walked through the dusty churchyard and out past the wrought-iron gate, he gave in to the desire to hear her voice again.

"Are you planning to return to England shortly?"

He expected her to answer in the affirmative and was startled when instead she said, "I haven't had an opportunity yet to decide what I will do."

Beneath her low, melodious words, Jordan heard a degree of firmness that made his eyes darken. He suspected she had already reached a decision, and could not imagine why she would deny it. What other option was open to her except to return to England? Unless she had relatives elsewhere . . .

They had reached the carriage. He handed her into it and waited while she smoothed her skirts and settled herself.

When she looked at him again with those huge green eyes empty of all expectation, he heard himself say, "If I can be of any help to you, please don't hesitate to call on me."

The formal words received no more than their appropriate response. Elizabeth smiled faintly and extended her hand. "Thank you, Mr. Nash. Everyone is being most kind."

7

He wanted to say that it was only natural for people to treat her gently; that she aroused that sort of behavior, but he stopped himself in time. The other couple had joined them.

Jeremy Wentworth nodded to him stiffly. Like most of the proper British gentlemen in the colony, he did not care for Jordan Nash.

The American was too bold, too inclined to go his own way regardless of what other people thought. He was known to hold some very peculiar ideas about how the natives should be treated.

Some even said he had spent time in the bush with the feared Ashante tribesmen, living as one of their warriors. Wentworth didn't really believe that, but looking at Nash he could see how the rumors might have started.

The man was dangerous. There was a primitive quality about him that challenged the very foundations of civilized authority.

Stepping into the carriage, Wentworth nodded to the driver. Jordan moved back as the horses lurched forward, heading swiftly down the path and out of sight.

As Elizabeth watched the churchyard fade from view behind her, the small plot of ground and the whitewashed building were eclipsed by the man who still held her attention.

She did not take her eyes from Jordan Nash until the carriage rounded a corner and he was lost from her sight.

The Wentworths glanced at each other. They had been married for twenty-five years and their understanding was complete. They no longer needed words to communicate.

Nan put her hand on top of the young girl's. "Please come home with us, dear. We don't like the idea of your staying on that boat by yourself."

Elizabeth repressed a smile. She doubted Captain Winslow would take kindly to hearing *Britannia's Pride* called a boat. It was in fact an oceangoing yacht that plied the route between England and Africa, dropping passengers off in Spain, Morocco, and, very occasionally, further south.

"Thank you, but I really will be fine. Besides, although the captain has been very understanding so far about the delay in removing our possessions, I really must get everything packed."

"But . . ." Nan began, uncertain how to phrase what was on her mind without appearing rude. "Don't you plan to make the return voyage?"

Elizabeth hesitated. She was no more anxious to reveal her intentions to the Wentworths than she had been to Jordan Nash. Less so, in fact.

Although the American could not even be considered an acquaintance, some instinct told her he would have understood the hitherto unsuspected need to take control of her own life that was swiftly dominating all her thoughts.

"I am not sure yet. At any rate, I think it best for me to go back to the ship. You have been very kind, but I cannot impose on your hospitality any longer."

The merest degree of coolness crept into her voice, signaling that much as she appreciated the Wentworths' help she still regarded them as strangers.

They might consider her a weak and frightened girl, but she had no intention of acting as one.

A faint glimmer of humor showed in her eyes when she perceived that her companions were just the least bit relieved by her refusal. They were genuinely caring people, but they also had responsibilities and worries of their own. They did not need any more.

A brief exchange followed as the Wentworths made a perfunctory attempt to change her mind. Convinced at last that she meant what she said, they subsided.

They had, after all, done everything they could. Lady Elizabeth's life was now in her own hands and she would do with it what she could.

She left them on the dock after warmly thanking them for all their assistance and promising to keep in touch. Stepping onto the deck of *Britannia's Pride*, she could not deny a surge of relief. For the first time since her father's death, she was alone.

There was no sign of the crew. She supposed that except for a skeleton staff, they were all on shore. That suited her well. She needed quiet to still the clamoring in her mind.

In the sitting room of the large cabin she had shared with Sir Alfred, she undid her bonnet and cape and set both down absently on an ornately carved chair. She was traveling without a maid, having been unable to find one willing to attempt such a rigorous journey.

Her father's valet had come as far as Casablanca, where he awaited their return. She would send a message telling him what had happened and providing the funds for his journey back to England.

That took care of the most immediate problem, but left her wondering what she was going to do about herself.

Logic dictated that she should remain right where she was. *Britannia's Pride* would sail again at the end of the week. Simply by doing nothing, she would be on the way home.

The mere thought made her shiver. She could not do that to herself. For the first time in her life, she was free. To give that up would be to destroy something essential in her soul that was just beginning to flower.

Some thoughtful member of the crew had left a carafe of chilled water on a tray in her bedroom. Elizabeth filled a tumbler and drank thirstily.

Lord, but it was hot! Her clothes clung to her. She

could feel the sweat trickling down her back. Her temples throbbed with pain and her legs felt weak.

Sitting down swiftly, she undid the small pearl buttons of her high-necked blouse and pulled it off. Underneath she wore a fine lawn camisole and the usual corset. She had laced it herself, so it was fairly loose, but still uncomfortable.

The bathrooms of *Britannia's Pride* boasted running water. Passengers could luxuriate in a full bath whenever the urge struck. It did now, forcibly.

Elizabeth wasted no time removing the rest of her clothes. The corset had left ugly red marks on her skin. She hated it, but was so inured to wearing it that it never occurred to her to leave it off.

Sinking into the cool water, she sighed with pleasure. The shock of the last twenty-four hours had worn her out.

She was tired in body and soul; so tired that she wondered how she was ever going to be able to sort through her thoughts and plan what she was to do.

Yet she had no choice. Whereas always before, every step she took was intended to fulfill her father's expectations, now for the first time she had to think of herself. It proved to be a difficult task.

She lay in the tub for a long time. The water grew tepid without her noticing. Through the open door of the bathroom, she could see some of the many bundles of supplies for the expedition her father had planned.

For years, he had dreamed of seeking out the lost city of the Mande, a loose confederation of immensely powerful tribes that had ranged far and wide over western Africa, carving out an empire whose extent was only beginning to be appreciated.

The Mande, according to legend, were masters at exploiting the wealth of their conquered lands. In the Gold Coast, they mined not only the precious metal that earned the region its name, but also diamonds which they used to decorate their idols.

Sir Alfred had become convinced through his research that a great statue of pure gold studded with diamonds remained hidden away in the Mande's fortress along the Volta River. It was his intention to find the idol and take it to England, where it would rest as a fitting testimony to his own greatness.

Elizabeth turned the matter over in her mind. The expedition was a thrilling departure from her humdrum life back in England, and the idol made as good an objective as any.

Why couldn't she simply go on as planned, taking advantage of the fact that everything was already in readiness?

Granted, women did not go off on expeditions into the African jungle. But perhaps that was only because it hadn't occurred to any of them to do so.

She, on the other hand, was quite taken with the idea.

Rising from the tub, she dried off hastily without looking at herself. Since coming to womanhood, her body had troubled her. A young male cousin had told her once that she resembled a stick. The barb had stung. Ever since, she had taken care to keep herself well concealed in bulky clothes that hid her slenderness.

Wrapped in a robe, she sat down at the dressing table and began brushing her waist-length brown hair while thinking over what might be involved in going through with her father's plans.

To begin with, she would need help. Not for a moment was she so foolish as to think she could attempt the journey without expert assistance. But from whom?

The answer presented itself all too easily. Although

she had been in the Gold Coast barely a week, she had already learned a great deal about its inhabitants.

Her father's illustrious reputation had made them welcome dinner guests at the homes of all the most important government and business personages.

There she had followed her usual practice of sitting quietly in the background while Sir Alfred held everyone's attention.

By doing so, she had quickly picked up a great deal of information about the activities and interests of the various people brought together in this outpost of British civilization perched on the curve of Africa's western coast.

Most of them had no objective except to line their own pockets. Whatever grandiose terms they used to describe their activities, that was what it came down to.

They saw Africa as a literally golden opportunity to achieve wealth that, had they remained at home, would have been beyond their wildest dreams.

The sole exception to this litany of greed seemed to be Jordan Nash. His motives eluded everyone's guess, but all the evidence suggested that he was both wealthy and willful.

He went where he would and did as he chose. For the last ten years, he had made periodic visits to the Gold Coast on his oceangoing yacht *Tara,* often leaving the ship docked at Accra and vanishing upriver for months at a time.

He had published several learned treatises on his findings. These were markedly different from the writings of such notable adventurers as Sir Richard Burton, David Livingstone, and John Speke, each of whom approached the subject from a preconceived set of biases. Nash had caused considerable controversy by claiming that African cultures were as deserving of respect as any other, and that the popular notion of white superiority was nothing more than a rationale for exploitation.

Yet as startling as his theories might be, his credibility could not be challenged. He was reputed to know the area better than any other white man. Much as she tried to think of someone else who might guide her, she kept coming back to him.

Stepping into fresh undergarments, Elizabeth glanced out the porthole. In the gathering dusk of early evening, she could make out the proud shape of the *Tara* swaying slightly on the current only a few hundred yards away.

While *Britannia's Pride* was a fine ship, which offered her passengers both comfort and safety, the *Tara* was in a different class altogether.

More than two hundred feet long and propelled by both steam and sail, the yacht was a magnificent testimony to the skill of the Yankee seamen who had built her, as well as eloquent proof of Jordan Nash's riches and power.

Elizabeth considered it thoughtfully. Clearly, she could not persuade him to help her by offers of money. However, she might have something else he would want.

Carefully hidden away in one of her father's valises was a yellowed and creased map drawn more than fifty years before by an explorer who claimed to have copied it from an earlier original, charted by Portuguese sailors in service to the renowned Prince Henry the Navigator.

The map purported to show the exact location of the golden idol of the Mande. If that claim was correct, it represented a treasure whose value went far beyond any monetary consideration. To the man who found the idol would go international acclaim and honor. Surely even Jordan Nash could not be immune to that?

Whatever his background, whatever hungers drove him, he would at least be tempted by the vision of what could be his if he agreed to help her.

Fastening the buttons of the simple long-sleeved dress she had selected, Elizabeth strode into what had been her father's bedchamber.

The sudden sight of his belongings, left just as he had last touched them, brought her up short. Despite the difficulties that had existed between them, she could not deny the abrupt upsurge of grief that threatened to overwhelm her.

To divert herself, she quickly found the valise and dug through it until her fingers closed on the small metal cylinder protecting the map. Drawing it out, she carefully unrolled the tissue-thin paper.

It was just as she remembered it from the one brief glimpse she had had in her father's study back in England.

By simply separating the top third of it with a small pair of scissors, she was able to leave the map sufficiently intact for a skilled eye to judge its worth, while tantalizingly denying the exact location of its ultimate objective.

Back in her own bedroom, she hid the smaller piece under a pile of her nightrobes. That done, she took a final look at herself in the mirror.

Her hair troubled her. Falling lankly to her waist, it made her look like a child. Swiftly, she coiled the brown strands into a heavy chignon at the nape of her neck.

Like almost everything in her small, subdued wardrobe, the gray poplin dress was fortuitously suitable for mourning. But it was also snugger than she remembered, revealing all too clearly the delicate curves of her body. Much as she disliked the voluminous cape, she put it on again.

The high-buttoned shoes she wore made no sound as

she left the cabin and went up on deck. Several crew members had returned. They murmured a few words of sympathy.

If any thought it strange for her to be going ashore by herself, they did not say so. Her long service to her father had cut her off from any real contact with other people, with the result that she seemed unapproachable.

None of the men who watched her go was willing to confront the wall of reserve surrounding her.

Elizabeth did not pause to consider that she might be behaving improperly. It was likely that Jordan Nash had brought guests along, since wealthy adventurers rarely traveled alone. She would be in the company of people of her own class, even if they were Americans.

Or so she thought. Nearing the *Tara,* she hesitated momentarily. Very few lights were showing. If there were many people on board, they must be clustered in a forward stateroom where she could make out the flicker of oil lamps.

Taking a deep breath, she marched up the gangplank. A quick glance around confirmed that the yacht was as well cared for as she had expected.

The long expanse of mahogany deck was polished to perfection, as were the brass railings and fixtures. Not a speck of dirt showed anywhere. Jordan Nash might be casual in his dress, but he apparently tolerated no laxity about his ship.

She had just turned to find her way to the stateroom and announce her presence when a movement in the shadows startled her. As she began to speak; the breath caught in her throat and her heart began to pound wildly. Out of the darkness stepped an immense, powerfully built black man.

He was just over six feet tall with dark brown skin and black, tightly curled hair worn very short. Set between a wide forehead and a broad, slightly flattened nose, ebony eyes regarded her sharply. Full lips were drawn in a hard, unrelenting line.

Although he wore khaki trousers and a shirt similar to Jordan's, there was no mistaking his true identity. Everything about him, from his fierce, proud bearing to the ease with which he held the rifle aimed at her, proclaimed him an Ashante warrior, one of that fierce tribe who for two hundred years had ruled not only much of the Gold Coast but vast lands in the interior and whose name alone was enough to strike terror in the hearts of Europeans.

Elizabeth tried to retreat, her eyes darting round for some avenue of escape, but there was none. A strangled cry escaped her as an ebony hand lashed out, seizing her in a grip of iron and yanking her forward remorselessly toward the stateroom.

Chapter Two

JORDAN HAD JUST SETTLED DOWN IN HIS FAVORITE wing chair with his feet propped up on the desk and a freshly lit cheroot in his hand when the door slammed open.

He did not move, but an eyebrow raised quizzically. "Trouble, Osei?"

"I'm not sure. I found this wandering around near the gangplank."

The warrior shoved Elizabeth forward, so that she fell heavily against the desk. Her hands shot out to absorb much of the impact, but she was still winded enough that it took a moment for her to catch her breath.

As she struggled to regain control of herself, Jordan surveyed her openly. He had not moved from his relaxed posture, yet he exuded an unmistakable sense of tightly coiled strength.

With a shock of belated recognition she realized that the man who had spoken to her so gently in the cemetery was in fact every bit as dangerous as the

Ashante who she had no doubt would have killed her without a qualm.

Their eyes met and clashed. His were narrowed and cold. Hers were wide and frightened, despite her best efforts to hide her dismay. Whatever she had expected when she set out to meet with him, it was not this.

For the first time in her life, she understood what it was to feel physically threatened. She was alone and helpless aboard his ship.

No one knew where she had gone or why. For reasons she could not begin to understand, she was being treated as a trespasser, perhaps even worse.

The shock of her father's death and the exhausting ordeal that followed had undermined her strength far more than she cared to admit. Tears glistened briefly in her eyes before the pride bred into her through generations of stalwart forebears came to her rescue.

Straightening, she pressed her hands tightly together to stop their stinging and stared at Jordan frostily. "Really, Mr. Nash, I had heard that the manners of Americans left much to be desired, but I still did not expect to be received like some hoodlum. What is the meaning of this disgraceful treatment?"

He did not answer at once. Instead, he stood up leisurely and put his cheroot in an ashtray, all the while continuing to subject her to his unrelenting scrutiny.

Elizabeth tried to keep her expression hard, but she knew she was not succeeding very well. The sight of Jordan clad only in snug-fitting trousers and an unbuttoned shirt that hung open to bare a goodly portion of his powerful chest proved immensely distracting.

As a consequence, she remained unaware of the astonishment that he was struggling to conceal. Her sudden appearance seemed the realization of a half-formed fantasy.

In the hours since the funeral, she had drifted repeatedly through his mind despite his best efforts to eject her. Giving up finally, he sat down to try to determine what could possibly be so intriguing about a plain, prudish English girl to whom he should not have given a second glance.

Instead of arriving at an answer, he got the problem itself, standing right in front of him with her eyes as dark as a storm-tossed sea and her cheeks becomingly flushed.

The sheer pleasure he felt at seeing her again shook him. He had known far too many women—all more beautiful than this waif—for whom he felt nothing more than desire and casual affection. Not one of them had ever captured his attention so suddenly and thoroughly. The sensation was unsettling, to say the least.

Angry at his own uncharacteristic susceptibility, he reacted defensively and lashed out at the cause. "I pegged you wrong, your ladyship. At the cemetery, I thought you looked like a typical stiff-necked Englishwoman, one of those whose emotions are as rigidly laced as her body. Little did I guess you would take it upon yourself to pay me a nocturnal visit."

Before Elizabeth could give vent to the outraged exclamation his insulting insinuations prompted, Jordan had turned to the black man. "Thank you for your vigilance, Osei, but I honestly don't think I'm in any danger from this one."

The warrior grinned knowingly. He turned to leave, the rifle held once again under his arm. In perfectly clipped British tones that deepened Elizabeth's already considerable confusion, he said, "It does appear that way. However, if you change your mind, don't hesitate to call. I'll be out on deck."

When the door had closed behind him, Jordan strolled over to a cabinet set in the wood-paneled wall. He opened it to reveal an array of crystal decanters and glasses.

As he poured two drinks, he said, "Osei is a good friend who, for reasons I won't go into, has also appointed himself my bodyguard. You're lucky he has a soft spot for women, or he would have killed you the instant you set foot on board."

"How forebearing of him," Elizabeth muttered. She was having trouble staying as alert as she knew she should be. Deadening weariness blunted the keen edge of her anger and outrage.

It had been a terrible mistake to seek Jordan out. What she had thought was a well-reasoned decision to take charge of her own life was in fact nothing more than a panicky response to her sudden emancipation. While she still believed her idea of continuing the expedition was sound, she was shocked by the naiveté that had led her to approach so ruthless and uncaring a man.

Dazedly, she tried to fathom how a callous adventurer who counted an Ashante warrior among his friends also came to possess an array of beautiful furnishings tastefully arranged in a room that was at once elegant and cheerful.

Unless she was very much mistaken, the desk on which he had so cavalierly rested his feet was Chippendale, in excellent condition despite such casual treatment. The breakfront opposite was Sheraton. Magnificent Oriental carpets covered the floor, their muted colors glowing warmly in the light from crystal and silver wall sconces.

At least she had been right when she guessed his assistance could not be bought with money. If the *Tara*'s stateroom was anything to go by, Jordan Nash was far richer than anyone suspected. She wanted to believe that his wealth was the source of his arrogance. If she could only label him a fatuous dilettante, she could dismiss him from her mind. The tiny voice that insisted he was anything but was most vexing.

21

Jordan approached her, offering a tumbler holding an inch of what she suspected was whiskey. Her nose wrinkled. "No thank you."

He smiled faintly. "It will do you good. For a few moments there you looked as though you were about to faint. Since I have an abhorrence of swooning women, I would prefer for you to drink this as a preventative."

"I have never fainted in my life," Elizabeth informed him stiffly, "nor have I ever drunk spirits. I do not intend to begin either practice now."

She turned away resolutely. His lack of manners was beyond belief. Not only had he not apologized for her odious reception, but he hadn't even bothered to button up his shirt.

Jordan shrugged. He set her drink on a table beside the overstuffed leather couch and took a sip of his own before saying, "Suit yourself, but I would appreciate it if you would sit down. How you can even stand upright in all those clothes is beyond me."

"Some of us have respect for our own modesty and that of others," Elizabeth sniffed. She hadn't really meant to sit down, but weariness got the better of her and she succumbed before she realized what she was doing. Annoyed, she muttered, "You are apparently unhindered by such concerns."

To reestablish, if only to herself, that she was no weak-willed woman susceptible to his whims, she directed a pointed stare at his bare chest while resolutely beating down the peculiar feelings that once again threatened to sweep over her.

To her surprise, he laughed throatily. "Should I conclude from that remark that you did not come here with designs on this poor body you are so anxious to have me cover up?"

Elizabeth stared at him for a long moment. Much as she regretted seeking him out, she was determined not

22

to retreat ignominiously. If nothing else could be salvaged from her disastrous visit, she would at least have the satisfaction of explaining her plan.

"Mr. Nash," she said quietly, "while I admit to being—shall we say—surprised by the manner in which you receive guests, I am once again sufficiently in control of myself to be unmoved by your efforts to shock me. I will not swoon, cry, retreat, or do any of the other things you are apparently trying to provoke. The sooner you realize that, the sooner we can get down to business."

It was, for her, a rather long speech and she concluded it with some doubt as to how it would be received. Jordan Nash did not impress her as the sort of man who took kindly to strong-willed women.

She had never thought of herself in such terms before, but found she rather liked the idea. After so many years of catering to her father's every whim, she was not about to let anyone else direct her actions.

He took another sip of his drink and studied her over the rim of the glass. She met his gaze unflinchingly, despite the painful twisting of her stomach.

Jordan suppressed a smile. She clearly did not realize that her brave words had been slightly slurred by exhaustion. Nevertheless, her valiant pride impressed him enough that he was willing to accord her the respect he would have given a man. Without taking his eyes from her, he inquired matter-of-factly, "What business did you have in mind?"

Elizabeth released her breath slowly, not wanting him to see how tensely she had awaited his response. Sitting straight-backed on the couch with her hands folded neatly in her lap, she began to explain the purpose of her visit.

"You may be aware that my father came here with the intention of taking an expedition upriver to search for the lost city of the Mande. It was his dream to find the golden idol reputed to be hidden in the ruins. I have decided to carry out his plans, but to do so I require a guide. From what I have heard about you, you are the logical choice for the job."

Whatever hope she had still nurtured that he might agree to her proposal evaporated as Jordan's gaze hardened with astonishment. "You can't be serious."

"I assure you I am. There is no reason I can think of to prevent me from going on."

"Maybe not, but I can think of at least a dozen. To begin with, has it escaped your notice that you happen to be a woman?"

Elizabeth flinched at his sarcasm but did not give way. "My father intended for me to accompany him, so he obviously thought me strong enough to handle any difficulties we might confront. Now I shall simply have to do so without him."

In truth, she did not believe her father had ever given a moment's thought to the advisability of taking a young woman along on such a trek, but she wasn't about to admit as much to Jordan.

Let him think Sir Alfred, who should after all have known her better than anyone else, had judged her capable of managing the journey.

The clout she had hoped her father's intentions would carry turned out not to exist. Jordan's mouth tightened ominously. "No man with half an ounce of sense would agree to take a white woman into the bush. You couldn't stand up to the strain. The mere idea is ludicrous."

His arrogant dismissal of her abilities enraged Elizabeth, but she would not give him the satisfaction of seeing how easily he could affect her. Instead, she took a firm grip on her temper and faced him with all the dignity her weariness would allow. "To you, perhaps, but not to me. I shall make this expedition, have no doubt of that. The only point in question is who shall be my guide."

Pausing deliberately, she added, "I have reason to believe you may be more interested than you know."

Jordan leaned back against the couch, one booted leg resting over the knee of the other. "What is that supposed to mean?"

"It means that if you will agree to lead me upriver, when we find the golden idol I will turn it over to you. All the credit for its discovery can go to you. It will bring you honor and acclaim far beyond anything mere money can grant."

She spoke confidently, certain that he would be forced to reevaluate her proposal. But instead Jordan merely shook his head incredulously.

"You astound me, Lady Elizabeth. Ignoring for just the moment your complete inability to even attempt such a trip, what on earth makes you believe you would find the lost city of the Mande, much less the idol itself?"

With just the merest hint of smugness, she played what she considered to be her trump card. "Because I have a map."

In the next instant, her self-assurance was severely dented as Jordan threw back his head and roared with laughter.

"A map! Oh, pardon me, that changes everything. Why didn't I ever think to get one of those? I could have gone into any market in the Gold Coast and bought maps purporting to show the location of the Mande's great city, not to mention the elephant's burial ground, the lost mines of King Solomon, and the true location of Noah's Ark, which apparently went aground far south of where most everyone thinks. Are you sure you wouldn't rather search for one of those? They are just as likely to be found."

Bitterly stung by his derision, Elizabeth jumped to her feet. Her hands were clenched at her sides and her eyes glittered as she snapped, "How dare you suggest that my father could have been fooled by a specious map! He spent decades researching the history of this area. Nothing was left to chance. By the time he set out on this expedition, he knew he had found the true location."

"He knew nothing," Jordan retorted, standing up more slowly but with rather more effect.

Hands on his lean hips, feet planted firmly apart, he towered over her. Elizabeth had to fight the urge to take a step back as he went on remorselessly.

"The great Sir Alfred spent his life making grandiose pronouncements from the safety of his study or lecture hall. Not once did he get out in the field to test his theories against reality. He simply deluded himself and others into believing he knew far more than he did."

His voice gentled slightly as he took in her ashen pallor. Silently, he rebuked himself for not remembering how much she had endured. More kindly, he said, "Grief can make people do strange things, Elizabeth. It's obvious that your father was the center of your life. With him gone, you can't be expected to be thinking rationally. The wisest course open to you is to go back to England, where there must be people who will look after you and help you through this difficult time."

Elizabeth opened her mouth to answer him, then abruptly shut it. Too many contradictory feelings were clamoring within her. She could hardly admit how far short she fell of his opinion of her.

Nor could she reconcile his sudden use of her Christian name with his earlier coldness. For just a moment, he had seemed to genuinely care about her in a way she found very difficult to reject.

Yet she managed to, simply because the alternatives were unthinkable. "Spare me your self-serving advice, Mr. Nash. It's obvious you can't bear the thought that my father discovered something you don't know about, any more than you can stand the idea of a woman carrying through his plans. But I will do precisely that. Now you will kindly excuse me. We have nothing more to say to each other."

Gathering up her skirts, Elizabeth turned smartly toward the door. She completed two, perhaps three steps, before a steely arm lashed out, wrapping around her waist so firmly as to knock the breath from her.

"You've got a temper, your ladyship," a drawling voice murmured in her ear. "You do your damnedest to hide it under those atrocious clothes and that frosty air, but it's still there all right."

"Let me go! You've no right to do this! If you don't stop immediately, I'll . . . I'll . . . "

"Do go on. This is just getting interesting." As he spoke, Jordan lifted her off her feet and carried her over to the couch, where he deposited her none too gently.

Staring down at her from his great height, he grinned complacently. "Feel free to scream. Osei will simply presume you're being properly punished for trespassing."

On the verge of doing just that, Elizabeth gritted her teeth. Not a sound escaped her, though the glare she shot him spoke volumes.

"That's it," Jordan mocked. "Hate me all you like. That rage I can feel inside you has to go somewhere or you're liable to burst out of that abominable corset you're wearing."

Sitting down across from her, he stretched out his long legs comfortably and regarded her over the bridge of his tanned fingers.

His expression was thoughtful as he mused, "I can't

help but wonder where all your anger comes from. Surely proper English ladies aren't supposed to be prey to such intense emotions?"

White-faced, she stared back at him. Was it only an accident that he seemed able to unerringly discern her most vulnerable points?

Too many times she had struggled to hold back the fury provoked by her father's uncaring disregard of her feelings and needs. Over and over, she had told herself that it was her role to obey him without thought of herself.

But no matter how often she repeated that silent litany, some portion of her remained unconvinced. Anger continued to both torment and shame her.

"Since you know nothing at all of propriety," she murmured shakily, "how can you presume to judge me?"

Jordan regarded her steadily. He was regretting having taunted her, even as he wondered what had driven him to it.

Granted, he couldn't claim to know much about women beyond their obvious uses in bed, but he had never before felt compelled to peel away the protective layers shielding another person's soul and to discover for himself what lay beneath.

Why would he attempt such an intimate act with Elizabeth Derrick?

Bewilderment at his own actions made him harsher than he intended. "I know stupidity when I encounter it, and that is exactly what this plan of yours reeks of. How you can think for one moment of going off into the bush is beyond me. Do you imagine it will be like an afternoon's punt on the Thames or some other such nonsense?"

Elizabeth had endured all she could. The relentless bombardment of shock, grief, and guilt had exhausted her strength. She had nothing left but a last, tenuous hold on her self-control, which his mockery abruptly snapped. A choked sob broke from her as she jumped up and ran for the door.

This time she was not hindered by any concern about making a good exit. All she thought of was to get away, to put as much distance as possible between herself and the insufferable Jordan Nash.

Her desperation caught him off guard. She got to the door before he could react and jerked it open, fleeing down the corridor and up the short flight of steps to the deck.

Osei was at the stern, too far away to prevent her from reaching the gangplank. She could hear Jordan's muttered curse right behind her as she leaped onto the wharf. Her heavy skirt made running difficult, but she managed as best she could. Until Jordan once again caught her.

His touch was totally different from what she had experienced before. Instead of the cruel strength he had used against her, there was only gentle determination to keep her from coming to any harm.

"Elizabeth," he murmured softly, drawing her still struggling body against his, "be sensible. I'm sorry I upset you, but I can't let you go wandering around the docks on your own. Let me take you back to wherever you're staying."

Blinded by tears whose cause she refused to acknowledge, she shook her head angrily. "That is the second time you have called me by my Christian name, Mr. Nash. I have not given you permission to do so. Therefore, pray desist, and while you are about it *let me go*."

This last was punctuated by a swift kick to his shin. Jordan yelped, more in surprise than pain, but refused to relinquish his hold.

He was getting used to the fact that beneath her pale, almost mousy exterior, Elizabeth Derrick possessed a fighting spirit he could not help but admire. Realizing that made him far better prepared to deal with her than he had been at first.

Holding on grimly, he managed to thwart her frantic efforts to break free, until at last her strength was exhausted and she subsided against him.

When he was certain she had accepted her inability to escape, he tilted her head back and compelled her to meet his eyes. Very quietly, not wanting to make her feel any worse than he already had, he asked, "Where are you staying?"

It occurred to Elizabeth not to tell him. But what was to be gained by that? She couldn't go on defying him when there was no doubt he would win in the end.

All her strength seemed to be gone. She was so very tired and hot . . . so disoriented, as though everything were whirling out of its appointed place and the whole world were splitting apart . . .

"On board *Britannia's Pride*."

Her words were little more than a whisper, but Jordan caught them. He stared down at her, taking in the extreme pallor of the delicate face lying against his shoulder, the unnatural brightness of the eyes she was struggling to keep open, and he cursed softly.

Strong arms lifted her, cradling her protectively. Before she could even think to protest, he strode off down the dock. They had gone only a few yards when he abruptly demanded, "Why are you still on the ship? Surely the Wentworths offered you their hospitality?"

She nodded wearily. "Yes, but I wanted to be by myself. I wanted to feel . . . free."

Elizabeth was only dimly aware of what she was saying. Her tongue seemed to be running away with itself. There was something about being held in a man's arms—or at least in this man's—that made her forget all about restraint and discretion.

30

Perhaps it was just the novelty of the experience. She couldn't remember ever being held by anyone, except perhaps by a serving maid when she was a child. Come to think of it, she couldn't remember even being touched very often.

In some never stated but nonetheless clear way her father had communicated his disapproval of such things. She seemed to have always known it was wrong to want any physical expression of affection.

Was that what this was? Surely not. Jordan Nash had no reason to feel the least affection for her. That knowledge unexpectedly pained her. She blinked hard, trying to force back the tears that threatened to fall.

Jordan stared down at her glumly. What had begun as an uncharacteristically chivalrous attempt to see her safely back to her lodgings was rapidly turning into something quite different. The feel of her body nestled in his arms was having an unexpected effect on his senses.

He told himself he was only surprised. She was much lighter than the bulky clothes had led him to believe and she fit so perfectly against him, as though there was nowhere she was better suited to be.

Grimly, he thought that the months of his self-imposed celibacy must have taken an even greater toll than he had thought if a sharp-tongued termagant who looked like an exhausted child could arouse him so effortlessly. He was in very real danger of taking advantage of her helplessness.

All the more determined to get her back to her ship as quickly as possible, Jordan hastened his pace. He strode up *Britannia's* gangplank and glanced around for some member of the crew or other passenger he could legitimately hand Elizabeth over to.

No one. They might have had the entire ship to

themselves for all the signs of life he could make out. Sighing, he tightened his hold on her. "Where is your cabin?"

From the depths of a near-dreamlike state that enveloped her as gently as his arms themselves, she managed to reply, "On the main deck, aft and to port."

He nodded and set off hurriedly. It was not difficult to find the stateroom. All the others were awaiting new occupants and were consequently standing open. Only one door was locked.

"Do you have the key?"

Elizabeth could not quite muster the strength to speak again, but she did manage to gesture to her reticule.

With a groan of mingled impatience and frustration, Jordan set her on her feet outside the stateroom and fumbled in the small bag until he found the object in question.

Swiftly unlocking the door, he lifted her again into his arms and stepped inside. A quick glance around was sufficient to point him in the right direction. He had seen the plain cotton petticoat she had left forgotten on the floor of her room.

Stepping over it, he lowered her gently onto the bed. She blinked up at him, seemingly unaware of her surroundings.

"Elizabeth," he murmured, "I know you're exhausted, but you can't sleep in all these clothes. You'd suffocate. Can you undress yourself?"

She nodded weakly and tried to undo the clasp holding her cape shut, but her fingers were stiff and after a few seconds, she gave up, letting her hands fall back into her lap.

"So sleepy . . ."

Jordan groaned more urgently. He couldn't believe

this was happening to him. How had he come to be in the bedroom of a stiff-necked, prudish Englishwoman who regarded him as an insufferable ruffian and would undoubtedly despise herself in the morning for accepting even the slightest help from him?

Not that he would still be around in the morning. He was getting out of there as quickly as possible. But first, he had to get her into bed.

"Sit up, Elizabeth . . . just a little more . . . that's it." The cape fell away, revealing the high neck of her dress fastened down the front with a multitude of tiny buttons. There was nothing for it but to undo them all.

Halfway through the process, Jordan paused. She really was much slenderer than he could have guessed. Her waist was delightfully wand-like and her hips were slimly curved. It was a pity she was flat-chested.

Sliding the dress from her, he quickly undid her many petticoats and tossed them aside. That left her corset, camisole, and bloomers. She could sleep in the last two, but the first had to go.

With unmistakable expertise, he undid the laces and eased the cumbersome garment from her. As he did so, he laid her again on her back. A sharp exclamation broke from him.

Far from being flat-chested, as he had believed, her breasts were gloriously high and full. Through the thin white cotton, he could clearly see the dark crests of her nipples. A film of sweat broke out on his forehead as he fought the almost irresistible urge to lower himself to her and claim the innocently beautiful body before him.

Though he knew himself to be out of practice, he did not doubt he could bring her to a peak of desire every bit as great as his own. Only the knowledge of her extreme innocence and vulnerability stopped him.

A jagged pulse beat in the shadowy hollow of his

cheek as he covered her swiftly and turned away, his lean fingers burning with the remembered touch of her flesh.

Stepping hurriedly through the door, he resisted the urge to look at her just once more as he closed it firmly behind him.

Chapter Three

ELIZABETH WOKE WITH A DELIGHTFUL SENSE OF well-being, so far beyond anything she had ever before experienced that she was reluctant to move for fear of disturbing it.

For long uncounted moments she lay on her back with her eyes closed, relishing the utter relaxation of her body. Only very gradually did memory return and with it shame.

There must be something terribly wrong with her. How else could she feel so good the day after her father's burial? Sitting up gingerly, she stared straight ahead, trying to track down the cause of her happiness.

She remembered coming back to the ship and changing her clothes, thinking about what she was going to do next, then setting out to see Jordan Nash. The echo of his insults made her flush. He had as good as called her father a fraud and herself an idiot.

Everything after that was rather blurred. She knew she had gotten very angry and had tried to escape. He had stopped her—once. The second time she had made it off the ship. But he had followed her.

A vivid flush spread across her cheeks. She could still feel the press of his body against hers and the tensile strength of his arms holding her so easily.

Elizabeth's head fell forward. She buried her face in her hands as a horrified moan broke from her.

He had carried her back to this very room, set her down on the bed, and . . .

She couldn't possibly have allowed such liberties. Yet she had. Self-conscious, prudish Elizabeth Derrick had permitted a man to remove almost all her clothing, to see her without the bulky camouflage she relied on to hide her deficiencies.

Not only had she allowed it; she had enjoyed it thoroughly. Even in her semiconscious state, she had taken great pleasure in his touch. Had he realized that?

If he had, how contemptuous he must be of her, and how she deserved his disgust. With her father barely in his grave, she had behaved like a wanton.

Humiliation seared her. She twisted on the bed, as though trying to escape from her own body. But there was no escape. Not this day or the next or the next, far into a dark and barren future.

She could not hope to get away from herself, but she could get away from Jordan Nash before he had any opportunity to taunt her for what she had done.

Jumping out of the bed, she paused only long enough to gather up the clothes left on the floor before quickly washing and dressing. Though her stomach growled urgently, she refused to acknowledge it.

Instead, she tossed her cape over her shoulders and hastened up on deck, exchanging polite greetings with the members of the crew she passed but avoiding any conversation that might delay her.

Not even the heat, already considerable despite the early hour, forced her to slow her pace as she walked quickly and determinedly in the direction of the cemetery.

Pausing only once, to buy flowers from an Englishwoman who had managed to create a little corner of Kent thousands of miles from home, she reached her father's grave out of breath and perspiring heavily.

With the weight of her clothes pulling her down, she sank to her knees beside the freshly turned earth. Her hands shook as she set the flowers in place, a silent and already wilting offer of repentence.

"I'm sorry," she whispered brokenly, unsure of exactly what she was apologizing for but knowing that it was vast.

She, the person charged with looking after his comfort and welfare, had failed him dreadfully. Moreover, she had neglected even to mourn, giving herself over instead to the shocking delight of a Jordan Nash's touch and care.

An anguished sob rose in her throat. She tried to force it back and found that she could not. Hot tears slid down her pale cheeks. For the first time in longer than she could remember, she began to truly cry.

She didn't do it gracefully. Each sob and tear was fiercely resisted, thereby multiplying its effect tenfold. What should have been a cathartic release was instead the final humiliation heaped on her already overburdened spirit.

Not for her the dignified sniffles she had heard occasionally from aristocratic belles momentarily thwarted in the pursuit of some whim. She sobbed noisily, her face turned red, and her nose ran.

Fumbling in her reticule for a handkerchief, she did not at first notice the man gazing down at her. When at last he swam into her watery line of vision, she gasped.

"Oh! I didn't realize . . . I thought there was no one else here."

"Obviously." He went down on his haunches beside her, far enough away so that there was nothing intrusive about his nearness but close enough to express the compassion she saw mirrored in his eyes.

He was almost as tall and well built as Jordan Nash, but otherwise bore no resemblance whatsoever to him. Whereas the American exuded a threatening sense of virility and determination, this man seemed the epitome of all that was gentle and noble.

His eyes, framed by pale lashes, were light brown. Impressive sideburns, slightly darker than his sun-bleached hair, set off fine-boned features with an aristocratic cast. A narrow mouth was partially concealed by a luxuriant moustache. He spoke softly, with the merest hint of an Etonian accent.

"Believe me, I had no intention of intruding. But I saw you from the roadway and I couldn't just . . ."

He didn't have to spell it out. Of course he couldn't just go on and ignore her. No proper Englishman would. And that was obviously what he was—well-bred, considerate, and decidedly handsome.

He looked rather like portraits she had seen of the late Prince Albert when he was a young man, and appeared to be in his late twenties, not much older than she was.

Her new acquaintance smiled gently. He held out a hand, unobtrusively helping her to her feet as he said, "I'm Nigel Chandler, by the way. Attached to the Colonial Administrator's office. I've been upriver the last few weeks and had only just got back last night when I heard the terrible news."

Still holding her hand, he added quietly, "I'm deuced sorry about your father. Sir Alfred was a great man. I was looking forward to meeting him."

Elizabeth swallowed hard. It was more imperative than ever that she get a grip on herself. Not for anything could she let this kind, sincere young man know that her tears had been caused far more by shame than by grief and that she did not truly share his view of her father.

"Uh . . . thank you," she murmured shakily. "If you don't mind, I'd like to leave here . . ."

"Of course. This must be dreadfully hard on you." Tucking her hand into the crook of his arm, he led her gently away. "Watch your step now. The ground is very uneven. Tends to blow about quite a bit during the dry season."

"Have you been in the Gold Coast long?" Elizabeth asked as they left the confines of the cemetery. Her voice was steadier but her throat still ached with unshed tears. It took all her willpower not to embarrass herself further.

"About two years, although frankly it seems longer." He smiled engagingly. "I came out here to survey the area for the Home Office. The job was expected to take about ten months to complete. Of course, it turned out to be far more complicated than anyone thought. Not until just recently have I felt I was making real progress."

"Then you must have traveled over a good portion of the colony, even into the bush?"

"Certainly. There's no other way to do the work. I suspect I've seen more of this country than just about any other white man."

Elizabeth could hardly believe her luck. She turned to look up at him, unconsciously giving him a brilliant smile. "Mr. Chandler, would I be right in presuming that you have experience leading expeditions upriver into Ashante country?"

"Why yes, of course. In fact, I had rather hoped to go along with your father. It would have been the highlight of my stay here." He sighed regretfully. "Quite a loss to science, your father. Pity there's no one to carry on with his work."

"I have been thinking the same thing. In fact, it has occurred to me that it would be a terrible shame to turn back this far along. Certainly my father wouldn't have wanted it. He was a great believer in completing whatever one started out to do."

"Yes, but . . . I mean, with his tragic end, you don't really have any alternative but to give up. Do you?"

"I might . . ." Elizabeth ventured cautiously, ". . . if I could find someone qualified to take over the leadership of the expedition."

Seeing Nigel's surprise, she went on more hurriedly. "After all, the supplies are ready, the bearers have been hired, everything is prepared and waiting. And I still have my father's map. That was the most important part."

"His map? Yes, I'd heard about that. He bought it from a man named Davies in London about two years ago, didn't he?"

She nodded hesitantly. "May I ask how you knew that?"

Nigel laughed modestly. "It's no great trick. I've always taken an interest in antiquities, so it was only natural that I follow your father's work. The last time I was in London, I went to hear him speak on ancient maps. During the course of the talk he mentioned his purchase from Davies."

"It was on his mind a great deal," Elizabeth murmured pensively, "particularly because of the tragedy that happened only a few days after he bought the map."

Nigel raised an eyebrow curiously, encouraging her to explain. "Mr. Davies was killed by a thief who broke into his shop. It was all so senseless. Something must have frightened the man off, because nothing was taken . . . except a life."

"How dreadful. Please don't think on it. You've had

quite enough to endure without my raising such un-happy memories."

In her highly susceptible state, his apology touched her deeply. On impulse, she allowed her fingers to tighten slightly against his arm. Nigel smiled down at her. There was nothing the least improper about his look. He clearly regarded her as a lady entitled to the full respect and consideration due her station.

Despite herself, Elizabeth could not help but con-trast his behavior to that of Jordan Nash. The Ameri-can had no idea at all of how to treat a lady, nor did he show any sign of caring. But in the handling of women he had to be regarded as an expert.

The mere thought of him was enough to make her blush. She had no idea how she would ever be able to face him again, but devoutly hoped the need would never arise. With Nigel's help, it might be possible for her to leave Accra without ever seeing Jordan again.

"Mr. Chandler," she began, "I do not wish to impose on you, but I would greatly appreciate your advice. Is there a chance you might be able to spare me some time today so that we could discuss what is to be done about the expedition?"

Clearly flattered to be asked for assistance, Nigel nodded quickly. "I would be honored to help you in any way I can, your ladyship. If you have no other plans for this morning, may I suggest that we proceed to the Club, where we can talk without disturbance?"

His eagerness convinced her that she had not mis-read his interest. With a slight smile, she agreed.

The Accra Club was housed in a palatial structure built more than a century before as one of a chain of fortifications put up by Europeans anxious to establish a toehold on the African continent. It had changed hands frequently among the English, Dutch, Portuguese, and Ashantes, the last group giving it up when they decided they preferred their grass huts.

In its present incarnation it was the focal point of what passed for society in the colony. She and Nigel stood for a moment in the entry hall to let their eyes adjust to the far dimmer light. Elizabeth had been to the Club before; it was impossible to spend any time in Accra without visiting there. But she was still startled by how meticulously a small fragment of England had been carved out of alien surroundings.

The only concession to the vast continent on which they happened to be perched were the mounted heads of lions, tigers, impalas, and elephants decorating the walls of the main lounge. They stared down balefully at the full Victorian complement of overstuffed furniture, fringed lamps, ornate carpets, cabinets, tables, potted palms, and bric-a-brac.

As Nigel instructed a native servant to bring them glasses of iced tea, Elizabeth took the opportunity to study her new acquaintance. Her first impressions of him held up well.

He reminded her of the young men who had come to visit her father, to sit almost literally at his feet while he declaimed his great insights into the history of man and the probable future.

She had had little direct contact with such guests, there being, after all, no real reason for them to notice her. But she had still formed certain conceptions of them that until recently had been the sum total of her knowledge about men other than her father.

Or was it still? Surely Jordan Nash could not be connected even by contrast to the earnest young gentlemen she remembered. He belonged to an entirely different frame of reference utterly beyond her ken but nonetheless fascinating to her.

She must stop thinking of him at once. Nigel had

been speaking for several minutes without her having any awareness of what was being said.

"I'm sorry, my mind seems to have wandered. Would you be so kind as to repeat that?"

He looked momentarily surprised as he realized he had not had her full attention. But true to the traditions of his upbringing, he recovered nicely. "Of course. I was just saying that this idea you have about carrying on with the expedition frankly fascinates me. If the map is as good as your father believed, it would be a shame to let it go to waste."

"I agree. In fact, the more I think on it, the more determined I am not to let that happen."

"You do realize, however, that there are enormous problems associated with such an endeavor?"

"Yes, but it seems to me that a great deal of the solution to those difficulties is to have the right people in charge. You did tell me you know the Ashante territory well?"

Nigel nodded, taking a sip of his tea before continuing. Droplets of it clung to his moustache as he said, "I know it well enough to understand the enormity of what your father intended. Not that I have any doubts about whether or not he would have succeeded. I'm just concerned that you not entrust such valuable information as is contained in the map to anyone who would misuse it."

Did Jordan Nash's ridicule constitute misuse? Granted, he had never actually seen the map, but he had still made his feelings quite clear. The memory of his derision stiffened her resolve. "I will be very cautious, Mr. Chandler. However, since you are experienced in the field of antiquities, I see no possible harm in showing you the map."

Her smile made it clear that mistrust simply could not enter into their dealings. They were from the same world, with the same standards and perceptions. How could she not trust him?

Nigel accepted her confidence gracefully. He paused only long enough to return the greetings of several acquaintances who had just entered the Club, before moving a bit closer to her.

"I would be honored to examine the map, your ladyship. May I ask where it is presently being kept?"

Elizabeth hesitated a moment. She could hardly tell him the vital piece of parchment was in the pocket of a dress she had haphazardly hung up in the closet that morning while her thoughts were very much elsewhere.

But there was no need to do so. Mr. Chandler could escort her back to *Britannia's Pride* and wait in the sitting room while she got the map.

He was immediately agreeable, but insisted on hiring a carriage for the trip. "You really must be more cautious about the heat, Lady Elizabeth. The ladies here find it best not to go anywhere on foot. During the better part of the day, they remain inside out of the sun and venture forth by carriage only very briefly in early evening."

Resisting the impulse to point out that she could not bear such a circumscribed life and that, furthermore, if they did indeed go on with the expedition she would be subjected to rigors far more strenuous than any to be found in Accra, Elizabeth allowed herself to be helped into a hired phaeton.

The impassive native driver was as capable at his job as all the other workers she had noted in the colony, but the pitted roadway caused the vehicle to bounce up and down jarringly.

Laced into her corset and engulfed in her concealing garments, she was hard-pressed to keep her balance. A tiny sigh of relief escaped her when they pulled up on the dock in front of *Britannia's Pride* and Nigel assisted her down.

Unaware of the restrictions customarily placed on gentlemen callers, since she had never had any, Elizabeth felt no reluctance about inviting Nigel into her stateroom. For once, her lack of beauty proved an asset.

Not for a moment did it occur to her that Mr. Chandler might have designs on her person. The very idea was lamentably ludicrous. After all, hadn't a vastly more virile and assertive man stripped her practically naked only the night before without attempting to have his way with her?

As Nigel seated himself on the overstuffed leather couch, she went to fetch the map. The sight of her bed, neatly made up by one of the crew, brought back disconcerting memories. A half-formed feeling of regret threatened to engulf her when she considered how innocently the previous night had ended.

Although she had only the dimmest notions of what submitting to a man might entail, Elizabeth found herself to be genuinely curious about it for the first time in her life. Shocked by her wayward thoughts, she found the map quickly and returned to the sitting room.

As she carefully removed it from the cylinder, Nigel leaned forward eagerly. He took it from her and unrolled the parchment, tilting it toward the light as he studied it.

A frown marred the smoothness of his brow. "But, Lady Elizabeth . . . the most important part is missing."

"Oh, heavens, I forgot. I separated it yesterday . . ." She broke off, not eager to explain why she had taken such an action. That would lead to talk of Jordan Nash, whom she wished most firmly to put from her mind.

"I see . . ." Nigel said slowly, though she suspected he did nothing of the sort. When he looked at her, his expression had altered slightly.

With a start, Elizabeth realized that he was regarding her warily. Too late she remembered that ladies were not supposed to be clever or farsighted. She had just shown herself to be both.

Since there was nothing to be done about it, she met his gaze calmly. It was in her mind to get the missing piece of the map for him to look at, but before she could do so, Nigel forestalled her.

"Very wise, Lady Elizabeth. There are many unscrupulous people in this part of the world. You do well to be cautious."

"Oh, but I didn't mean to withhold it from you, Mr. Chandler. I only intended to . . ."

He waved her protest aside, apparently convinced she was merely being polite. "I understand your reluctance completely, your ladyship. In your position I would do exactly the same. At any rate, I should be able to evaluate the map from this portion."

Since he seemed determined to misconstrue her motives, Elizabeth gave up the effort to correct him and lapsed into silence while he studied the parchment.

She quickly concluded that whatever hidden character deficiencies he might possess, her new acquaintance was the furthest thing from impetuous. He scrutinized the document thoroughly, evaluating the paper, ink, and writing as rigorously as the indicated route itself.

At length, he looked up and smiled thinly. "I admit to being surprised, Lady Elizabeth. Not for a moment did I imagine your father could have been cheated, but with matters such as this, one never knows for sure. At any rate, I am now convinced this map is genuine.

If the remaining portion is as accurate as what I have already seen, it may very well lead to the lost city of the Mande and the golden idol."

Barely able to contain her excitement, Elizabeth held herself absolutely still as she asked, "Does that mean you would be willing to undertake the expedition?"

"It most certainly does. I would be honored to carry out Sir Alfred's plans. If you will entrust the map to me, I will do my utmost to find the idol and bring it to you, either in Accra, if you wish to remain here, or in England."

"Oh, but . . . I must not have made myself clear. While I realize that I could not possibly lead such an expedition, I certainly intend to be part of it. There will be no need to bring the idol to me anywhere, since I will be with you every step of the way."

Under other circumstances, the young Englishman's expression would have been comical. His mouth dropped open and his pale eyes fairly bulged. He shook himself dazedly, as though trying to throw off a great shock.

"I beg your pardon, your ladyship, but you can't possibly be serious . . ."

"I'm afraid she is," a mocking voice interrupted. "And the sooner you realize that, Chandler, the better for all concerned."

Elizabeth jumped up, the color fading from her face as Jordan Nash strode into the room. The man she had hoped never to have to confront again stared at her boldly, his hard mouth curved in a sardonic smile as his crystal blue eyes ran over her unrelentingly.

"You look in fighting form once again, Elizabeth. Marvelous what a good night's sleep will do for you." Mercilessly, he added, "I'll have to remember that."

Considering that she had never before had the opportunity to be anything other than even-tempered and compliant, Elizabeth was finding she had a remarkably short fuse where the American was concerned.

With no pretext of courtesy, she exclaimed, "There is no reason for you to remember anything! We have nothing to say to each other, Mr. Nash. Good day."

Her scathing rejection left him unmoved. Ignoring the utter lack of welcome, he settled himself in a chair across from Nigel, crossed one long khaki-clad leg over the other and observed the Englishman tauntingly.

"What a coincidence finding you here, Chandler. When I came by earlier and discovered her ladyship's absence, I presumed she was visiting the Wentworths or engaged in some other suitable occupation. How unfortunate that she should have encountered you."

"Mr. Nash!" Elizabeth burst out angrily. "You may feel perfectly free to behave odiously on your own ship, but here such rudeness is not tolerated. Mr. Chandler is my guest, you most certainly are not. If you insist on staying against my expressed wishes, you will at least have the decency to conduct yourself properly."

"There is no reason for him to stay," Nigel declared, rising swiftly to confront Jordan. "His behavior to me is of no account, but a gentleman can hardly stand by and allow a lady to be discomfited. You are leaving, Mr. Nash, whether you wish it or not."

Shocked by Nigel's unexpected and highly inappropriate challenge, Elizabeth sucked in her breath anxiously. The young Englishman was certainly in good shape, but he was nowhere near a match for Jordan.

Not only was the American far larger and more muscular, but he possessed a degree of ruthlessness that made her fear he could kill a man without the slightest hesitation.

Her eyes darted from one man to the other as she

tried to decide how to calm the situation before it erupted into violence. To her astonishment, that proved not to be necessary.

After regarding Nigel steadily for several moments, Jordan responded to the verbal gauntlet with the deep, hearty laugh she had already come to loathe.

"Such chivalry!" he jeered. "Next you will be telling me you will go to any lengths to protect her ladyship *and* her precious map."

His gaze shifted to her, impaling her mercilessly. "You do still have the map? If you'd given it to him already, I'm sure he would have been on his way."

"That's enough," Nigel snapped. "You've already said far too much. I have no doubt as to why you are pursuing her ladyship and I will tell you right now that I have no intention of allowing her to fall into your hands."

"Her ladyship," Jordan parroted mockingly, "might not find that such a terrible fate."

Elizabeth could not listen to anything more. She stormed over to the door and jerked it open. "Get out! You are a despicable, loathsome cur and if you come near me again, I will report you to the colonial authorities. Surely your presence does not have to be tolerated here by me or anyone else."

Nigel gazed at her admiringly, but it was on Jordan that her attention was focused. He stood up leisurely and walked toward her, apparently unperturbed by her denunciation.

"Have it your way, Liz, but be warned. If you go off with this pompous idiot, you'll be heading straight for trouble. Before I get you out of it, you'll have to ask damn nicely."

Wrenching her eyes from him, she stood stone-faced, refusing to acknowledge in the slightest that she heard him or was even aware of his presence.

Jordan shrugged disparagingly. He cast a last mocking glance back at Nigel before ambling out of the room. As he passed Elizabeth, he paused and bent close to her, low enough to speak without the Englishman's being able to overhear.

"I liked you better last night, Liz, when you were all soft and warm in my arms. Remember that when you need my help."

Then he was gone, leaving her to stare after him, wide-eyed with astonishment. Never in her life had she encountered anyone so insufferable and infuriating. Horse whipping was too good for him. He was rude, overbearing, and beneath contempt.

Then why did she catch herself wondering when she would see him again?

Chapter Four

STANDING ON THE DECK OF THE COASTAL STEAMER bound for the mouth of the Volta River, Elizabeth gazed out at the slowly passing vista. In the last few hours, the shoreline had changed dramatically. Upon first leaving Accra the day before, they had passed miles of dense forests that seemed to have no end. Only gradually did she realize that the thick undergrowth was giving way to the savannah that lay on either side of the great river Volta.

Where before there had been an impenetrable wall of massive, vine-draped trees, she could now see long, dark lagoons framed by white sand beaches against which the surf crashed in cream-crested swells.

For almost a week, colonial officials had held up her departure for no better reason than their own reluctance to allow a white woman into the bush. Only when at last, in a burst of uncharacteristic sternness, she reminded them that they had no authority to restrict her movements, were the obstructions to the expedition finally removed.

That, however, did not put an end to the heated

lectures she received from everyone she came in contact with.

The captain of *Britannia's Pride* fairly pleaded with her to remain on board for the return voyage. The Anglican priest who had buried her father made it clear he expected to have to do the same for her if she carried out her crazy scheme. The Wentworths marshaled all their friends to talk some sense into her and were astounded when they failed.

Through it all Nigel had been a bulwark of strength and understanding. After making one attempt to convince her she should not go along, he accepted her determination to do so and did not try again to dissuade her. Instead, he threw himself into the preparations with a vigor she could only applaud.

As busy as she was during the final days in Accra, it did not escape Elizabeth's notice that neither Jordan Nash nor the *Tara* was anywhere in evidence. Her discreet inquiries revealed that he had sailed for parts unknown the morning after their last meeting.

The stab of dismay she felt upon learning he was gone baffled her. If there was ever a man she should want to see the back of, it was the infuriating American. Yet try though she might to convince herself she should be delighted by his departure, she could not shake the sense that they had unfinished business which sooner or later would have to be resolved.

Thankfully, there were far more pleasant matters to occupy her attention. Once the sad job of sorting through her father's belongings was completed, she gave herself up completely to the excitement of the expedition.

An offshore breeze ruffled the strands of hair peeking from beneath her straw bonnet. Her navy serge cape fluttered gently, as did the wide skirt of her matching dress.

The layers of outer clothing, underwear, and corset

kept her body tightly cocooned, so that only her face felt the cooler air. But she was nonetheless invigorated by it.

Everything she saw seemed new and marvelous, perhaps because for the first time she was truly seeing for herself rather than through the filter of her father's domination.

Nigel could barely persuade her to come away from the railing long enough to have an early supper. Only his good-humored coaxing drew her inside.

"I promise the view will still be there when we get back. But meanwhile it will do you no harm to eat a proper meal. Once we get into the bush, decent food will be scarce."

"Surely we have packed ample provisions," she remarked, as he pulled out a chair for her to be seated in the small dining saloon where the few other Europeans making the journey were already eating.

The amount of equipment they were taking along had been the only bone of contention between them. She had insisted the number of bearers they had hired could not possibly manage so great a burden.

Nigel had maintained that to allow them to do less work than was customary would invite laziness and disrespect. Reluctantly, Elizabeth had given in, but only after insisting on an increase in wages.

"I certainly hope so, but it's impossible to be sure. Dried foodstuffs can suddenly start to spoil out here, or be lost in a capsizing canoe or some other accident. But even if they remain edible, their attraction will soon pall. We'll make every effort to shoot fresh meat. However, I wouldn't like to have to count on a hunt being successful."

"I'm sure you're an excellent shot. But even if you weren't, there doesn't seem to be any lack of food among the natives. Perhaps they could show us where to find it."

About to swallow a spoonful of curry-flavored chicken stew, Nigel paused. "Forgive me, Lady Elizabeth, but what you are suggesting would be highly inappropriate. It isn't possible for us to learn anything from the natives. We are, after all, the superior race. The responsibility for teaching and guiding is ours."

"The white man's burden?"

"Why yes, I suppose Kipling did put it best. The Creator saw fit to endow us with certain qualities he did not give to other people. So we must do our best to help those less fortunate."

"I've heard that same explanation for colonialism many times before, but I must confess I still don't fully understand it. Weren't there native peoples living in this area long before white men came here?"

"Of course."

"Then doesn't that mean they were able to get along perfectly well without our help? From what I can see, they've provided for themselves and their children more than amply without our assistance."

Nigel smiled indulgently. He put down his spoon and set himself to the task of clarifying the matter in terms a woman might be able to understand.

"There can be no doubt that the natives have attained a marginal standard of living. However, their inherent limitations are such that left to themselves they can exist only on the most primitive level. All the finer expressions of civilization—art, music, philosophy—are denied them."

Elizabeth looked at him doubtfully. "I thought the Ashantes and other tribes in this area were very religious. Isn't that a form of philosophy?"

"Yes, I suppose it could be considered that way. But the natives here are Moslem. They only adopted the teachings of a more advanced race."

"You mean they were without religion before then?"

Nigel nodded disparagingly. "Oh, they had some sort of pagan beliefs, but that can hardly be considered."

"I understood they worshipped a deity called Nyame, whose attributes don't really seem all that different from those of our own god."

Putting down his fork, Nigel stared at her in amazement. "Where on earth did you hear that?"

A bit reluctantly, Elizabeth admitted, "I read it in a book."

"And what else did this learned treatise have to say?"

"Only that the Ashantes believe each person is born with a *ntoro* or spirit that is a tiny portion of the Creator imparted to every individual. That struck me as a rather lovely thought."

"Anything else?"

"Not on the subject of religion. There doesn't seem to be a great deal of information about that, perhaps because we Europeans have no interest in the beliefs of other people. But the author did mention that the Ashantes have a very well-developed government headquartered at their capital in Kumasi, where the Asantehene rules over them all. He sounds rather like our own sovereign."

A low laugh broke from Nigel as he shook his head disbelievingly. "Forgive me for speaking bluntly, Lady Elizabeth, but I can't imagine anyone having been more misled about the state of affairs here. I've spent the last two years in this part of the world and I can assure you the Ashantes and all the other African tribes are nothing but a pack of savages. They're ignorant, benighted pagans who, left to themselves, live little better than animals. It's up to us, as the superior race, to rescue them from their spiritual wasteland."

"Is that what we are doing here, rescuing them?"

"Of course. Why else would we be here?"

"To make money?"

Nigel's eyebrows shot up. He could not suppress a stern response. "Lady Elizabeth, I must say again that you have severely misunderstood the situation. Considering the terrible risk we run in coming out here and the trials we endure to try to help our less fortunate brethren, I don't believe anyone could begrudge us a few small comforts. No amount of payment could ever compensate for the benefits of civilization which we bring. What we receive in return is little enough."

Elizabeth glanced down at her plate. Tempted though she was to pursue the topic, she knew it would not be wise to do so. The result could only be contention between them at a time when they needed to work together comfortably. Nonetheless, she could not help but think that Nigel had severely understated the vast wealth Africa was giving up.

How many hundreds of thousands of human beings had been shipped to foreign lands during the terrible days of the slave trade? How many tons of gold and precious stones adorned the elite of Europe and the Americas? How much sheer blood, sweat and toil went to fill the insatiable appetite for raw materials needed to fuel the industries of the mother country?

Nigel spoke of civilization where before there had been none. Perhaps he was right. Yet her instincts told her that men like the Ashante warrior Osei, whose fierce pride and intelligence still lingered in her memory, were hardly the deprived primitives some wished to believe.

Beyond the narrow confines of the colonial foothold, she sensed there was a vast, teeming land full of wonders that only a handful of whites had ever seen. Her determination to be one of that lucky few became even greater as the steamer made its way around the sandbars and shifting mudbanks that marked the delta of the river Volta to dock at the trading village of Ada, which would be her jumping-off point into the secret heart of Africa.

Even at the height of the dry season, the river cut an impressive swath through the bush that framed both banks. Along either side of it were thatched huts raised up on stilts. Nearby were the fields where rice, sorghum, millet, maize, and yams would be cultivated later in the year after the rains had come. Small herds of goats, sheep, and dwarf cattle could be seen. They were among the few domesticated animals that lived in an area infested by the dread tsetse fly, and as such they were regarded as precious.

Numerous canoes were clustered around the dock. Elizabeth supposed the smaller ones were used for fishing on the lagoons, while the massive, thirty-foot-long craft served for journeys upriver.

A large crowd had gathered to see the steamer arrive. She hastily averted her eyes from the bare-breasted women who clothed only the lower halves of their bodies in swathes of brilliant blue, green, yellow, and red fabric. The children wore even less, both boys and girls running about naked.

The older men favored a garment similar to Roman togas, draped over the left shoulder and allowed to fall loosely to midcalf. But the young warriors strutted about clad only in breechcloths with weapons draped over broad shoulders that bore elaborate tattoo marks.

Some of the warriors carried a huge green parasol beneath which an immensely dignified old man stood waiting.

"That's the village chief," Nigel explained. "Technically, we have to ask his permission before we can embark on the river. But that won't be any problem since we've brought plenty of presents to sweeten his disposition."

Elizabeth hoped he was right. The chief looked

harmless enough, but the heavy gold bracelets and chains adorning his body and the gold-leaf crown on his head signified that he was a man of considerable wealth. Their presents just might not come up to snuff.

As they left the steamer, the crowd closed in around them, forming a chanting, dancing escort. Elizabeth quickly found herself the object of great curiosity and speculation. The women were clearly bewildered by her appearance. A few made tentative efforts to touch her, but relented when it became obvious she did not welcome their overtures.

Nigel did his best to protect her, but in the press of humanity it was near to impossible. By the time they reached the chief, her knees were shaking and her throat was dry.

As the bundles were unpacked the crowd began to ooh and aah. Among the assortment of clothing, tools, adornments, and the copper wire used as currency, the clear favorite was the half-dozen umbrellas opened with great flourish and presented to the chief and his top advisers.

Though they looked ugly next to the gaily decorated parasols, the ease with which they could be collapsed caught everyone's fancy. Elizabeth was willing to bet that within a few days the struts would be broken from constant use, but it was unlikely anyone would mind. The amused looks she caught made it clear their offerings were viewed as nothing more than toys.

Beside the chief stood a tall, somber-faced young man holding a gilded wand that was the badge of his office as linguist. When the initial excitement had died down a bit, he stepped forward and addressed Nigel.

"Chief Nana Kofi Adahene welcomes you. The talking drums have brought word of your expedition and of the white woman with you."

The translator glanced at Elizabeth before matter-of-factly inquiring, "Is there truly a female under all those clothes?"

Such frank curiosity made her gasp. Nigel stepped in quickly to ease the situation. "Lady Elizabeth is the daughter of Sir Alfred Derrick, a great British historian who longed to explore your land. Tragically, he died before the expedition could begin. Out of respect for him, her ladyship has decided to continue his quest."

When this was explained to the chief, the old man nodded sagely. "It is good for children to honor their parents. But is there no son to undertake this effort?"

When Elizabeth understood the question, she shook her head, a gesture which needed no translation. The chief smiled sympathetically. "Then I suppose the daughter will have to do. Good luck to her and to you all."

That was the signal for the visitors to be taken off to guest huts where they would rest until embarking on the river the following day. Elizabeth was initially relieved to discover that separate quarters had been provided for her, but that relief faded as she discovered privacy did not quite make up for the apprehension she felt at being separated from the others.

Nigel seemed to think nothing of it, clearly presuming her modesty would be offended by any other arrangement. But as she stepped inside her hut, she found herself wishing social decorum could have been at least temporarily overlooked.

Glancing around warily, she was relieved to see that the packed dirt floor was swept free of debris and covered with clean mats. A small cot had been set up for her. Beside it was the valise holding her change of clothes and a bucket of water.

Much as she longed to strip off her sticky garments and bath herself thoroughly, she did not dare do so. Only a cloth flap protected her from anyone who might be passing by.

Reluctantly, she had to be satisfied with removing her cape and shoes. Stretched out on the cot, she tried vainly to rest. Tomorrow, she would need every bit of strength she could muster. But even knowing that, sleep would not come.

As night settled over the village, she discovered that all her half-formed ideas about what the African bush would be like were wrong.

To begin with, it wasn't quiet. Barely had darkness descended when a veritable cacophony of hoots, whistles, thrills, chirps, and howls filled the air. She could cope well enough with those; it was the ominous rustles and slithers that made her heart thump wildly.

Every story she had ever heard about wild beasts passed through her mind. Was that a lion she heard roaring not more than a few feet away? Could a snake crawl up the legs of her cot? Did poisonous insects move about at night, waiting to bite the unwary?

As though the noise weren't enough, the heat was remorseless. Beneath her heavy clothes, her body itched and prickled. Her whalebone corset had become an instrument of torture.

Far into the night, Elizabeth at last gave up. Rising shakily, she stripped off her dress and removed the restrictive garment before reclothing herself. Justifying such boldness on the grounds that some concessions had to be made to her surroundings, she managed to drift into an uneasy sleep that ended before dawn when the village once again came to life.

After swallowing the daily dose of quinine, which was her only protection against the ever-present threat of malaria, she smoothed the wrinkles from her clothes as best she could and rewound her hair into a neat bun. Determined to ignore her weariness, she left the hut and glanced around curiously. Though it was still early, everyone was already hard at work.

Groups of men were departing to fish in the lagoons, leaving behind women busy pounding maize and millet gathered during the last harvest. Children were scampering around, the littlest ones playing; the older boys and girls helping their elders by looking after the precious livestock.

Near the center of the village compound, she found Nigel enjoying breakfast while talking with the headman who would be in charge of their bearers.

"Good morning," he said, rising as she joined them. "Sleep well?"

"Off and on." Elizabeth peered into the pot dubiously. "What's that?"

"Breakfast."

"Could you be more specific?"

"I rather think it would be better if I weren't. Let's just say it's nourishing and practically tasteless."

"I'm really not hungry."

"Uh . . . actually it would be a good idea to find your appetite. You see our breakfast was prepared by one of the chief's wives." He grinned apologetically. "Wouldn't do to insult the cuisine."

Elizabeth sighed resignedly. Seating herself on the stump of a tree, she accepted a small hollowed-out gourd full of the white mushy substance. There were no spoons, but her finger proved adept enough.

With some difficulty, she managed to swallow a mouthful, only to discover that whatever she was eating really wasn't bad. When she said as much, Nigel gazed at her admiringly.

"I must say, your ladyship, you're holding up very well. The pundits in Accra who believed you'd come scampering back are in for a disappointment."

"Was there really much speculation about that?"

"It went a bit further than mere conjecture," Nigel admitted sheepishly. "I suppose there's no harm in telling you now that a betting pool was actually formed at the Club based on exactly how long you would last out here."

Whatever Elizabeth was eating went down the wrong way. She coughed and was forced to set the bowl aside carefully. Whatever doubts her restless night had given her abruptly vanished. Not for anything in the world would she slink back to Accra and let her smugly pompous critics believe they had been right.

"I hope," she said steadily, "that you are not involved in this wagering, Mr. Chandler."

The merest suspicion of a smile curved his mouth. "My money has been on you from the beginning, your ladyship."

A soft sigh of relief escaped her. "I am delighted to hear it. Now shall we forget about our fellow countrymen and get on to the matter at hand?"

Nigel agreed at once, clearly glad to drop the subject. He introduced the headman, Kwesi, an Ashante who was almost as large and powerfully built as Jordan Nash's friend and who possessed an innate air of command vital to anyone who aspired to lead other men.

If Kwesi thought it strange that a white woman would not only be going along on the expedition but would also possess the most vital part of the map, he kept his opinions to himself. In her presence, he was dignified and correct.

Elizabeth realized at once that it would be a mistake to think of him as a servant, something Nigel didn't seem to appreciate. The headman was clearly accustomed to both wielding authority and shouldering responsibility.

Which was just as well considering that once they left the village, their survival would be in his hands. Notwithstanding all of Nigel's pronouncements to the contrary, in the bush they would be the weaker race, as ill-suited to the rigors of their environment as Kwesi or someone like him would be if plunked down in the middle of Kensington or Mayfair.

Their utter dependency on the Ashante did not seem to trouble Nigel in the least. Yet studying the imperturbable black man, Elizabeth could not help but wonder exactly what they were letting themselves in for.

A strange sense of foreboding moved through her as she watched the dozen or so bearers loading their supplies into the canoes. Something about the men caught her attention, but it took a while to figure out the precise cause of her discomfort.

Drawing Nigel aside, she said, "Does it strike you at all odd that every one of the men who will be coming with us is Ashante?"

Startled, he shook his head. "Wherever did you get that idea?"

"Because they all have the same kind of tattoos on their shoulders as the warriors here in the village."

"Do they? By Jove, I hadn't noticed. Well yes, now that you point it out, I guess they are all from the same tribe. But that isn't surprising. After all, it only stands to reason that Kwesi would hire his relatives and friends for the job. Keep it in the family, so to speak."

The explanation was so reasonable that Elizabeth felt a rush of embarrassment over her suspicions, ill-formed as they were. Without further comment, she allowed one of the bearers to assist her into the first canoe where, after some considerable effort, she managed to confine her cumbersome skirts sufficiently to sit down.

Moments later, all was ready. Kwesi shouted an order. The rhythmic beat of drums set the pace for the rowers who quickly moved the canoes out into deeper water.

As the crowd on the dock cheered, Elizabeth took a final glance at the Union Jack flying over the coastal steamer, knowing it was the last reminder of home she would have for a long time.

The drums sounded more urgently, the canoes picked up speed, and the shouts of the villagers drifted away on the wind. She turned her gaze upriver and did not look back.

For three days they remained on the river, traveling through all the daylight hours and stopping to camp only when darkness finally overcame them.

Elizabeth quickly became inured to constant dampness, cramped legs, and enervating weariness caused by the unrelenting heat and the remorseless barrage of sights and sounds.

She had passed into a world that bore no relationship whatsoever to anything she knew. Time itself seemed to take on a different meaning as hour drifted into hour and day merged with day in a seamless flow.

Only a few events stood out in her mind. As the expedition rounded a bend in the river, they came upon a troupe of monkeys that fled back into the protection of the trees, hurling shrill insults behind them.

Early the first evening, they encountered a herd of rhinoceros cooling themselves in the mud along the riverbank. The massive beasts were unlike anything Elizabeth had ever seen. She found their slow, ponderous movements fascinating and would have liked to observe them at length. But Kwesi kept the canoes moving onward to the landfall where they could camp with relative safety.

Waking the next morning, after a stiflingly hot night in her tiny tent, she stumbled out to find an elephant nibbling placidly at a clump of leaves only a few yards away. It rolled a huge eye at her before apparently deciding she was not worth its notice and returning to its snack.

The sheer abundance and variety of life astonished her. Her neck began to ache from being so constantly swiveled back and forth. While Nigel's interest in the flora and fauna extended no further than whatever might supplement their food stores, Elizabeth was enthralled by everything.

Even the normally taciturn Kwesi unbent enough to enjoy her enthusiasm. Late on the third day, just before landfall, he signaled for silence and drew her attention to a magnificent leopard drinking at the water's edge.

As she stared in fascination, she became aware of the headman watching her. For just an instant it seemed that his imperturbable look gave way to a flicker of regret.

Elizabeth told herself she must have imagined it. He could hardly be considered responsible for the fact that she sweltered night and day in her heavy clothes, that insects feasted on what small portion of her skin was exposed, or that she was so tired even the effort of eating was almost too much for her.

If he had simply shown concern, she would have understood. After all, an expedition moved only as quickly as its slowest member. If her strength gave out, she would hold them back. But regret made no sense.

Long after they camped for the night, Elizabeth continued to dwell on what she thought she had seen. Her exhausted mind must be tricking her. She was giving far too much importance to what in all likelihood had never even occurred.

Yet the feeling would not go away. As she began her preparations for bed, it grew within her steadily. Washing out the heavy navy-blue dress she was rapidly coming to hate, she thought of other unexplained incidences that had struck her during their days on the river.

As foolish as it sounded, she had several times wondered if they were being followed. How else to explain why she kept seeing the same three warriors popping up at various points along their route to observe them from the riverbank?

Though she was tempted to mention it to Nigel, she held off. Like every other European she had so far met, he shared the belief that all natives looked essentially alike. He would never accept the notion that she could identify three individuals seen for only a few moments at a distance.

Laying out the gray dress she would wear the next day, she shook her head wearily. The journey was proving far more arduous than she had imagined. A life lacking in all indulgence had made her fitter than many other women. But she was nonetheless ill-equipped for the rigors of the bush.

Ruefully, she admitted that her clothes could not be less appropriate to the environment. Because of them, more even than the journey itself, she was beginning to experience real physical discomfort.

If only there was someone she could turn to for guidance. But Nigel—being a proper English gentleman—would be acutely embarrassed by any mention of her bodily needs, and there was no one else she could even think of approaching.

Common sense decreed that modesty had to give way to self-preservation. By keeping the flap of her tent securely closed, despite the lack of fresh air that caused, she could justify sleeping in only her pantaloons and camisole.

Lying down on her cot, Elizabeth folded her arms beneath her head and stared up at the canvas ceiling of her tent. The night sounds that had at first been so terrifying were already comfortably familiar. Though she was hot, worn out, and aching in every muscle, she managed at last to slip into sleep.

Her rest did not last long. The pale silver moon had barely sunk below the tops of the trees when something startled her into wakefulness. She sat bolt upright, listening intently.

Nothing. She must have imagined it. An impatient sigh escaped her. About to lie down again, she stopped. The sound came again, this time closer and more clearly.

Someone was moving around right outside her tent. Very carefully, Elizabeth swung her legs off the cot and stood up. It was probably just one of the bearers making a necessary trip into the bushes, or an animal searching for scraps left over from dinner. But it did no harm to check.

Cautiously untying the flap, she opened it just an inch and peered out. She could make out the shape of Nigel's tent on the opposite side of the encampment and the bundles of supplies suspended by nets from the trees to keep them from animals.

But where were Kwesi and the bearers? They customarily slept around the campfire, but though she strained her eyes to see through the darkness, there was no sign of them.

Had she and Nigel been abandoned in the bush to fend for themselves? The mere thought was enough to make fear tighten her throat, but she rejected it quickly. If Kwesi had intended such a treacherous action, he would certainly have taken the supplies with him. As it was, only the men were missing.

Or so she thought. As she let the flap open a bit more, a shape suddenly came at her out of the darkness. Elizabeth did not even have a chance to scream before she was roughly seized in a grip of steel as a hard hand slammed down over her nose and mouth, cutting off all air to her lungs.

She fought vainly through long, terrifying moments until blackness began to close in around her and she felt herself sinking helplessly down a long echoing tunnel into unconsciousness.

When she came to, she was lying on the hard ground with her hands tied behind her and her ankles bound together. There was a throbbing pain in her head and her chest ached from the effort to breath.

So great was her shock at finding herself in such a state that it did not at first occur to her that she was still clad only in her camisole and pantaloons. When it did so, a horrified gasp broke from her.

It was bad enough that she should be so exposed beneath the cloak of darkness. But while she was unconscious, torches had been lit in the camp, fully revealing her to the gaze of anyone who happened by.

Tears of mortification burned her eyes. She tried to turn over, to at least hide the shape of her breasts, but found that she could not. She was too tightly bound even to move.

Her efforts to conceal herself roused the attention of the man beside her. Struggling to raise his head, Nigel called to her. "Lady Elizabeth . . ."

"What? Oh, Nigel, not you too! Whatever is happening to us?"

"I don't know, but whatever it is that scoundrel Kwesi is behind it. He came into my tent and trapped me while I was asleep."

His petulant, almost whining tone grated on her already overstrained nerves. She winced, glad that the darkness at least hid that much.

"Do you have any idea why he should do such an outrageous thing?"

"No, but the man must be a fool if he thinks he can get away with it. The colonial authorities won't stand for this for an instant. He'll be hunted down like a dog and hung in the Accra square. I only hope I'm there to see it."

Even under the circumstances, the extreme hatred and vengefulness she heard in his voice was a shock. Swiftly, Elizabeth said, "Please don't talk about people dying, not even whoever is responsible for this. Let's just concentrate on getting away alive."

Nigel shook his head angrily and looked about to launch into a bloodthirsty tirade when the sudden appearance of the headman silenced him. As Elizabeth turned bright red with embarrassment, Kwesi knelt down beside her and regarded her steadily.

"Your advice is sound, Lady Elizabeth, but ill-founded. There will be no escape."

Staring into the impenetrable black eyes she struggled to speak. "Why . . . how could you . . . what is to be gained by this?"

Kwesi laughed. "A great deal. Didn't anyone tell you that the Ashantes are the slave dealers of Africa? In centuries gone by, we sold war captives to the whites. Now we sell to the Arabs, and a few other discerning buyers who know the worth of our merchandise."

As the full import of his words sunk in, Elizabeth turned ashen. Embarrassment, shock, disbelief all fled before the overwhelming horror suddenly thrust before her. "Y-you intend to *sell* us?"

The headman grinned heartlessly. "I wish I could, but who would buy an idiot Englishman like Mr. Chandler? He is of no use. You, on the other hand . . ."

A lean black finger reached out to gently brush aside the heavy weight of her hair that had fallen across her face. Very softly, he promised, "You will bring an excellent price, enough to keep the families of every man here in comfort for several years."

Nigel had heard enough. Struggling futilely against his bonds, he screamed, "You bastard! Call me an idiot, will you, when you're the one who's criminally stupid. No one would dare purchase an English noblewoman in this day and age when the consequences of such infamy are only too clear. You've slit your throat for nothing, and I shall greatly enjoy watching you bleed to death!"

Far from being angered by the outburst, Kwesi merely shrugged dismissively. "Your concern about the success of my business venture is appreciated, Mr. Chandler. However, be assured I do not take risks imprudently. A buyer has already been found for her ladyship. He awaits her right now."

A despairing sob broke from Elizabeth, only to be stifled instantly as her pride came to the fore. She did not make another sound as she was yanked to her feet and tossed over Kwesi's broad shoulder.

Her long, unbound hair trailed into the dust, obscuring her vision. Nigel's curses faded behind her as she was carried swiftly across the campsite. New voices penetrated the haze of her shock and horror, the deep voices of men who broke off their conversation as Kwesi approached.

"Here she is," the headman announced, dropping her unceremoniously onto the ground. "More or less in one piece, as promised."

"You've done an excellent job. My thanks."

Fighting against the waves of terror that threatened to engulf her, Elizabeth hesitantly pushed her hair aside and raised her head. Her heart was pounding wildly and her breath caught in her throat as she took in the sight of dusty brown boots set firmly apart, with khaki trousers tucked into their tops.

Biting her lower lip, she forced herself to raise her eyes further, taking in the expanse of long, sinewy legs, narrow hips, and a taut waist that widened into a powerful chest and shoulders.

Heedless of the bright rim of blood blossoming against her small white teeth, she dared to look upon the face of this man who had just purchased her as his slave.

Jordan Nash met her gaze unflinchingly, a rakish grin on his rugged face and an unholy gleam in his remorseless eyes.

Chapter Five

"You!"

"In the flesh, my lady. Although not to quite the same degree as yourself." Bending down beside her, Jordan let his eyes run over her slender body appraisingly. "Quite a fetching outfit, Liz. You must wear it more often."

"You despicable, loathsome, vile . . ."

"Now, now, Liz, get a grip on yourself. I realize events have taken an unexpected turn, but where's that stiff-lipped English propriety we hear so much about?"

Trussed up as she was, she had only words to give vent to her extreme sense of outrage. Without pausing to wonder how such appellations had crept into her vocabulary, she blurted, "You cur! Miscreant! Swine!"

"That's enough," Jordan said sternly. "This happens to be a largely Moslem country and they don't take kindly to anyone's being likened to a pig. Besides," he added, picking her up despite her fierce efforts to twist away, "women are expected to be compliant and submissive, and slaves even more so. If you don't start behaving right now, I'll be forced to thrash you just to preserve my honor."

"Honor! A jackass has more honor! You're nothing but a . . ."

Whatever Elizabeth meant to say was never uttered as without warning Jordan brought his mouth down on hers, silencing her in the most effective way possible.

She was dimly aware of the approving laughter of the other men witnessing her humiliation. But all thought of them faded before the onslaught of what was happening to her. Having never before felt the touch of another's lips against her own, she was totally unprepared for their effect.

Waves of heat and cold surged through her. What little strength remained in her drained away. A treacherous languor spread from the tips of her bare toes to the top of her tousled head.

The unbridled rage his effrontery had sparked turned to cinders on the fire of a far different blaze. She moaned deep in her throat, helpless to prevent the sound. As though of their own accord, her lips parted beneath his, becoming soft and pliant to his touch.

Jordan growled hungrily. The sight of her nearly naked and utterly vulnerable on the ground at his feet had stirred a fierce desire he could scarcely credit. It contrasted sharply with the sudden upsurge of protectiveness that made him want to shelter her from all who might hurt her, even himself.

For the first time in his highly eventful life, he genuinely regretted the morals he could not shed. While they might not be as rigid as the principles other men claimed to follow, they had served him well so far and he was not about to abandon them.

That did not mean, however, that they couldn't be bent a little.

Striding across the encampment, he entered Elizabeth's tent and dumped her on the cot. Towering over her, hands on his lean hips, he smiled mockingly.

"I might have known you'd be a fighter, Liz. All the better. No man wants an easy conquest."

Stunned by the overwhelming effect of his kiss, she said the first thing that came into her mind. "Don't call me Liz!"

"Who's to stop me? After all, I own you now."

"No one can own another person!"

" 'Course they can. Happens all the time out here. Especially to women."

That brought her up short. She was only too aware that he was right. For their own self-interest, colonial authorities turned a blind eye to the trade in human beings that went on all around them. Even in the supposedly enlightened year of 1890, so long as those put up for sale were black or brown, no one cared.

But she was white, for heaven's sake, and the daughter of an English lord. This couldn't be happening to her!

When she said as much to Jordan, his amusement only increased. "But it has happened, Liz. I paid mighty well for you and I intend to get my money's worth."

Without giving her a chance to respond, he sat down beside her on the cot and looked her over unabashedly. "You're a hot-tempered little thing and for all that touch-me-not air you affect, there's passion in you. This just may turn out to not be a bad bargain after all."

A despairing gasp broke from her as he suddenly leaned forward, trapping her between his powerful arms and quickly pinning her beneath him.

As his mouth moved again to claim hers, he murmured, "It can't be very comfortable for you to lie on your hands like that. So suppose we agree that you won't fight me and in return I'll untie you?"

"Never! I'll never stop fighting you, you . . ."

"I believe we've already covered my character quite thoroughly. It's time for pleasanter things."

So saying, he took her mouth without the slightest concession to her innocence. Caught unawares, Elizabeth was stunned by the sudden piercing thrust of his tongue. Not even his first kiss had prepared her for the devastating sensations he now provoked. They both repulsed and thrilled her.

His invasion was so complete that for long moments she could not even think to resist him. He was free to savor her fully, probing the moist sweetness without hesitation.

Only when her abhorrence gave way to shocking pleasure did she abruptly return to her senses and begin to fight in earnest.

Bound as she was, there was little she could do. Jordan lifted his head long enough to laugh at her efforts before returning to savor the prize that lay so helplessly before him. Or so he thought. When sharp little teeth snapped down on him, he realized just how wrong he could be.

"Ouch! You little hellcat, that hurt!"

"Too bad," Elizabeth muttered coldly, trying hard to look as though she felt nothing but disgust at his actions. "You deserved it."

Jordan stared at her narrowly. Part of him admired her courage and resistance. But another, primitively male part felt only rage. How dare she challenge him when she was utterly at his mercy and powerless to prevent anything he might chose to do.

"You think so?" he growled. "Then you can't complain if in return I treat you as I see fit."

Before she could even attempt to move, his burnished hands lashed out. Seized just beneath her breasts, she was jerked face down onto his lap. Holding her in place with one arm, he undid the cord from around her hands long enough to yank them in front of her where they were swiftly resecured.

"Now, my lady, you are in for a salutary lesson on what happens to slaves who dare to resist their masters."

Without pausing to think about the full enormity of what he was doing, Jordan pulled down her white cotton pantaloons. He barely paused to notice how lovely she was before his open hand struck her softly rounded bottom.

A loud crack resounded through the tent, accompanied by a strangled yelp of shock and pain. About to bring his hand down again, Jordan hesitated. Hard on the release of his anger came shame that he could hurt someone so much weaker.

Even as he tried to tell himself she had brought about her own punishment, he knew he could not continue it. As his arm lowered again, his fingers spread out over her reddened flesh, unconsciously caressing the curve of her buttocks and upper thighs.

His touch was gentle, his expression bemused. He could not remember ever before feeling so intensely and contradictorily about any woman, much less a slip of a girl who didn't have the common sense God gave a gnat.

Suddenly impatient with both himself and her, he jerked his hand away and pulled both Elizabeth and her pantaloons upright until she stood facing him. "Why did you have to come out here anyway? Didn't you realize the trouble you were asking for?"

Elizabeth stared back at him blankly. Luminous with unshed tears, her sea-green eyes appeared enormous in her ashen face. The stupefying impact of his actions had driven out all emotion. She was beyond anger or fear, beyond even the most fundamental instinct of self-preservation.

Since earliest childhood, no one had seen her unclothed except herself. No other's hands had touched her bare skin. She had existed behind a wall of prudery so complete as to become part of her.

With that wall suddenly rent in two, sensations she had never before so much as imagined poured in upon her. She was engulfed by emotions she could not identify, choked by feelings she could not put a name to, smothered by yearnings she could hardly credit.

Such an onslaught was great enough to overcome even her valiant spirit. Instinctively, Elizabeth retreated into herself, seeking some quiet corner of her mind where she could regain her composure and recover her strength.

Jordan stared down at her with growing concern. He realized what was happening and knew he had to stop it immediately.

Gripping her shoulders beneath the thin straps of the camisole, he shook her hard. "It won't work, Liz. I won't let you get away like this. You have to face up to what's happening whether you want to or not."

When she still did not respond, he lowered her onto the cot and swiftly undid her hands and feet. Dipping his bandana into the pail of water beside the cot and gently bathing her ashen face, he murmured, "Listen to me, Liz. Those men out there regard you as my property now. Not one of them will dare to touch you. Just go along with me and you'll come through this fine."

The words were not as gentle as he had intended, but it was his tone that really mattered. The genuine regret he felt was unmistakable. It penetrated even the cocoon of shock enveloping her.

She blinked, her eyes refocusing as she stared at him dazedly. "Jordan . . ."

"That's my girl. Just take it easy. Everything will be okay."

"W-why . . . why did you hit me?"

A dull flush suffused his high-boned cheeks. "All I did was spank you. There's a difference." He wasn't clear what the distinction might be, but he couldn't bear the thought that he had struck a woman. Defensively, he said, "Hasn't anyone ever tanned your bottom before?"

Elizabeth shook her head. His nearness and the gentleness of his touch as he continued to bathe her face made it impossible for her to respond more lucidly.

"Well, maybe if somebody had, you wouldn't be so headstrong and impulsive. That idiot Chandler should have his head examined for agreeing to bring you along."

Nigel. She had forgotten all about him. Was he still lying out there trussed up like a chicken for the roasting or had he been . . . ? "What are you going to do with him?"

Jordan frowned. He didn't much care for her obvious anxiousness about the other man. Reluctantly, he said, "Not what I'd like to. He'll have to come along with us, otherwise he'd just go scampering back to Accra and alert the colonial authorities to what's going on."

Sitting up shakily, Elizabeth forced herself to meet his gaze. So softly that he had to lean forward to hear her, she asked, "What *is* going on?"

"The search for the golden idol of the Mande, of course. Your father was right about its existence, although I didn't realize that until I learned he'd bought Davies' map." Standing up, Jordan glanced around the small tent. "Where is it?"

"W-where is what . . .?"

"The map, of course. And don't try to pretend you

haven't got it. The only reason Chandler brought you along was because he couldn't get the map any other way."

"I don't know what you're talking about. You made such fun of the map that I decided it must be worthless so I got rid of it."

"Elizabeth, I am not a particularly patient man. Stop this nonsense and tell me where it is."

"Mr. Nash, I have already pointed out to you that you do not have permission to address me so familiarly. Kindly desist from doing so."

"Liz, you managed to address me as Jordan a few moments ago. Kindly continue doing so. Unless you prefer what is after all a more appropriate form of address, namely 'master.' "

"Master! Why, you overblown lout! If you think for one moment that I'll . . ."

Not at all displeased by her outrage, which he greatly preferred to the dejection he had briefly sensed in her, Jordan grinned infuriatingly. "Your vocabulary will have to be broadened if you expect to set me back on my heels. Let's see now, what could you call me? Most of the phrases I can think of are too harsh for your dulcet tones." He considered for a moment before cheerfully suggesting, "How about son-of-a-bitch?"

"Son of . . . I most certainly will not call you that!"

"Why not?"

Loath to admit that she was simply too imbued with decency to do so, Elizabeth took refuge in dissembling. "Because," she informed him tartly, "I am unacquainted with your mother and therefore can make no judgment as to her character."

A deep chuckle began in Jordan's burnished throat, visible through the open collar of his khaki shirt. It spread upward quickly, emerging as a full-blown laugh. When he was at last able to speak again, he said, "Fair enough. I'll make you a deal. I'll tell you about my mother and you tell me about the map."

Since she suspected there was little chance of keeping the parchment from him, Elizabeth agreed, but with a stipulation. "You first."

The delectable picture she made predisposed Jordan to agree. Her hair tumbled around her creamy shoulders, half veiling, half revealing the ripe curve of her breasts, her narrow waist, and the swell of her slender hips. Her legs were long and slim, ending in delicately curved calves and ankles.

Since seeing her on the boat, he had known she was far lovelier than the image she presented to the world. But alone with her in the tent, his sense of proprietorship was asserting itself.

Whether she cared to admit it or not, she belonged to him. While the remnants of her shock kept her from realizing the full extent of her deshabille and taking steps to remedy it, he intended to enjoy the sight of his newest and certainly most interesting possession.

Seating himself on a camp stool, he set himself to satisfy her curiosity. "My mother lives in Boston where she manages half-a-dozen charities and a good chunk of what passes for polite society."

His eyes were gentle as he added, "Considering that she first set foot in the new world when she was fifteen, after traveling from Ireland in steerage, she hasn't done too badly for herself. Father's family was mortified when he insisted on marrying the woman they thought he should have kept only as a mistress. But her proclivity for producing healthy sons and daughters won them over."

Despite herself, Elizabeth could not refrain from asking, "How many did she have?"

"Eight, including me. Two of my brothers help my father run the family's shipbuilding and trading business, two others are involved in railroads, and one owns a steel mill. My sisters are both married, one to a pillar of the New York community and the other, Kathleen—who has the misfortune to be most like me—to a former gunfighter turned Texas rancher." Barely pausing for breath, he demanded, "Now will you tell me where the map is?"

"Wait a minute. You can't just start to describe your family and then break off. They sound fascinating."

"They're wonderful and on my trips home we all get along splendidly. However, right now I have far more pressing concerns. The map . . ."

Elizabeth hesitated. His large and obviously loving family was so different from anything she had known that she wanted to hear much more about it. But she sensed he had said all he was going to, at least for the moment.

"It's in my valise, in a metal cylinder."

Jordan moved quickly to open the bag and retrieve the map. As he glanced at it, his face darkened ominously. "The most important part is missing. What happened to it?"

"I . . . I cut it in two before I went to see you on board the *Tara*. I thought if I could interest you in leading the expedition, it wouldn't be a good idea to give you the entire map. Otherwise, you would simply leave me behind."

"So when I refused to have anything to do with the venture, you used the same ploy with Chandler?"

She nodded reluctantly. It was impossible to discern his thoughts, but she guessed he wasn't amused. In an effort to make him understand, she said, "I could think of no other way to ensure that the expedition would not proceed without me."

"And you were bound and determined not to let that happen?"

Elizabeth raised her head, meeting his eyes unflinchingly. "For the first time in my life, I had a chance to do something just for myself, and no one was going to rob me of it."

Jordan sighed. He ran a hand over his face wearily. Her determination was admirable, but nonetheless foolhardy. "Did it ever occur to you that you might be placing yourself in grave danger?"

"I knew the journey would be strenuous . . ."

"That's an understatement, but not what I was referring to. I meant that your insistence in going along on the expedition made you an easy target for any unscrupulous person who wanted to take advantage of your helplessness."

The look she shot him made it clear who she thought was a more likely candidate for such behavior. "Think the worst of me if it makes you feel any better," he snapped, "but I only have your welfare in mind. If I could, I'd send you straight back to Accra. Unfortunately, you'd cause as much trouble there as Chandler, so you'll have to come along. But I'll do everything possible to keep you safe."

"How touching," Elizabeth snapped. "From what I've seen of your protection so far, I would be better off entrusting myself to a pit of vipers."

She didn't mean to speak quite so harshly, but the full import of her situation was only beginning to sink in and it shook her to the core.

She was alone with a man who operated outside all the rules and boundaries of the only world she knew. A man who clearly preferred the society of those she had been raised to regard as savages. Who seemed perfectly at home in a wild, untamed land. Who didn't hesitate to go after what he wanted, whether a treasure map, a golden idol, or a woman.

He frightened her badly, almost as much as she was beginning to frighten herself.

"Vipers?" Jordan repeated. "Is that what you think? Well, far be it from me to disappoint you."

Rising, he crossed the tent in a single stride and loomed over her. "Let's get something straight right now, Liz. No one is going to help you. As far as they're all concerned, you're my property. The only difference between you and a horse or dog is that you're not as useful. So if you have any sense at all, you will do your best to keep me satisfied. Otherwise, I might be tempted to sell you to somebody else or simply leave you behind to die."

What little color had returned to her face quickly vanished. Even as she told herself he was only trying to frighten her, to punish her for lashing out at him, she couldn't shake the sense of dread his words evoked.

Jordan Nash was too complex a man to deal with lightly. On the one hand, he possessed all the gentleness and consideration that were the gift of his loving parents and family. But he was also accustomed to living by his own rules in a harsh and violent world.

Until she could be more certain of how he really intended to treat her, Elizabeth thought it prudent not to risk angering him further. Quietly, she said, "The rest of the map is under the false bottom of my valise."

Jordan stared at her for a moment, taken aback by her abrupt change of attitude. Uncertain as to how permanent it might be, he considered warning her further.

Only the ashen pallor of her skin and slight trembling of her shoulders stopped him. She had already endured a great deal; there would be time to enjoy her obedience later.

To find the remainder of the parchment, he had to tip all the contents out of the bag. They fell in a frothy mess onto the dirt floor. With a cry, Elizabeth sprang from the cot.

Rationally, she knew it was absurd to be concerned about her clothes getting dirty when there were so many more serious worries to occupy her. But the very direness of her situation made her take refuge in the mundane.

"Stop that! Don't you have any idea how hard it is to keep clean out here?"

Jordan stared at her in surprise. It took him a moment to realize she was serious. A wry grin curved his mouth as he considered that her docility had not lasted long.

"With the clothes you insist on wearing, it's no wonder you've been having trouble. But that's going to change, starting right now."

Not bothering to explain, he dug into the bag until he located the missing piece. Pulling it out, he surveyed it carefully before nodding. "This is it, all right. The same map I tried to buy from Davies."

"You tried?" Forgetting all about the garments strewn on the ground, Elizabeth stared at him warily. It had not occurred to her that he had attempted to get the map before.

Still studying the scrap of parchment, Jordan nodded. "That's right. I went to London to purchase it from Davies. But I was too late. By the time I got there, the map had been sold and Davies was dead. I couldn't even find out who had bought it, until I heard you and Chandler talking on board the *Britannia's Pride*."

Very slowly, Elizabeth said, "Davies was killed by an intruder who broke into his shop and ransacked it. The police speculated he was looking for something of great value, but no one could figure out exactly what."

"Could have been a lot of things. Davies traded in antiquities from all over the world. Egyptian papyrii, Mesopotamian stelae, Cretan artifacts all passed through his hands. A lot of his stuff was fake, but every once in a while he came across something genuinely valuable. Like this map."

"Valuable enough for someone to kill for?"

"That depends. Some people believe a magnificent golden idol that symbolizes the strength and pride of a race is worth any number of lives."

Elizabeth did not dare to ask him if he was one of those believers. She was afraid his answer might shatter what was left of her composure, particularly in light of the fact that she had just become aware of how skimpily clad she was.

Stepping back hastily to the bed, she seized the sheet and wrapped it around herself. Jordan's laughter did not improve her disposition. Angrily, she demanded, "Will you please leave while I dress myself?"

"That depends."

Knowing he was baiting her but unable to prevent it, she faced him stiffly. "On what?"

"On what you intend to put on, of course. If you go on dressing as you have these last few days, you'll collapse in no time."

"Surely you don't expect me to remain like this!"

A maddening smile lit his eyes. "That's a tempting idea, but I'm not eager to share your charms quite so generously with the other men. You can cover yourself modestly enough in far fewer clothes than you're used to."

"Your concept of modesty is obviously not the same as mine."

He shrugged uncaringly. "Be that as it may, you will wear what I've brought along for you. Everything else is just so much excess baggage and gets left right here."

"But my dresses, petticoats, capes . . . I can't just forget them."

"You can and will. I won't have any fainting women on my hands."

Before Elizabeth could attempt to stop him, Jordan scooped up her clothes and threw them outside the hut. He glanced round the small hut to make sure he had missed nothing before an omission struck him and he turned back to her. "Where's your corset?"

She blushed painfully. Not once had she heard any other man mention such an intimate female garment, much less demand to have it handed over. Worse yet, she could not comply. He had caught her without the one item no decent woman would be seen without.

"I . . . don't have one."

"Of course you do. I saw it the night I undressed you."

"Must you remind me of that?"

"If it will stop you from lying to me. Now where is it?"

"I told you . . . I don't have it. I . . . got rid of it . . . in Ada."

Jordan stared at her for a long moment, as though deciding whether or not to believe her. Slowly, distrust gave way to admiring amusement. "There's hope for you after all, Liz. If you could decide on your own to get rid of that instrument of torture, you just may make it through this okay."

Although she suspected he meant to compliment her, his patronizing tone was not to be borne. "I will dress myself as I see fit. Not as you or anyone else dictates."

His eyes softened, becoming almost gentle as he surveyed her thoughtfully. "More of your hard-won freedom, Liz?"

She couldn't answer him. He had come too close to the most vulnerable core of her being. Turning away, she drew the sheet more tightly around herself. "Please leave me."

Jordan caught the note of desperation in her voice. Wisely, he chose to heed it. "Of course. Nevertheless, you will have to wait a moment while I get you some clothes."

Since he had disposed of all her garments, Elizabeth had no choice but to obey. She stood stiffly in the center of the tent while he went off to fetch whatever it was he had in mind for her to wear.

When he returned and she saw what he held in his hands, her mouth dropped open. "This is a joke!"

He grinned unrepentantly. "No, actually this is a shirt and this is a pair of trousers. They will protect you from the sun and insects but still allow you to move about comfortably. Your boots you may keep, along with such undergarments as you now have on. But that's all."

"I can't possibly wear men's clothes."

"Of course not, you aren't big enough. These were made for a boy and should fit you nicely."

Elizabeth was getting rather tired of standing around with her mouth hanging open, but she couldn't seem to put a stop to it. Not so long as Jordan kept throwing her one incredible shock after another.

Absolutely no lady worthy of the name wore trousers. Granted, certain feminists had tried to make a fashion of bloomers several years back, but the ridicule and censure they received quickly did their efforts in. The style remained current only among music hall actresses and others who were no better than they had to be.

She had not managed to get out so much as a single word in protest before he placed the odious clothes in her hands and said sternly, "It's really very simple, Liz. You either wear these or stay in what you have on."

"That's no choice at all!"

He grinned infuriatingly. "I know." Pulling open the tent flap, he added, "I'll be right outside, Liz. So don't get any clever ideas about trying to escape. You wouldn't get two feet and when I caught you I really would thrash you."

On that note, Jordan sensibly chose to withdraw, leaving Elizabeth to stare after him in helpless rage.

The moment she was alone in the tent, her first thought was to rip the clothes to shreds and throw them in his face. But common sense stopped her. She had already learned that he was not a man to challenge lightly.

Jordan was perfectly capable of leaving her in nothing more than her camisole and pantaloons, at least until he was certain she regretted her hasty action.

Grimly, she held out the shirt and trousers and looked them over carefully. For all their casualness, they were as carefully made as Jordan's own clothes and looked as though they would fit her well.

But then why shouldn't they when the man who had picked them out knew the shape of her body better than any other?

Gritting her teeth, Elizabeth stepped into the trousers and pulled them up around her slender hips. The sight of her legs covered but still clearly delineated struck her as very odd. She looked away hastily as she donned the shirt.

The cool, crisp fabric felt good against her skin. She was relieved to note that it was loose enough to at least partially conceal the shape of her breasts. Tucking it into the slacks, she took a few tentative steps, trying to become accustomed to her new garb.

It felt very . . . light. The air reached right through to her skin. The sense of restraint that permeated every article of women's clothing was missing. She could move easily and freely.

Unwilling to admit that Jordan might have done her a favor, Elizabeth glanced warily toward the tent flap. She doubted he would give her much longer. Men like him had no respect for a woman's privacy.

A rueful smile curved her mouth as her own thoughts echoed in her mind. What did she know of men like him? Less than nothing. He was utterly outside her experience. But it seemed that fate had decreed he was not to remain so.

Her hand shook only slightly as she opened the tent flap and stepped out to join him.

Chapter Six

JORDAN STOOD WITH HIS BACK TO THE TENT LOOKING
out over the encampment. The torches still burned but
the early light of predawn made them unnecessary. He
was gratified to see that much had already been accomplished.

Chandler's tent lay in a heap on the ground, along
with most of the Englishman's possessions and a good
part of the supplies he had brought along. Elizabeth's
tent and belongings would soon join the pile.

With the ground so dry, there would be no difficulty
igniting the bonfire that would destroy all trace of the
expedition. The previously overburdened bearers
would be free to take up their true roles, warrior
escorts for what promised to be a difficult and dangerous journey.

Not for the first time, he debated the wisdom of
taking a woman along. It would be hard enough on
men trained to the rigors of the bush, but for Elizabeth . . .

Perhaps it was just as well that there was no alternative. He could justify his refusal to send her back to Accra on the grounds that she would undoubtedly notify the authorities of what had happened and bring a squadron of British soldiers down on them. The fact that he hated the mere thought of being separated from her didn't come into it.

His fascination with her rankled. If he had to feel anything at all, why couldn't it be the simple desire and affection he had known for other women? Why did he have to so admire her spirit and courage?

Jordan laughed wryly. He wasn't being honest with himself. His feelings went a damn sight further than admiration.

Something far more basic made him want to throw her down on the nearest flat surface and make long, passionate love to her until all her defenses were stripped away and he held her warm and ardent in his arms.

Being no stranger to carnal desire, he could understand that urge well enough. What he couldn't accept was the even stronger need to get to know her as one person to another.

He wanted to talk with her, to question her about her life, her hopes, her dreams, and to tell her all about his. And he wanted to make her laugh, to banish the sadness that never seemed to lurk far beneath her surface.

Instead, he had so far only managed to frighten and enrage her. For a man who had never before had any difficulty winning over a woman, he was making a bad job of it.

A sound behind him made Jordan turn. Elizabeth had left the tent and was gazing at the ruins of the campsite, her face pale and her eyes dark with apprehension.

Try though he did, he couldn't stop his gaze from running over her. The boyish clothes she wore in no way hid the femininity of her form.

Free of its usual restraints, her tall, slender body was as beautiful as he had known it would be. A tremor ran through him as he struggled against the urge to draw her to him and touch her as fully as he wished.

With her golden-brown hair tumbling around her shoulders and her moss-green eyes as wide and wary as a startled fawn's, she looked like a wood nymph come to life. Yet there was nothing ethereal or fragile about her. The proud, graceful carriage of her body spoke of vibrant feminine strength that entranced him.

Under his scrutiny, she flushed. Her eyes grazed past him to focus on some point over his left shoulder. A slender hand touched a strand of her hair.

"I can't find my pins. They were in the valise you emptied."

Her words were simple enough, but Jordan had trouble understanding them. He was too absorbed by the delightful picture she made to be more than dimly aware of them.

"Pins?"

"Ivory pins to put my hair up. Surely you don't expect me to leave it hanging down like this?"

The faint note of tartness in her voice penetrated his abstraction. He shook his head. "No, of course not. They must be around here somewhere."

A quick check of the ground right outside the tent turned up the missing pins. As he handed them to her, their fingers brushed.

Elizabeth stiffened. Even so slight a touch set off complex feelings within her. Torn between the desire to be held tight against him and the equally powerful urge to flee, she could barely remember the prosaic chore requiring her attention. Only with difficulty did she recollect herself enough to ask, "Will you hold them for me, please?"

Jordan nodded bemusedly. As he held the pins out for her one by one, he could not help but notice how her upraised arms stretched the fabric of her shirt tautly over her full, high breasts.

Irresistibly, his gaze drifted upward to the smooth cleft of her throat visible through the open collar, the delicate line of her jaw, the ripe fullness of her mouth . . .

His stomach twisted painfully. It was all too easy to remember how her lips had felt beneath his own. But was the memory correct? Had he really sensed the first stirrings of response in her just before she realized what was happening and retaliated so effectively?

There was only one way to find out. He wanted badly to kiss her again. Yet he couldn't bear the thought of the hurt and anger that would most likely follow. For the moment at least he would have to be content simply to keep her close beside him.

"That's all of them," Elizabeth murmured. "Thank you."

"What? Oh, you're welcome." With her hair up, she looked even lovelier. The slender line of her throat and jaw were clearly evident, as was the hollow between her collarbones where he guessed his lips would fit perfectly.

Staring into her eyes, he swallowed hard. Only through an enormous effort of will did he remember what he was supposed to be doing.

Impatient with himself, he gestured to a knapsack leaning against the side of the tent. "That's yours. There's a change of clothes, a first-aid kit, and a few other necessities. If you need anything else, put it in now. But remember, on this trek we all carry our own belongings. No exceptions will be made for you."

"I didn't expect any," Elizabeth muttered. It hadn't

occurred to her that she would be expected to perform such common labor, but now that he mentioned it, she wasn't surprised.

Despite the gentleness she had glimpsed in him, she could hardly think of him as chivalrous. He was a ruthless, determined man used to getting his own way and not inclined to grant anyone quarter.

Wary of what other unsuitable occupations he might have in mind for her, she decided not to make a fuss about the bag. It wasn't precisely heavy, but neither did it feel like something she would want to carry any distance.

Prudently adding only a few items she considered essential, she hoisted it over her shoulder and followed Jordan back to the center of the camp.

The bonfire had just been lit upon Kwesi's direction and was being carefully watched by the men who would stay to make sure it burned out completely, so as not to endanger the tinder-dry forest.

Elizabeth refused to look at the headman, whom she now regarded as an enemy. But she could not ignore the tall, composed man beside him.

Osei had shed his European clothes for the breechcloth of an Ashante warrior. The traditional tribal tattoos shone clearly against the ebony skin of his shoulders and chest. He carried a Winchester repeating rifle slung over his shoulder, the same one Elizabeth had seen him with on board the *Tara*. It contrasted sharply with the spears carried by the rest of the warriors.

Most startling to her eyes was the large amulet of beaten gold suspended from a thong around Osei's neck. She suspected that it held great significance, and that it explained the deference Kwesi showed him. The headman spoke in Oji, the language of the Ashantes and their subject tribes. He was apparently requesting instructions, which he received before bowing and taking himself off toward the canoes waiting on the river.

Only then did Osei acknowledge her presence. The merest flicker of his eyes took in her greatly changed appearance. A hint of a smile curved his full mouth. He said something to Jordan in the same language Kwesi had used. Both men laughed.

Elizabeth's face flamed. She knew they were talking about her and was powerless to do anything about it. Angrily, she looked away. A gasp escaped her as her gaze fell on Nigel, still tied up and lying on the ground.

Without pausing to think of the consequences, she ran over to the Englishman and knelt down by his side. Angry red splotches showed against his pale skin. Dust and sweat streaked his face. He seemed to be having trouble breathing, though whether that was from physical discomfort or extreme rage she could not tell.

Slipping an arm around his shoulders, she gently eased him upright. "Here, let me help you . . . that's better . . . Are you all right? They didn't . . . do anything to you, did they?"

Nigel didn't answer directly. Instead he launched into a stream of bitter invective. "Bloodthirsty savages. Ought to be roasted over a slow fire. Hanging's too good for them." Leaning heavily against her, he glared furiously. "They can't get away with this. No one can kidnap a Crown official and escape unpunished. If it's the last thing I do, I'll make them pay."

In the midst of this tirade, it occurred to Elizabeth that he was showing remarkably little concern about her own well-being. For all he knew, Jordan might have done something terrible to her.

Nigel's preoccupation with himself surprised her. Yet under such trying circumstances, she supposed a lapse in the usual gentlemanly conduct had to be excused.

Struggling to hold Nigel upright, she did not at first realize that Jordan and Osei had both followed her. Only when a heavy hand came down on her shoulder did she become aware of their presence.

"Get up," Jordan ordered harshly. Giving her no time to either object or obey, he hauled her to her feet and shook her hard.

"Slaves do not go wandering off on their own, Elizabeth. You would do well to remember that. Unless I give you permission to do otherwise, stay clear of Chandler."

His sneering reference to her presumed status enraged her. A slim, booted foot lashed out, catching him just below the knee. "Don't you tell me what to do, you blackguard! I wouldn't keep a dog tied up like that, much less a human being. Let him go at once!"

Jordan's eyes glittered ominously. His grip on her shoulder tightened. He was about to say something when Osei's laughter stopped him.

The black man shook his head ruefully. "As I told you a few moments ago, my friend, Lady Elizabeth's willingness to wear more sensible clothes only indicates that she is intelligent, not submissive. If you're really going to try to turn her into a good slave, I suggest you guard your back. She's liable to stick something sharp in it!"

"Nothing she did would surprise me," Jordan growled. He was grateful to his friend for making a joke out of Elizabeth's disobedience and thereby saving him from the necessity of punishing her in order to protect his honor. For all his anger, he wasn't absolutely sure he would have been able to do so and was glad to have been spared finding out.

"But she's right about Chandler," he went on, still holding on to the squirming, irate woman who glared at him defiantly. "If we leave him like that, he'll lose the circulation in his hands and feet."

96

"And if we untie him, what guarantee is there that he won't try to escape?"

"Perhaps he'll give us his word," Jordan suggested facetiously.

"There is no white man alive whose word I would trust."

"You trust mine."

"That is different, as you well know. Your Ashante warrior training and the bond of our brotherhood far outweigh the color of your skin."

As she listened to the exchange between the two men, Elizabeth's head swiveled back and forth from one to the other. Did Osei really mean that Jordan had undergone initiation into the elite cadre of Ashante warriors whose fierceness struck terror into the hearts of even the best-trained British soldiers?

It didn't seem possible, yet what other explanation was there for the clearcut distinction Osei made between Jordan and every other white? Baffled, she forgot her anger long enough to wish that she could learn more about the enigmatic man who held her captive.

"Different or not," Jordan was saying, "I agree with you about not trusting Chandler. However, I don't think he's stupid enough to wander off on his own."

Glancing down at the other man, he said scornfully, "You wouldn't survive more than a few hours alone in the bush. So if you have any hope of saving your life, you'll stick with us and do as you're told."

"I'm not suicidal," Nigel snapped. "But I still say you won't get away with this. I fully intend to be there when you're caught and executed."

Jordan laughed mockingly. "Go right on thinking that. Your anger will goad you into keeping up with us."

Leaving Osei to untie the Englishman, he shoved Elizabeth toward one of the canoes. As she started to protest, he raised a hand warningly. "You've already said and done more than enough to justify being punished. If you open your mouth again without permission, I promise you'll regret it."

"Of all the overbearing, autocratic . . ."

"Quiet!"

"No! You can't make me keep silent. I'll say exactly what I think and nothing will stop me . . ."

"Are you really so hungry for my kisses that you deliberately provoke them?"

Elizabeth broke off abruptly. Staring at him through her thick lashes, she tried to discern whether or not he was serious. "K-kisses . . .?"

"Certainly. What better way is there to put a lid on that temper of yours?"

Ignoring the sudden rocking of the canoe as they stepped into it, he leaned toward her. "I thought you would have realized that by now, but perhaps you need a reminder."

"No, I don't! I remember just fine."

"You're sure?"

"Absolutely."

"Oh, well, maybe later."

"It'll be a cold day in hell before I let you . . ."

"Elizabeth, you're talking again."

Her mouth snapped shut. Not for anything would she give him an excuse to inflict more of that devastatingly sensual assault on her. She remained resolutely silent as the remaining canoes were quickly filled and the journey upriver was resumed.

For hours they traveled without pause through countryside that became progressively more withered and sere. Elizabeth lost count of the number of trees with dying branches being sacrificed so that the rest might survive. The lush undergrowth was beginning to thin out in patches and even the trailing vines that hung over the river looked shriveled from lack of moisture.

From time to time, she caught sight of animals driven to the banks in search of water. Some fled back into the thicket as the humans passed, but others were too listless to do more than remain where they were.

By midmorning the fierce heat of the sun had parched her throat and made her head throb. She longed for a cool drink and a chance to stretch her cramped legs, but she wouldn't ask Jordan for anything.

He sat right behind her in the canoe, rowing smoothly along with the half-dozen warriors who shared the craft. If the heat or the relentless pace they maintained bothered him, he gave no sign.

Out of the corner of her eye, she could see his burnished hands holding the paddle. His forearms were left bare by the rolled-up sleeves of his workshirt. They were darkly tanned and covered in black curling hairs. Smooth muscles rippled with each stroke. Each breath she drew made her more vividly aware of his intrinsically male scent of soap, tobacco and healthy sweat.

Elizabeth's head began to swim. She told herself it was because of heat and thirst, and gritted her teeth against the urge to ask him if they could stop for a short time.

To distract herself from her plight, she concentrated all the more intently on the passing scene. Only gradually did she notice that colors and shapes were beginning to blur and that there was a buzzing sound in her ears.

"Elizabeth."

"W-what—what is it?" Her voice sounded strangely thick. She couldn't quite seem to make her tongue work properly.

"Here, put this on or you'll get sunstroke."

That struck her as funny. She tried to find some way to tell him she thought she already had it, but the words wouldn't form. When she stared dumbly at the broad-brimmed cotton hat he handed her, Jordan cursed softly.

"Lean on me."

She shook her head automatically, even as her body collapsed into weariness and sagged against him.

"That's a good girl. Now sip this slowly."

Cool water touched her lips. Elizabeth swallowed once, then again. A line of shade appeared above her eyes as Jordan slipped the hat in place.

Vaguely, as though from a great distance, she heard him muttering, "I should have known you weren't ready for this. You're too damned delicate."

Gently, he turned her so that she was lying in his arms looking up at him. "We have to put as much distance as possible between us and that campsite. In a day or two we can slow the pace, but for the moment speed is critical. Do you understand?"

Mutely, she nodded. Whatever he was saying didn't seem anywhere near as important as the strength of his arms around her and the hardness of his body close against her own. A soft sigh escaped her as she gave in to the irresistible need for comfort and closed her eyes.

Jordan stared down at her guardedly. He was both worried about her and wary of the effect she had on him. Reluctantly, he accepted his need to hold her.

Easing her into his arms with her head resting against his chest, he picked up the paddle again and resumed rowing. Elizabeth didn't stir. The rhythmic motions of his powerful body rocked her even more deeply asleep.

When she did finally awake it was late afternoon and the canoes were pulling into the shore. She raised her head slowly, surprised to discover that she felt much better.

Glancing up, she noticed that Jordan had fastened an extra shirt to a pole and placed it over her to provide a sunscreen. His thoughtfulness was disconcerting. With her strength restored, she wanted to think of him only as a ruthless captor, not as a gentle man capable of such consideration.

As the prow of the canoe struck bottom, she was thrown hard against him. Instantly, his arm tightened around her. Seeing that she was awake, he asked, "Are you all right?"

"Yes, of course, I'm fine." The touch of his skin burned through her shirt to sear her skin with a heat that had nothing to do with the temperature. Sitting up quickly, she struggled to regain her composure and to remember her manners. "Thank you for letting me sleep."

Jordan laughed shortly. "I didn't have much choice. Another few minutes and you would have passed out."

Elizabeth couldn't deny it, but neither did she need to be reminded of her weakness. Stiffly, she said, "I need some time to become acclimated. In a few days, I'll have as much stamina as any of you."

Though he looked doubtful, he didn't press the point. Instead, he merely nodded and stepped lithely from the canoe, holding out a hand to help her do the same.

As they walked up the bank, Jordan said, "Since you're the only one of us who got any rest today, you can help with the cooking."

If he expected her to object, he was disappointed. One of her few recreations at home had been to prepare exotic dishes for herself and the family servants, all of whom had known her from the time she was born.

Many long winter afternoons had been spent in the big kitchen that was the only cheery spot in the London house, trying out new recipes and experimenting with rare ingredients. More often than not, the results had been delicious.

She was rightly confident of her ability to concoct at least a passable meal under any conditions, and she didn't mind letting Jordan know about it.

He left her near the bundles of food supplies brought up from the canoes and went off to join the men who were working with machetes to enlarge the campsite. As he slashed and cut through the thick tangle of shrubs that came almost to the water's edge, he managed to keep a close eye on her. The sight of her sitting cross-legged on the ground wrung a rueful grin from him.

She looked surprisingly at home amid surroundings that would have had almost any other woman of her background swooning in horror. Such adaptability and resiliency made him admire her all the more, and further increased his determination to keep her safe against all odds.

The task of combing through what was left of the expedition's food stores and putting them together with supplies brought by the Ashantes so absorbed Elizabeth that when she finally looked up again she was startled to find several simple shelters scattered around the campsite.

Constructed from tall brush grass interwoven over a structure of poles carried along for that purpose, they looked rather more comfortable than the stifling hot tents whose loss she could not honestly regret.

A heavy stack of dried wood suddenly dropped on the ground inches from her hands. She looked up in surprise, thinking Jordan was responsible and intending to reprimand him.

The words caught in her throat. A near-naked warrior armed with a spear loomed over her. Though he was not as big or powerfully built as Osei or Kwesi, his fierce demeanor made him seem every bit as threatening.

Her stomach clenched painfully as terror darted through her, but she refused to give any sign of it. Instead she met his gaze coolly. From the corner of her eye, she could see Jordan standing nearby, taking in the scene.

The fact that he did not raise a hand to help her only added to Elizabeth's determination not to show her fear. Concentrating strictly on the warrior, she did not notice that Jordan had taken a step forward, poised to move instantly should the need arise.

For a long, seemingly endless moment, the Ashante held her gaze before he abruptly laughed. Dropping down on his knees beside her, he matter-of-factly set about digging a shallow pit in which he laid a web of sticks and twigs. Banking the sides he used a tinder and flint to ignite the fire.

As Elizabeth attempted to thank him, he got up, dusted off his hands, and said something to Jordan, who nodded good-naturedly. When the warrior had gone off to join the others, he strolled over to the fire and met her outraged glare complacently.

"An oyke says that if your cooking skills equal your courage, we will eat well tonight."

Tossing a handful of groundnuts into a pot, she muttered, "I hope you all choke."

Settling down on his haunches, Jordan peered warily at the stew she was concocting. What he saw reassured him. Mixed with rice, water, pellets of beef broth, and spices, the dried vegetables and meats that would have to be their diet until they could hunt smelled quite appetizing.

Even as he wondered how she had managed such a feat, he couldn't resist teasing her a bit. "Now, now, Liz, you don't mean that surely. After all, if the men discover you can't cook, they'll expect me to find some other use for you."

"I'm not afraid of rowing, if that's what you mean. I'll take my turn with the oars like everyone else."

"Uh . . . that isn't quite what I had in mind."

Despite herself, Elizabeth's curiosity impelled her to glance at him. What she saw brought a fiery blush to her cheeks and made her hastily lower her eyes. Jordan's mocking smile made it clear what other occupation he meant.

Telling herself she should feel only outrage and disgust at such effrontery, she nonetheless could not prevent a tiny quiver of pleasure from running through her.

It seemed unbelievable that plain, straitlaced Elizabeth Derrick should be the object of a man's baser desires. Yet perhaps it wasn't so strange when she considered that the days since her father's death had wrought tremendous changes in her.

More than just her corset had been left behind at Ada. Along with it had gone just about all her preconceptions about what she could or could not do.

The world did not screech to a halt simply because she dressed like a boy and suffered herself to be kissed like a woman. And although she could have done without that spanking, it had proven that certain notions of propriety could be entirely disregarded without dire consequences.

For all that she was stranded in the midst of the African bush with a ruthless captor whose intentions were still largely unknown, she felt remarkably free. The irony of it struck her and, without knowing that she did so, she smiled.

"What," Jordan demanded suspiciously, "is so amusing?"

Elizabeth shook her head, trying hard not to laugh. "I don't think you would understand."

"Try me."

There was no mistaking that the words were an order. Though she was tempted to ignore them, prudence dictated that she respond.

"To put it mildly, I am not accustomed to gentlemen making improper suggestions to me. Are you sure you're not very hard up for feminine companionship?"

Jordan glanced at her narrowly. The mild asperity of her tone did not please him. She might have been reprimanding a mischievous little boy. Crossly, he demanded, "Are you fishing for compliments?"

Elizabeth thought about that for a moment. Perhaps she was. Certainly they had not been in any great supply during her life. A bit of flattery might go down very well indeed. "Yes . . . maybe I am. But then considering my glamorous dress and elegant occupation, how could you fail to compliment me?"

His annoyance faded away, replaced by wry amusement. "I admit you don't look as though you've just stepped out of *Godey's Lady's Book,* but then I've never shared prevailing notions about what makes a woman attractive."

Even as she marveled at her own daring, Elizabeth could not resist the urge to ask, "How do your preferences differ from those of classic beauty?"

Settling more comfortably beside her with his long body stretched out near the cooking fire and his head propped up on one hand, he studied her for a moment before responding. "I suppose what it comes down to is that I don't like women who are so wrapped up in artifice that they seem to have lost track of themselves as human beings. So many of the fair sex insist on being treated like dolls instead of women. Being around them gets to be very tedious."

"Is that why you left Boston?"

"Partly. With the exception of my mother and sisters, there didn't seem to be a lady in the city who had an idea in her head beyond fashion, gossip, and the next day's entertainment. After a couple of years of that, I decamped for greener pastures."

"You were lucky you could do so," Elizabeth said rather wistfully. "For women who are dissatisfied with their lot, it is far more difficult to make any change, let alone one so dramatic."

"You realize you are a rather glaring exception to that?"

She flushed slightly. "Yes, I suppose I am. But that is only because I have been caught up in rather extraordinary circumstances. If my father hadn't decided to come here, I would undoubtedly still be in England caring for him."

Biting her lower lip, she glanced at Jordan. Against the burnished tan of his skin, his crystal blue eyes were startlingly light. A lock of thick black hair fell across his forehead.

Despite the grueling pace they had set that day, he looked as strong and determined as ever. Yet there was something about him she had not seen before, a degree of gentleness that gave her confidence.

So softly that he had to lean forward to hear her, she murmured, "It must seem strange to you that I haven't grieved more."

Jordan caught her apprehension and responded instinctively. A large hand covered hers, its gentle warmth coaxing her into meeting his eyes. "While Sir Alfred was alive, you gave him everything possible. Now that he is gone, you owe no duty except to yourself."

"But he was my father . . ."

"Was he? Or did he just happen to sire you and then take advantage of that fact for his own convenience?"

"I'm not sure I understand the difference."

"Then let me give you an example: my parents did their best to prepare their children for the world, but they never tried to keep us from it. They encouraged all their sons and daughters to live their lives to the fullest, even if that meant going far from home. It's that kind of unselfishness that makes a good parent."

Elizabeth had never thought in such terms, but she had no difficulty understanding what he meant. Her father had been the epitome of selfishness, never showing the slightest concern for her well-being.

It occurred to her that she ought to hate him for that, but all she could manage was vague sadness for what might have been. The events of the present and the uncertainties of the future were far too exciting to allow her to dwell on the past.

A teasing gleam shone in her eyes as she asked, "When you told your parents that you were leaving home, did you explain it was because you were bored by the ladies of Boston?"

Jordan laughed, relieved by the quick reassertion of her good humor. "No, but I suspect they guessed as much. My father had done a fair amount of wandering in his day. When I told him my plans, all he did was give me a piece of advice."

"What was that?"

"Never to set out on a journey without first shucking all my preconceptions and prejudices. If I went with the belief that my race or culture was superior to everyone else's, I would miss a great deal and ruin a good adventure before it even started."

"You took his advice, didn't you? That's why Osei calls you his brother."

"Yes, he does me that honor."

Elizabeth regarded him quizzically. "Kwesi shows

him great deference and you clearly hold him in high regard. Why?"

He hesitated a moment before apparently deciding there was no harm in answering. "Because Osei is an Ashante prince, the eldest son of the Asantehene. He was sent on this quest for the golden idol by his father. The Ashantes are convinced they are direct descendents of the Mande. It is vitally important to them to preserve such a unique part of their heritage. If the idol is stolen by the whites, it will be taken as proof that the gods have turned against the Ashantes and that the whites are destined to win the conflict between them. That's why the British authorities are determined to find it first."

"You mean Nigel . . . ?"

"Only made use of your desire to continue the expedition to further his own ends. He is under contract to the Colonial Administration, which has hired him to find the idol and take it to Accra for eventual removal to London."

Elizabeth didn't know whether or not to believe him. She wanted to think that the young Englishman was as noble and high-minded as all of his kind were supposed to be, but she was beginning to wonder.

Nigel's lack of interest in her welfare had shaken her faith in him. Perhaps, like Jordan, she would do well to forget her preconceptions.

A short time later he went off to help the men construct a perimeter fence to protect them from roaming animals. Barely had he gone than Nigel came over and sat down next to her, his expression one of great concern and indignity.

"It's outrageous that you should be doing this work, Lady Elizabeth. At least let me help you."

"Thank you, but that really isn't necessary. I'm fine."

"Your courage is admirable, but you cannot mislead

me. I am only too well aware of what an ordeal this is for you." Lowering his voice, he muttered, "Never fear. Jordan Nash will be brought to justice. I promise you that."

The idea of Jordan falling into the hands of the colonial authorities sent a quiver of horror racing through her. Stiffly, she said, "I shall be quite satisfied if we simply come out of this safely. Nothing more is necessary."

"Of course you are too tenderhearted to think on vengeance. Forgive me for mentioning it."

Elizabeth nodded curtly, wishing he would leave. She didn't like the way his eyes kept running over her, as though he could not control his fascination with her new garb and what it revealed of her body. When the men began to return, she was undeniably relieved.

Their appreciation of the hearty stew was complete and unfeigned. In her pleasure at their compliments, she was able to forget her concerns about Nigel. He was far from her mind by the time the remains of the meal were cleared away and the camp settled down for the night.

As the warriors began to retire to the grass shelters, she glanced around warily. It occurred to her that she had no idea where she was to sleep. The thought of spending the night by herself in such strange surroundings was not appealing, but then neither was the only possible alternative.

Despite the easy camaraderie she had shared earlier with Jordan, he was a highly virile man who had made no secret of his desire for her. To share his quarters might be to invite something for which she was still completely unprepared.

Yet, as it turned out, she had no choice. As the warriors on the first watch took up their positions around the perimeter fence, Jordan touched her shoulder lightly.

"You look done in, Elizabeth. Time for bed."

Wearier than she had ever been in her life, she still felt compelled to object. "I'd rather stay here by the fire. The smoke keeps the bugs off."

"Not really. There isn't enough of it for that. You'll be better off in the hut."

"*Which* hut?"

He grinned, obviously enjoying her discomfiture. "Why, mine, of course. After all, you do belong to me."

"Don't say that! I won't have you speak of me in such a way."

Something of her fatigue-induced fear must have reached him, for instead of being angered by her outburst, Jordan simply raised her gently to her feet and spoke to her softly. "Take it easy, Liz. We're both tired and we've got another tough day tomorrow. So let's just call it a night, what do you say?"

What could she say? It wasn't as though she had any alternatives. As he lifted her into his arms and strode across the camp, she lay against him unresistingly. All the fight seemed to have gone out of her. She couldn't even protest when he set her down on a soft reed mat and pulled off her boots before lowering himself beside her.

The distant roar of a lion jerked her back into full consciousness, but only briefly. Jordan drew her to him, holding her gently, his big hands softly stroking her back.

His tender caress and the soothing words he murmured did their work. She drifted off to sleep in his arms, aware only of a feeling of security and peace greater than any she had ever known.

Chaper Seven

Breakfast the next morning was frugal at best. Water and rice made a tepid mush that was eaten strictly to fill their stomachs. Looking over the food stores, Elizabeth knew they would have to find game soon or face real hunger.

Many of the supplies the Ashantes had tried to salvage from the expedition were already spoiled. They were left behind for scavengers as the canoes were reloaded and the party prepared to set out again.

Standing on the riverbank, she did her best not to think of the previous night. It would not do to remember how comfortably she had lain in Jordan's arms or how reluctant she had been to leave them when dawn at last broke over the bush. Better to concentrate on the day ahead and what promised to be yet another test of her strength and endurance.

That expectation proved to be true before the first paddle was dipped into the water. While the canoes were still being loaded, a blood-chilling scream ripped the air. Elizabeth, like everyone else, turned in its direction.

Her heart leaped into her throat as she saw Nigel being dragged into the water by an immense crocodile whose powerful jaws were closed around the calf of his leg.

The beast, at least fourteen feet long, was heavily armored from its vicious snout to its thrashing tail. The warriors who fearlessly rushed forward with their spears to try to drive it off were completely ineffective. The steel tips of their weapons might have been feathers for all the notice given them by the hideous animal.

Elizabeth wanted desperately to look away, but shock froze her in place. The terrible stories she had heard in Accra of men swallowed whole by crocodiles were suddenly horrifyingly real. Nigel's screams continued to rend the air as he was dragged remorselessly toward the edge of the river and certain death.

At immense risk to themselves, the warriors grabbed hold of the Englishman, trying to pull him back while thrusting their spears again and again at the impervious animal—until Jordan shouted at them to get back. Within seconds of the attack, he had reached Nigel's side, his Winchester rifle loaded and at the ready.

His command distracted the beast, who loosened his grip just enough for his intended victim to be yanked away. A bestial roar of anger signaled its new target. Rising up out of the water, it lumbered toward Jordan, its powerful tail thrashing relentlessly and its great jaws snapping open and shut with clear intent.

Elizabeth dropped the small bundle she clutched and, without a thought of her own safety, raced toward Jordan. She knew only that she had to try to distract the beast long enough for him to escape. But before she could run more than a few yards, Osei gripped her tightly.

"No! He has the only clear shot. Let him be."

"He'll be killed! Let me go!" Struggling desperately, she succeeded only in bruising herself as the warrior held her helpless. She could not even turn her head away as the scene was played out before her in agonizing slow motion.

Jordan stood absolutely still, making no effort to flee as the beast lurched toward him at a speed that was astonishing for so large an animal. Its fetid breath must have touched his face before he at last secured the gun against his shoulder and with agonizing slowness squeezed the trigger.

Fragments of the crocodile's brain splattered against the nearby thorn bushes. It fell forward with a sickening thud, landing directly in front of Jordan's feet.

Slowly, with the caution so great an animal deserved, the warriors approached until they formed a circle around the kill. Their spears were raised high as cheers broke from them.

Jordan looked unimpressed by his feat. He took careful aim at the beast and shot it again, something Elizabeth could not understand until Osei explained that even presumably dead crocodiles had been known to suddenly revive and deal savagely with the unwary.

Not until that was clearly no longer a possibility did he accept the warriors' congratulations, along with those of Osei, who at last let Elizabeth go and hurried over to join the other men.

Only she and Nigel remained outside the elated circle. The Englishman was slumped on the ground where he had fallen when the crocodile let go. White-faced and dazed, he was rubbing his badly bruised leg, which miraculously was still intact.

With the help of several warriors, he was able to

make it to one of the canoes, where he promptly hung his head over the side and retched. Elizabeth was tempted to follow suit but managed to fight down the urge.

She prudently did not watch as the remains of the crocodile were skinned and the portions that could be used for food were carefully cut away. When Jordan came to her side, she was staring down at the ground, once again clutching her bundle and trembling visibly.

A burnished, blood-stained hand tilted her chin back. Wide-eyed, she gazed into eyes still hard with the implacable determination to kill. Instead of trying to brush off their danger, as she had half-expected him to, Jordan said, "Learn from this, Liz. Chandler was warned to stay with the rest of the group. He chose not to obey and almost got himself killed. Don't you make the same mistake."

In vain, she searched his face for some sign of the gentleness he had shown her the night before. There was none. He looked for all the world as though her death would be only a minor inconvenience.

Her throat was tight with unshed tears as she mutely nodded. Jordan continued to hold her a moment longer, as though wanting to convince himself of her submission. Abruptly, he let her go and turned away to the canoe.

A short time later they were back on the river, once again heading north as though nothing had happened to delay their departure. Only the pale chunks of meat hanging on poles to dry in the sun and Nigel's sporadic groans drifting over the water were left to remind Elizabeth of why she suddenly felt so desolate and alone.

The feeling stayed with her throughout the grueling hours that followed. A rhythmic chant rang out as the large oars rose and fell swiftly, cleaving the water with steady strokes. One purpose dominated all: to cover as many miles as possible before dark.

Crouched in the prow of the first canoe, with her legs tucked up under her and her head weighed down by the combined pressure of her heavy hair and cumbersome hat, Elizabeth struggled to stay awake. For reasons she did not begin to understand, it was important for her to show Jordan that she could be as impervious as he himself.

Only once, when they stopped briefly in the middle of the river to wipe the sweat from their faces and drink from the water pouches, did she allow her eyes to meet his. The bleak look she encountered surprised her. It seemed to have no source she could understand.

Though he might think very badly of Nigel, she could not believe he regretted saving his life. What then was responsible for the somberness she sensed in him?

The answer was not forthcoming. Once again, the rowers resumed their swift pace and Elizabeth drifted back to her thoughts. She tried not to be overly conscious of the man seated directly behind her, but soon found that was impossible. Try though she did, she could not ignore Jordan's effect on her.

All her senses were acutely tuned to his presence. She was vividly aware of his every movement, of the warmth of his body emanating through the sweat-stained khaki, and of his intrinsically male scent filling her breath.

She ached to reach out to him, to feel the powerful ripple of his muscles and the firm smoothness of his skin. Unbidden, she remembered the rhythmic sound of his heartbeat under her cheek the night before. The memory made her hands clench, the nails digging into her palms sharply enough to draw blood.

Despite all her preoccupation, she managed to

weather that day's journey far better than she had the last. By the time they pulled over to the shore to spend the night, she was still alert enough to be dismayed by her dirty, bedraggled state.

Glancing down at her shirt and pants streaked with dust and mud, she realized that she looked every bit as bad as she felt. Yet the mere thought of trying to bathe unnerved her.

After experiencing the dangers that lurked beneath the seemingly calm surface of the river, she had a far different attitude toward Africa in general and the expedition in particular. Jordan's contention that it was insanity for her to embark on such a journey now seemed perfectly just.

That did not, however, change the fact that she was filthy and that her badly dented morale needed a boost. Finding Jordan once again among the men clearing away the underbrush, she approached him tentatively.

"Uh . . . do you think there might be some way for me to tidy up?"

He lowered his machete and stared at her in bemusement. Thick, damp curls clung to his head. Sweat poured down his face, pooling in the hollow at the base of his throat before vanishing beneath his shirt. Not an inch of him was free of dust, dried blood, mud, or river slime.

Her request seemed to astound him. Long moments passed before he gathered himself to respond. "Tidy up? Next you'll be asking why I didn't bring along a lady's maid."

That was unfair. She had not made so much as a murmur of complaint during the long, exhausting day and had done what she could to help by keeping the water pouches full and the sunshade in place. The implication that she was a weak, self-indulgent female was not to be borne.

Sudden tears blurred her vision. She was hot, filthy,

116

and worn out, and she hadn't yet recovered from the terrifying events of that morning. Her defenses were at an all-time low. Before he could discover that and mock her even further, she turned away.

"Elizabeth, come back here!"

The contrite sound of his voice did not stop her. She stomped off angrily, determined to find some exhausting occupation that would drain what little was left of her strength and make her forget all about him.

Hacking the crocodile meat into stew-sized pieces seemed as good a diversion as any. She went at it with a will, taking out all her frustrations on the toughened slabs. But she had managed only a few wallops with the ax Anoyke had lent her when a powerful hand seized her wrist.

"The croc's already dead," Jordan murmured. "There's no need to kill it all over again." As she tried to twist away from him, he calmly removed the ax from her hand and said, "Besides, I thought you'd like to know I found a pool near here where you can bathe."

Elizabeth stared at him suspiciously, hardly daring to believe what she was hearing. "A pool?"

"That's right. Most of them will be dry until the rains come, but this one must be fed by an underground stream because it's still full. Want to give it a try?"

"Yes, of course!" In her pleasure at the thought of being clean again, she forgot to be angry with him. Quickly gathering up a towel, soap, and fresh clothes, she followed him from camp.

The trail he had blazed was rough but passable. Arriving at the lagoon surrounded by thick bushes and draped with trailing vines, she laughed delightedly. "This is marvelous!"

Jordan smiled indulgently. Leaning against an acacia tree, he checked his rifle to make sure the safety catch was off, then took a cheroot from his shirt pocket and lit it leisurely. "I'm glad you think so. Go ahead and enjoy yourself."

Elizabeth's eyes widened. Surely he didn't mean to . . . "I-I will . . . as soon as you leave."

"Not on your life. And that's exactly what it would be. Or have you already forgotten what happened this morning?"

She looked at him in horror. "You mean there could be a crocodile in there . . .?"

"No, it's too small even for a little one. But that doesn't mean you can stay out here by yourself. If a snake didn't get you, a lion or leopard would. Not to mention marauding elephants, irate hippos, short-tempered rhinos . . ."

"I see. Actually, being dirty really isn't so bad."

Intending to beat a hasty retreat from the pool that no longer looked anything like the sylvan oasis she had first imagined, Elizabeth was stopped by an amused chuckle.

"Maybe I exaggerated a little," Jordan admitted. "But the fact remains, it isn't a good idea for anyone to be out in the bush alone. While you bathe, I'll keep watch. Then you can return the favor." Looking her up and down speculatively, he asked, "You can handle a gun, can't you?"

As it happened she could. A friend of her father's had insisted on teaching her when he learned she was going along on the expedition. Contrary to both his and her own expectations, she had quickly become a more than respectable shot.

The gun was no problem. However, getting undressed in front of him was quite a different matter. No matter how inviting the water or how desperate her need for a bath, she could not do what he apparently expected.

"We don't have all day," he reminded her.

She glanced from him to the water and back again. "I can't . . ."

"Can't what?"

"You know perfectly well what. I can't disrobe in front of you."

"Oh, is that all?"

"All?"

"I thought there might actually be something wrong."

"There most certainly is. You may have the modesty of a goat, but I . . ."

"Goat? That's going a bit far, don't you think?"

"If the shoe fits . . ."

"Perhaps you're right." With the cheroot clamped between his teeth, he began to unfasten his shirt. "If you don't want to go first, I'll be happy to."

"You wouldn't dare."

"Want to bet?"

Not particularly. The swift work he was making of his buttons convinced her he meant what he said. Turning away hastily, she marched over to the edge of the pool and dropped her belongings.

"Oh, all right. But at least turn around."

"Only until you're in the water."

"Not a second before."

"Yes, ma'am." Grinning infuriatingly, he presented her with his back. Elizabeth kept a close eye on it as she quickly stripped off her clothes and lowered herself into the water.

The deliciously cool wetness brought a gasp of delight. Forgetting her chagrin of a moment before, she cupped her hands and splashed her heated face and shoulders before dunking her hair.

Her unconsciously childlike antics made Jordan grin. Taking a seat on a rock overlooking the pond, he indulged in as clear a view of her as the opaque water permitted. "Having fun?"

"Yes," Elizabeth admitted, rather surprised to find herself not particularly self-conscious in front of him. Granted she was actually better covered than she would be in a fashionably low-cut evening gown. But the circumstances made all the difference. Their isolation by the secluded pond seemed to wrap them in a private world all their own. Softly, she said, "It feels wonderful."

"Doesn't look too bad either."

Knowing full well that he was not referring to the water, Elizabeth lowered her eyes. She busied herself shampooing her long hair, unaware that her raised arms exposed the soft swell of her breasts to his appreciative eyes.

Jordan stirred restlessly, wondering just how much more he could take. The sight of her naked before him, covered only by the gently lapping water, was painfully arousing. His desire was hard and fierce.

A low curse rose in him, only to be bitten back. It would be churlish to make her aware of his predicament. In her innocence, she might well interpret frustration for displeasure and her happiness in the bath would be spoiled. Stalwartly, he resolved to bear his discomfort as well as he could.

When her hair was clean, Elizabeth swam some little distance away and soaped herself thoroughly beneath the water. She would liked to have stayed longer, but thinking the tense set of Jordan's features meant he was as anxious for a bath as she had been, she resolved not to linger.

Swimming back to him, she reached for her towel. "If you'd turn around again . . ."

When he had done so, she quickly dried herself, then reached for her clean clothes. She had just stepped into a pair of fresh pantaloons when a motion in the underbrush caught her eye. Elizabeth froze in horror as a dark green snake several yards long, with a body as thick as a man's calf, raised its head and eyed her chillingly.

"*J-Jordan . . .*"

"What is it?"

"Could you . . . That is, I think I need some help . . ."

He sighed impatiently. "You'll have to manage your clothes yourself, Elizabeth. There's a limit to how much any man can stand."

"I didn't mean that . . . I meant . . ."

The terror in her voice finally reached him. His shoulders stiffened as very slowly he turned his head just enough to catch sight of the snake. "Don't move."

"I had no intention of doing so."

"Good. Stay right where you are and everything will be fine . . ." As he spoke, he straightened carefully, inch by inch. The viper hissed at them, but made no attempt to strike. "He won't attack unless he feels really provoked, so just take a step backward . . . Careful . . ."

Obeying the reassuring sound of his voice as much as the words themselves, Elizabeth did as he said. Step by step, she eased herself away from the snake who continued to stare at her balefully until it became convinced she meant it no harm. Then, with a flick of its huge body, it vanished into the bush.

Jordan's arms were around her instantly, holding her as the strength went out of her legs and she collapsed against him.

"My God," she blurted, "it's one thing after another around here!"

A deep laugh rumbled in his chest. His embrace tightened, making her suddenly aware of her nakedness. The thin pantaloons hid very little and were certainly no protection from the powerful male body pressed so intimately against her own.

"Elizabeth . . ." His voice was hungry, his eyes

even more so. Big hands rough with calluses stroked her bare back between her shoulder blades and down the ultrasensitive ridge of her spine.

He shifted slightly, drawing her even closer so that the hard columns of his thighs pressed against her soft abdomen. The thick mat of dark hair on his chest teased the tips of her breasts.

She was engulfed in the touch, sight, sound, and scent of him, immersed in a world of pure sensuality, shorn of reason and doubt. When his mouth lowered gently to hers she met him without restraint, glorying in the fierce need that could no longer be denied.

Chapter Eight

JORDAN'S KISS WAS LONG AND ARDENT. NIBBLING lightly at her lower lip, he tugged at it gently before soothing the delicate inner flesh with the hot, wet stroke of his tongue. As he traced the ridge of her teeth, Elizabeth moaned. Her hands slid under his shirt, savoring the hard strength of muscle and sinew.

His skin was rough silk, warm and damp with perspiration. Beneath her touch, he trembled uncontrollably. Exalted by the knowledge that she could affect him as deeply as he did her, she was emboldened to meet his caresses with a degree of daring she would not have thought possible.

Her mouth parted willingly, accepting the thrusting urgency of his tongue. When she touched it with her own, a ragged groan tore from him, further fuel for the heady sense of power beginning to glow within her.

They sank together to the ground as fluidly as dancers in an age-old *pas de deux*. Even in the midst of passion so intense that it turned his eyes to burning slivers torn from the cobalt sky and brought a flush to his high-boned cheeks, Jordan's control remained absolute.

Holding his weight above her, he gently traced the smooth line of her throat with his mouth to the curve of her shoulders and beyond. Her skin tasted of sun-warmed water, lemon soap, and her own intrinsic flavor.

The cleft between her breasts received the lingering touch of his lips and tongue before he tenderly cupped her breasts in his hands, tracing their fullness with his ardent mouth.

Beneath him, pressed between his powerful body and the warm earth, Elizabeth writhed helplessly. Her slim legs, clad only in the pantaloons that were her sole covering, opened of their own accord. Deep within her, in some secret part of herself whose existence she had never before suspected, she grew hot and moist.

As he tenderly drew a straining nipple within his mouth, she cried out. Her eyes opened wide, taking in the radiant sky above the feathery branches of the acacia trees, the flash of a ringtailed monkey peering down at them curiously, the riotous orange and red and blue of a kingfisher bird alighting by the pool.

All her senses were more vividly alive than ever before, and by their very brilliance her perceptions melted into each other. She could feel the vast expanse of the sky, hear the coolness of the water, smell the rippling waves of passion coursing through them both.

Jordan's big hands gently gripped her waist, his fingers slipping beneath the waistband of her pantaloons to caress the flat plane of her abdomen. Slowly he circled the indentation of her navel before reaching further to brush the soft tangle of golden-brown curls between her thighs.

. When she instinctively flinched from so intimate a

touch, he soothed her with words that made her cheeks burn, even as she could not deny the pleasure they brought.

"Please, Elizabeth, don't draw away . . . I want to know every inch of you . . . your breasts are so lovely . . . high and full and sensitive to my slightest touch . . . I love the color of your nipples . . . like spun honey . . . your waist is so small and your hips curve so enticingly . . ."

Between ragged murmurings, his mouth savored each part of her he praised. Helpless before the on-slaught of sensations so intense as to make everything she had known before pale into nothingness, Elizabeth gave up her brief resistance and sank again into the cocoon of voluptuous delight he was weaving around her.

No thought remained in her mind except to return the pleasure he was so ardently bestowing. Her hands pulled urgently at his open shirt until he obligingly shrugged it off. A soft gasp escaped her. This close, she could see that the broad sweep of his shoulders bore the same tribal marking Osei wore.

Her fingers trembled as she traced the hard ridge of raised skin down across his chest until it vanished into the thick mat of curling hair. Surprise whirled through her, but whatever questions she might have asked had to give way before the sheer erotic delight of discovering his body.

He was so astonishingly different from her! Her hands, wandering over his chest, tracing the line of his ribs, stroking up along his back, encountered only taut, virile strength.

In vivid contrast to her own body, there was not the slightest hint of softness in him. Directly beneath his skin, she could feel the hardness of bone and sinew. Power radiated from him, making her vividly aware of her own vulnerability.

It was an awareness Jordan shared. In the midst of passion greater than he had ever believed possible, he hesitated. The astonishment evident in her wide, dazzled eyes and the trembling of her full mouth made him acutely conscious of how helpless she was before him. Not because he would ever use his greater strength to force her to accept him, but because she lacked the experience to withstand the natural effect of his skilled caresses, made all the more potent by his own rampant desire.

To take advantage of her in such a state would be the height of callousness. The darker side of himself urged him to forget that and take what she so ardently offered. But Jordan was a man of honor. He could not disregard his protective feelings toward another human being no matter what the cost to himself.

Slowly, fighting against the most fundamental desires of his heart and body, he sat up. His breath came in harsh gasps as he turned slightly away so she would not see how shaken he was. "I'm sorry," he muttered huskily. "This shouldn't have happened."

Elizabeth stared at him in disbelief. He couldn't be serious. Though the riotous clamoring of her senses made reasonable thought all but impossible, she knew without doubt that the last few minutes had been the best of her life. She regretted nothing, except that he had stopped.

Hang the stupid social conventions that soiled what to her at least was gloriously beautiful! Racked by desire so intense as to be painful and choked by tears of hurt and frustration, she tried vainly to cover herself. The near nakedness that a moment before had seemed right and natural was now shameful.

Her hands trembled as she reached for her camisole and fumbled into it. She could not look at Jordan. Surely he must despise her for her licentiousness, so utterly at odds with the behavior of women such as his

126

mother and sisters. Or perhaps he simply thought her a frustrated old maid, easy prey for any man's touch.

Too late she remembered what he had said about men not liking easy conquests. Her soft, ripe mouth trembled as she reflected that she had come within a hair's breadth of being exactly that. But never again. She had learned a harsh lesson she would not soon forget.

Tightly, against the pain of unshed tears, she murmured, "I'm going back to camp. I'll ask Osei to send someone over here to keep watch while you bathe."

Jordan stood up, keeping his back turned while she finished fastening her shirt and slacks and pulling on her boots. Not until she tried to walk off did he stop her. "We'll go together. By this time you should know it's too dangerous around here for you to be alone."

His voice was low and tinged with something that sounded very much like regret, but Elizabeth didn't notice. She was too caught up in her own distress to recognize his.

She wanted to argue, to tell him she didn't need his or any man's protection. But the hurt inside her was too great. She could only nod numbly and suffer his silent presence beside her until they were once again back at the camp and could go their separate ways.

Even then there was little solace to be found in the routine of fixing dinner. She kept her mind rigorously blank as she chopped up the remainder of the crocodile meat and set it to fry in palm oil while putting the rice on to cook.

The food was as good as anyone could have managed under the circumstances, but it stuck in her throat. She ate only a few bites before giving up. Without looking at Jordan, she murmured her goodnights and sought the privacy of the small grass hut where her belongings were stowed.

Dropping a cowhide flap over the entrance, she sat

down heavily on the rush mat and rested her head in her hands. Worn out, bewildered, and tormented by needs she could not begin to understand, she wept quietly. Conscious of the men just outside, she could not give way to the full fury of her hurt and pain. Most of it had to remain bottled up inside her, where it quickly festered.

Damn him! What right did he have to play with her like that? To treat her as though she was an object for his amusement instead of a human being with feelings every bit as real as his own? Didn't he know how badly he had made her want him? Didn't he care?

Rubbing her eyes with the knuckles of her hands, she let the anger boil up in her. At first, it was all directed at Jordan. He had taken advantage of her inexperience; he had led her along until she was in a painful state of need; he had turned his back on the newly awakened woman in her, making a mockery of her desire for him.

But was all the blame entirely his? Hadn't she been remarkably naive and foolish? Self-loathing churned within her as she thought of how easily she had fallen under his control. How ludicrous he must find her. How absurdly weak and womanish.

It was her femininity that had led her into such a trap. For the first time in her life, she had dared to be something other than a colorless neuter, and for her pains, she had been slapped down hard.

Infuriated at her own weakness, Elizabeth frantically sought for some way to lash out at it. Her eyes fell on the pack lying nearby. With shaking hands, she reached inside for the compact kit of necessities she had added to the clothes and other equipment Jordan had supplied.

There was a small mirror and a pair of scissors inside. Barely hesitating, she yanked both out and stared at herself in the glass. The drawn, anguished face that stared back at her confirmed every unhappy thought whirling through her mind.

She was weak, stupid, helpless. Prey to emotions she could not control. Susceptible to the whims of men. Lacking in reason and even common sense. All because of her womanhood.

No wonder men despised her sex. No wonder she and all the others like her were made to take a back seat to the great events of the world. How else when their very appearance branded them weak and incapable?

Rage bubbled up in her. Without pausing to think, she seized the most visible object of her femininity, her long, glistening hair, and began to whack at it with the small scissors.

It was tough going but by dint of great determination and persistence she managed to laboriously snip off strand after strand. A pile of brown-gold silk began to accumulate at her feet.

Only once did she pause to consider the enormity of what she was doing. Glancing down at the coils of hair lying in the dust, she choked back a sob. It was too late for regrets. Gritting her teeth, she continued stubbornly until nothing remained but a short mass of curls clinging to her head.

With the scissors still clutched in her hand, Elizabeth gazed at herself in the mirror. What she saw stunned her. Far from the sexless caricature she had expected, an undeniably lovely young woman stared back at her.

The downy soft mass of hair glistening with the gold of the sun framed delicate features dominated by enormous sea-green eyes. Whereas before she had always thought her face thin and unappealing, she could now see that it was a perfect oval set off by a slim, straight nose, full mouth, and gently rounded chin. Her skin, warmed by the tropical sun, was lightly splattered with freckles that could not detract from its peaches-and-cream smoothness.

She was . . . not beautiful, surely. That was impossible. Or was it? The longer she stared at herself, the stronger the feeling grew that she was at last seeing the woman she had always been meant to be.

Slowly, Elizabeth lowered the scissors. They dropped unnoticed onto the rush mat. Could that lovely, graceful creature who seemed part wood sprite and part water nymph truly be her?

It didn't seem possible, yet the evidence of the mirror was unmistakable. The plain, almost homely image she had always had of herself was cracking wide open. If she had been so wrong about that, was there any chance she was equally in error about the rest of herself?

Hesitantly, she glanced down at her body. The shock of her encounter with Jordan and its aftermath had stripped away her preconceptions. For the first time, she really looked at the lines and curves of her form without automatically regretting their failure to conform to accepted standards of beauty.

Was this the same body she had felt compelled to keep bound by a corset and muffled by layers of clothes? Why had she never realized that though she was undeniably slender, there was nothing displeasing about her shape? Her long legs, slim hips, small waist, and high, firm breasts all fit together perfectly.

Dazedly, she shook her head, only to repeat the gesture as an alluring sense of lightness settled over her. With the weight of her hair gone, she felt unchained. The last fetters linkng her to another life were dropping away.

In the aftermath of her father's death, she had

learned to trust her own mind. Now she was realizing that her body merited the same faith.

Elation filled her, every bit as strongly as the despair of only moments before. She wasn't pitiable in any way. On the contrary, she was strong and beautiful, with a great deal to offer any man. If Jordan Nash didn't happen to recognize that, too bad for him.

A chuckle of pure delight rippled from her. She picked up the mirror again, staring at herself as she wondered how she could have been so destroyed by his actions at the pool. Granted, they had seemed callous at the time. But with her newfound confidence, she could acknowledge that perhaps he had motivations beyond her immediate understanding.

It wasn't outside the bounds of possibility that Jordan had recognized the potential in her before she did herself. Another man might have been tempted to play Pygmalion to her Galatea, and by so doing to deny her the glorious experience of self-realization.

But Jordan had not. He had left her to come to terms with herself on her own, just as he had refrained from taking advantage of the sensuality she was only beginning to understand.

A warm smile curved her mouth, as the rage she had felt for him only a short time before gave way to far tenderer feelings. Though she was exhausted by the emotional turmoil of the day, she hastily tidied up the grass enclosure before lying down on the rush mat.

Her ears strained for any sound of his approach even as her eyes irresistibly fluttered shut. She was asleep before she could do more than hope that he meant to join her.

Waking far in the night, Elizabeth turned over uneasily. It was very hot. The parched air seemed to crackle with an electrical charge. Far off in the distance, a lion roared.

Instinctively, she reached out a hand for Jordan, seeking the comfort of his nearness. But her fingers encountered nothing. She was alone in the hut. Sitting up, she looked around hesitantly. There was no sign of his belongings or any other indication that he had come near her after she fell asleep.

A ragged sigh escaped her. He had clearly decided to bed down elsewhere. She supposed she should be relieved. After all, he had originally insisted on her sharing his hut to enforce his ownership of her. By removing himself, he seemed to acknowledge her independence. So why wasn't she glad?

Because you miss him, you ninny, her irate mind informed her. *You like the way he feels against you, hard and solid and reassuring. You like the sound of his voice, the smell of his skin, the rise and fall of his breathing. And you like thinking about what's going to happen between the two of you. Don't try to pretend otherwise.*

Her conscience sounded remarkably like a tart-tongued nanny, Elizabeth thought sourly. But maybe it was right. She did miss Jordan. Opening the flap of the hut, she wondered where he was.

The campfire had been carefully extinguished and the moon had already set, so it was difficult to see. By straining her eyes to absorb as much starlight as possible, she could make out the other grass huts encircling the campsite. Most of their flaps were up, revealing the shapes of slumbering men.

One of them must be Jordan, but she couldn't begin to guess which. And one must be Nigel, whom she felt a bit bad about ignoring. Even if his motives had not been the best, he was still an Englishman in need of help.

Since his brush with the crocodile, he had been quiet and withdrawn. Tomorrow she should try to draw him out, to convince him they really weren't all that badly off and that he should take a more charitable view of Jordan and the others.

Feeling better for having resolved to do that, she left the hut quietly to answer a call of nature. Mindful of the ever-present dangers lurking in the bush, she went only as far as modesty required. When she came back, she was far sleepier than before and more than ready to return to her mat.

Only the realization that one of the grass huts was now empty stopped her. Glancing around, she wondered who else might be up and about. Probably just someone off on the same errand as herself.

About to reenter her hut, Elizabeth paused. A man was moving among the bundles of supplies near the beached canoes. He was shorter than either the Ashante warriors or Jordan, and dressed in a light-hued khaki shirt and trousers.

Nigel! Was he mad? He had given Jordan his word he wouldn't try to escape. Yet what other construction could be put on his proximity to the canoes, or to the nervous look he cast over his shoulder as he carefully undid the mooring lines and pushed one of the craft back into the water.

She had to stop him. If he was found, he would be severely punished. The Ashantes were merciless to those they considered betrayers, and she did not doubt Jordan would be equally as ruthless. Nigel was risking his life in an insane venture that could only lead to his own death.

Hastening forward, she got within several yards of him before he realized her presence. When he did, his head shot up and an angry snarl twisted his lips.

"What the hell are you doing here?"

The angry hiss jarred Elizabeth. She had hardly expected him to be pleased, but neither had she counted on the unbridled rage emanating from him.

"I came to stop you," she whispered anxiously. "If

you go through with this, you'll only harm yourself."

"If you think you're going to keep me here, you're crazy," Nigel snarled. "I'm not staying around for Nash and his friends to decide to cut my throat. I'd rather take my chances out there." He gestured toward the dark expanse of the river and the savannah on either side.

"You're mad! You admitted yourself you couldn't last more than a few hours without supplies or bearers."

"I said what Nash wanted to hear, that's all. There's no reason I can't make it back to Accra, and when I do you can bet I won't waste any time setting the dogs on your American friend and his cronies. They'll be stew meat before a fortnight's passed."

Elizabeth's stomach clenched painfully. He meant what he said. Nigel was really so deluded as to believe he could match the extraordinary survival skills of Jordan and the Ashantes.

She had to stop him, as much for his own sake as for the men he intended to betray. But how? Any attempt to reason with him was clearly out of the question. Nigel was glaring at her with narrowed eyes.

The mooring rope twisted in his hands. He took a step nearer, spurring her to action.

Opening her mouth to scream, she was abruptly stopped by his lightning-fast reflexes. Lunging forward, Nigel clamped a hard hand over her mouth while pulling her tight against his body. Trapping her flailing arms with one of his, he laughed cruelly.

"The playing fields of Eton may not seem like a harsh training ground to you, my lady, but believe me they leave very little room for error. I am not about to let you ruin my plans just when they are on the verge of realization. You're coming with me."

Elizabeth gazed at him in horror. He meant what he said. He actually intended to take her along on a demented flight into deadly danger. Twisting frantically, she tried to break free of him, without success.

His hands tightened on her mercilessly. Tying a bandana around her mouth so tightly that the cloth dug into her skin, he flung her to the ground with sufficient force to knock the breath from her.

As she lay dazed and hurting, he quickly pulled her arms behind her back and looped the rope around her wrists and ankles. His pale eyes gleamed as he pulled it taut, forcing her spine to arch until she thought it would surely snap.

An anguished moan broke from her, caused as much by her acute physical discomfort as by the realization of how foolish she had been to go anywhere near him. She should have woken the entire camp the moment she had seen him trying to escape. Instead, she had attempted to protect him, with the result that now she was in graver danger than ever before in her life.

Tears misted her eyes as she considered the foolishness of her good intentions. But it was too late for regrets. Nigel had hoisted her into the canoe and followed quickly, throwing in the few supplies he had managed to select before quickly shoving off from the shore and plunging them both into the forbidding darkness of the African night.

Elizabeth lost track of how far they traveled. The hours blurred one into the other. She tried to sleep to conserve her strength, but could not. The steady throbbing of her bound limbs gave way slowly to numbness that in its own way was all the more agonizing.

She was trussed up as helpless as an animal being readied for the slaughter. Lying on the floor of the canoe, she could not protect herself from the sharp edges of the wood or the water that sloshed repeatedly over the sides.

Quickly soaked to the skin, she had to watch helplessly as her shirt and trousers clung to her body, clearly outlining her delicate curves. In his hurry to get away, Nigel had so far ignored her. But as the miles lengthened between the campsite and themselves, he felt confident enough to slightly slow his pace.

Glancing down at her, his pale eyes narrowed. Leisurely he raked the slender lines of her legs and hips upward toward the high, firm breasts straining against the thin fabric of her camisole and shirt. A chilling smile curved his narrow mouth.

"Well, well, it looks as though the ugly duckling has turned into a swan. No wonder Nash was so anxious to keep you to himself."

Elizabeth did not respond. She turned her face away, fighting against the almost suffocating waves of panic sweeping over her. The look she had just seen in Nigel's eyes bore no resemblance to Jordan's appreciative appraisal of her. Whereas he had shown only healthy male enjoyment, Nigel evinced violence and a potential for cruelty that made her throat tighten with fear. When a booted foot poked into her ribs, she flinched but refused to turn her head.

He laughed callously. "You'll soon change your tune, that is if you want to stay alive. Without me, you'll be lion bait. I don't suppose you've ever thought about what it actually means to be eaten by a wild animal. Maybe you should, your ladyship. Annoy me and I just might stake you out on the ground for any marauder who happens by."

Despite herself, she could not resist the urge to answer him as he deserved. "Did you also learn this behavior on the playing fields of Eton, Mr. Chandler? Or was that part of your education acquired elsewhere?"

He laughed harshly. "No, as a matter of fact you were right the first time. I found out quickly what it

136

meant to be the poor relation of a wealthy family. Oh, they sent me to the best schools all right, but beyond that they wouldn't lift a finger. I had to earn every penny for myself, no matter how hard. While my cousins were getting fancy court appointments, I was slogging it out as a junior barrister. Not for me, thank you very much. Africa will be my fortune, especially once I've got hold of the golden idol."

"You can't seriously expect to get away with this. Kidnapping is a capital offense. You'll hang."

"On whose say-so? Yours? I doubt it." Wiping the sweat from his brow, Nigel looked down at her mockingly. "I'll be a hero, Lady Elizabeth. The brave young Englishman who went into the African bush and found a great archaeological treasure. Even though I'm essentially penniless, did I make any attempt to sell it? No, I brought it home for the greater glory of the empire. The public will love it and I'll be set for life."

"Life in prison, perhaps, if you're lucky."

"Not likely, considering that you're the only person who could testify against me and I can destroy your credibility simply by announcing that you went with the Ashantes and Nash voluntarily, that you were in fact his willing mistress. Not a court in England would believe anything you say after that."

Elizabeth opened her mouth to respond, only to think better of it. Even if he did allow her to live, which she seriously doubted, he was right about her word carrying no weight in court.

By her insistence on going into the bush, she had placed herself outside the bounds of proper behavior and made herself automatically suspect. The moment Nigel raised the possibility that she had been Jordan's mistress, she would be condemned.

A painful smile twisted her lips. How ironic to be damned for something she fervently wished was in fact true. But it was too late for thoughts of what might have been.

Despite Nigel's seeming assurance that she could do him no harm, she did not believe for a moment that he would take the risk of letting her speak out. Just now he needed her because she knew where the idol was. But once he found the golden statue, her usefulness would be over.

And until then . . . ? The look in his eyes made her shiver. Not even the enervating heat of the river could prevent the wave of coldness that washed over her. She trembled inwardly, closing her eyes against the tears she was determined would not fall.

Toward dawn, they stopped. Nigel pulled the canoe up on shore and carefully hid it amid the foliage before hoisting the rifle he had stolen over his shoulder. Yanking Elizabeth to her feet, he undid her bonds, then watched with amusement as her numbed limbs gave way and she sank to the ground.

"Get up." To add emphasis to his command, he kicked her sharply in the side.

Clutching her bruised ribs, she managed to stagger to her feet, only to realize that the situation was even worse than she had feared. Nigel gestured to the bundle of supplies as he said, "You're going to earn your keep, your ladyship. Put that on your back."

The relentless glare he shot her made it clear it would do no good to argue. Preferring to save her strength, she did as he said. The bag was heavy, but not unbearably so. She was able to stand upright under its load.

At least at first. But as weary mile followed mile, the weight seemed to increase by leaps and bounds. A pain started in the small of her back, spreading quickly outward until it radiated through her arms and legs like hot piercing needles. Sweat poured down her face, almost blinding her. Her lips grew quickly parched and her breath came in shallow pants.

When she staggered, the rope Nigel had tied around her neck tightened remorselessly. He yanked her forward again, refusing to give her even a moment to rest.

"You can rest tonight," he snarled, "after you've set up the camp, fixed dinner and . . ."—deliberately, he let his eyes run over her—". . . seen to my other needs."

Drawing air into her dusty lungs, Elizabeth managed to answer him defiantly. "Will you add rape to your other crimes, Mr. Chandler? Because that's what it will be."

He jerked the rope again, snarling angrily. "Will it? Not if you hope for the slightest consideration from me. Perhaps I should refrain from feeding you until you show me what Nash taught you about pleasing men."

"Go right ahead. If I don't eat, I won't be able to walk. Then where will you be?"

"You have a point. I'll have to get you to tell me the location of the idol sooner than I had planned."

"I'll tell you nothing!"

"So you say now, but we'll see." Ominously, he added, "I haven't spent all these years out here without learning a few things about persuasion. There are a couple of techniques that were used on captured natives during the last uprising a few years back. I'm sure you'll find them instructive."

Bile rose in Elizabeth's throat. She told herself his threats were empty; he was after all an Englishman of good background. Such men did not go around torturing and raping women. Or did they?

What did she really know about how men behaved beyond the sacred shores of Britain? From time to time she had heard whispers of atrocities committed in

Ireland and elsewhere that she had refused to credit. Now she had to wonder.

Certainly most of her countrymen were decent, honorable souls. Yet there could be exceptions, and Nigel might well be one of them. Especially if he was as desperate as he seemed.

Refusing to think about what she would suffer if he carried out his threats, she concentrated all her strength on putting one foot in front of the other. Only by dint of extreme effort was she able to stay upright and follow him. Even so, her pace was frequently slower than his, so that the rope was stretched taut between them and her throat became so chafed that it bled.

At midafternoon, just when she thought she could not take another step, he surprised her by suddenly stopping. Reaching down to rub the calf of his injured leg, he said, "We'll stay here until morning. Put that pack down and get a fire going."

Silently, Elizabeth obeyed. Slumped on the ground, still holding the leash fastened around her throat, Nigel watched her every movement. He spoke only once, to ask, "What the hell did you do to your hair?"

In a voice made weak by extreme exhaustion, she murmured, "I cut it."

"That's obvious. Why?"

"Because it was too hot."

"Oh . . . I don't like it."

Tempted to point out that she considered that good news, she prudently kept silent instead. During their long trek through the bush, she had decided that Nigel was a bully who would seize any excuse to attack someone weaker than himself.

While she could, she would endure his taunts and save her strength for what she was certain would be the inevitable struggle against him.

It came sooner than she had expected. After a

sparse meal of rice and dried strips of beef, of which she was allowed to eat only a tiny fraction, he stood and stretched leisurely. "Tomorrow, when I'm sure we've gotten away clean, I'll hunt. Wouldn't mind getting myself a croc. Nash thinks he's such a good shot, but I can outhit him any day."

His boasting brought a sick coldness to Elizabeth's stomach. All too clearly she remembered how Jordan had risked his life to save the other man. He must be cursing himself now, and perhaps her as well.

For the first time, she wondered if he thought she had gone with Nigel willingly. Much as she rebelled at the notion, she could not deny the possibility.

The absence of both captives would lead to certain inevitable conclusions. Although she suspected Jordan was enraged by her, that did not make her long any the less for his presence. Especially when Nigel flung a rush mat onto the ground and gestured to it.

"Lie down."

Drawing on all her courage, she shook her head. "I'll stay where I am."

"What makes you think you have a choice?"

When she refused to answer, he yanked on the leash so sharply that she lost her balance and sprawled on the ground. Dust filled her mouth as she looked up at him, seeing the maddened glint in his eye.

"Don't you dare disobey me," he snarled. "I could kill you in an instant, and maybe I will if you don't behave properly. Now get on the mat."

Slowly, Elizabeth rose. Her legs would barely hold her. Desperately, she glanced round for some weapon, anything that might give her a chance against him.

"All right, but let me add some wood to the fire first to keep it going, otherwise animals are likely to come nearer."

Reluctantly, Nigel nodded. He kept hold of the rope while she picked up a sturdy stick and held it to the fire as though feeding it in slowly. When she took longer than he thought she should, he jerked the leash again impatiently.

"Hurry up. I'm anxious to sample what you gave Nash."

Whatever lingering indecision she felt vanished at that moment. Without hesitation, she grasped the stick in both hands and turned, thrusting the burning tip toward Nigel.

He screamed and dropped the rope, his arms darting up to protect his face. Panic tempted her to try to flee, but she resisted it, knowing that he would only follow. Her sole hope lay in stopping him right then and there.

Far in the back of her mind, she understood what that meant. The only way she could stop him was to kill him. The mere thought was enough to sicken her, but not to make her weaken. Every instinct for survival that she possessed came stunningly to the fore, blocking out all other considerations.

Swinging the burning brand back and forth, she managed to keep him sufficiently off balance so that he could not reach for his gun. But Nigel's instincts were every bit as good as her own, and they did not desert him.

With a vicious snarl, he hurled himself at her, grasping her around the waist and throwing them both to the ground. Elizabeth tried desperately to hold onto the stick, but failed. It rolled away, far enough so that she could not reach it, but still near enough to singe the soft skin of her hand.

She cried out in mingled pain and anguish, knowing that her last chance was gone. Nigel loomed above her, his face twisted into a hideous mask that did not even appear human. Brutally, he dug his knee into her stomach so that she could not breathe.

A black void dotted by spinning lights reached out to her. Valiantly, she fought against it, knowing that once she lost consciousness she would lose everything. Lying limply under him, she let her eyes close, praying he would think she had given up.

He laughed fiendishly, his hands reaching for the buttons of her blouse even as her burned hand groped again for the stick. Just as her fingers brushed it, a shot rang out.

Elizabeth's eyes opened wide in shock as Nigel abruptly went still above her. All the color drained from his face. Fumbling, he reached for his left shoulder. The hand he pressed to it came away red with blood. A stunned moan broke from him as he crumpled to the ground.

Sitting up hastily, she stared at him in disbelief. The man who an instant before had been an implacable menace now lay helpless before her, unable even to reach for the rifle on his back.

Not that he would have had any chance to use it. As she gazed wide-eyed, Jordan stepped from the bush, the smoking Winchester in his hands and Osei right beside him.

Chapter Nine

ELIZABETH STOOD UP SLOWLY. SHE COULD SENSE the barely contained rage in Jordan and was wary of it. It didn't make any difference that he had no reason to be angry at her. Until he knew that, she would be wise to go very cautiously.

As he and Osei stepped into the small clearing accompanied by the rest of the warriors, she stood frozen in place. Her burned hand throbbed even more than the rest of her aching, battered body, but she ignored it. All her attention was focused on Jordan.

He wore only boots and khaki trousers she suspected he had pulled on hastily. His bare chest glistened with sweat. The tribal markings stood out clearly against the darkly tanned skin. As he moved, his clearly defined muscles rippled sinuously.

Elizabeth forced herself to meet his eyes. Not for a moment would she let him think she felt any shame or guilt. Soon enough he would have to face the evidence of her innocence, but in the meantime she would not stand for any abuse.

"Don't say anything," Jordan snarled before she could even attempt to do so. "I'm angry enough right now to snap your head off. Just keep quiet until I've cooled down some."

Before she could respond, he turned to Nigel, who had been hoisted to his feet by the warriors and stood with his head slumped and blood still dripping from his shoulder.

"I thought about killing you," Jordan said very softly in a voice that sent shivers of fear down Elizabeth's back. "It would have been easy enough to do, given your . . . preoccupation."

Raising his head, Nigel glared at him balefully. His face was a sickly gray but his eyes still burned with rage. "Why didn't you?"

"Because Osei reminded me that you may still be useful. You have him to thank for your life."

Nigel's lips curled back in an ugly snarl. He wasn't about to thank a black man for anything. "You're as bad as any damn native," he jeered, "and you'll end the same way, dead!"

"You speak very boldly for a man in your position. Perhaps I should kill you after all."

What little color remained in Nigel's face vanished. He saw the implacable will in Jordan's face and tried not to believe it, but the meaning was unmistakable. Hastily, he mumbled, "Y-you said I might still be useful . . ."

"Osei said that. It's up to him to decide."

Nigel glanced at the warrior unwillingly. Clearly, it had never occurred to him that his life would be in the hands of that despised race of people he considered so inferior to himself. The stunning reversal of his position struck him hard. He stared wide-eyed as Osei calmly deliberated his fate.

"We are not like you, Mr. Chandler," the Ashante prince said quietly. "We do not kill arbitrarily. You will be taken to the capital at Kumasi to be judged by my father, the Asantehene. Your past crimes against my people will be considered, along with your intention to loot the golden idol. Only then will judgment be rendered."

Gesturing to several of the warriors, he said, "Guard him well. Tomorrow you will set off for the capital. I will have messages for you to take to my father."

The men nodded eagerly, glad of the opportunity to deliver one of the enemy to their king. They seized Nigel none too gently and dragged him off to a corner of the clearing.

When they had gone, Osei regarded Elizabeth quietly. With his eyes still on her, he asked Jordan, "What about the woman?"

Her heart caught in her throat as she waited for his reply. Jordan took his time, looking her over coldly before he at last said, "She is my responsibility. I will see to her punishment."

The black man glanced at him shrewdly. "That is your right. But I caution against hasty judgment." He looked back at Elizabeth for a moment, his full mouth curving in a surprisingly gentle smile, before he went off to join the other men.

Jordan stared at her, frowning. "I can't believe you've fooled Osei. He's smarter than any two men I know."

"Perhaps it's you who have been fooled," she ventured quietly. "Appearances are not always what they seem."

A mocking glare twisted his features. "I saw clearly enough. You were on the ground with Chandler, letting him put his hands on you, not offering up any resistance that I could see."

"Look again."

The very calmness of her voice forced him to com-

146

ply. Hesitantly, not wanting to believe what he saw, Jordan let his eyes wander over her. As Elizabeth watched, the color fled from beneath his tan, only to be replaced by the dark flush of anger.

His relief at the realization that she had not been a willing participant in the escape gave way instantly to rage as he took in the extent of her suffering. Big, capable hands trembled as he reached for her.

"E-Elizabeth . . ."

Nestled in his arms, safe against the broad expanse of his chest, she gladly yielded to his care. With a muffled curse, Jordan lifted her bruised body and carried her to the edge of the clearing, where he gently propped her against a tree.

His voice shook as he said, "Stay there. I'll be right back. Don't move."

She had no intention of doing so. Beyond the fact that the last of her strength had abruptly vanished, the fierce gentleness of his gaze was far too compelling to deny. With a soft sigh, she settled back against the broad trunk and closed her eyes.

He was back within minutes. Dropping his pack on the ground, he pulled out a rush mat and laid it down before gently lifting Elizabeth onto the softer surface. As he used a small knife to cut the rope from around her neck, a jagged pulse beat in the hollow of his cheek.

The force with which he threw the loathsome leash into the undergrowth was eloquent proof of his rage, but the hands that carefully touched her bruised throat could not have been more gentle.

"Hold still now," he murmured, using a cool cloth to wipe the burning sweat and grime from her face. When that was done, he applied a soothing ointment to her throat and to the burn on her hand, which he stared at narrowly.

"How did this happen?"

Somewhat reluctantly, Elizabeth told him. She concluded by explaining, "I was trying to reach the stick when you fired. I didn't realize there was any chance of help and I thought if I couldn't stop him myself, he would . . ." She broke off, unable to continue. The vision of Nigel looming above her was still too vivid. Helplessly, she felt tears rising in her sea-green eyes.

The look on Jordan's face was not pleasant. He was a man torn between rage and compassion. Compassion won. Turning his back on the corner of the camp where Nigel lay, he drew Elizabeth closer. Patting her shoulders a bit awkwardly, he murmured, "Don't think about it any more. It's all over. You're safe now. I won't let anything happen to you."

Though he was new to the role of comforter and protector, he found he took to it naturally. The feel of her nestled in his arms evoked powerful instincts he could not deny. They were linked to but far more complex than the simplistic sensations of carnal desire. While he still raged inwardly at the knowledge that another man had tried to possess her, he focused all his attention on blotting the memory from her mind.

The soft murmur of his voice reached Elizabeth even through the haze of remembered terror. Slowly, as though hardly daring to do so, she relaxed. The tension went out of her limbs. Her head rested against his shoulder as he gently tended her other cuts and bruises. Before he was done she had fallen asleep as suddenly as a worn-out child.

Jordan lowered her carefully to the mat, brushing away a fly that tried to settle on her nose. He could not bring himself to let go of her entirely. Positioning her burned hand beside her, he kept hold of the other.

The rage that had held him in a vise since realizing that she was gone was slowly giving way to gratitude for her safety. Despite his strong desire to hurt Nigel badly, he was still able to put that aside and to think of other things.

Chief among them, her hair. Bemusedly, he reached out to touch it. The soft tendrils of golden-brown silk tickled his fingers. He smiled unwillingly. It didn't take any great imagination to guess what had prompted her to hack it off. Much as he regretted having so upset her, he could not quarrel with the results.

She was even lovelier than he had dreamt she could be. The delicate line of her throat, clearly revealed for the first time, fascinated him. Skin lightly kissed by the sun was still so translucent that he could make out the feathery tracing of blue veins carrying her life's blood.

Carefully, so as not to wake her, he leaned forward to press his lips to the pulse beating just beneath her jaw. The sensations that simple caress provoked were so powerful as to make him tremble. He had to be grateful for Elizabeth's unawareness, as waves of almost desperate need washed over him.

Oblivious to the emotional storm she so effortlessly unleashed, she sighed in her sleep and moved closer to him. Jordan stifled a groan. More than anything in the world, he wanted to sweep her up in his arms and carry her away to some secluded place where they could discover each other as man and woman were meant to from the beginning.

But he was not free to indulge any such fantasies. Beyond his responsibilities to Osei and the other men, there was the simple fact that Elizabeth was in no condition to be confronted by his passion. The more he studied her, the more aware he became of the extent of her injuries.

Beyond the rope burns marking her throat and wrists, and the burn on her hand, he could see numerous scratches and bruises that were mute testament to all she had endured since the previous night.

He suspected other lacerations and abrasions must lie beneath her clothes, but short of stripping her he had no way of determining that. He would have to wait until she regained enough strength to understand that she had to let him tend all her hurts.

Letting go of Elizabeth, he stood up and glanced around. The Ashantes had wasted no time setting up camp. Half-a-dozen grass huts were already in place, a fire was burning, and several of the younger men were preparing supper.

Nigel was tied to the trunk of a tree in a sitting position, his injured shoulder roughly bandaged but no other effort made to see to his well-being. Jordan knew he had to keep his distance from him. If he got near the Englishman again, he would be in danger of preempting the Asantehene's privilege of administering justice. That was something no warrior, not even one whose skin was white, could do.

Even so, the urge to make Nigel suffer every bit as much as Elizabeth had was almost irresistible. It clawed at him throughout the few remaining hours of daylight as he automatically swallowed the food put before him and shared the muted conversation of the weary men.

His only comfort came from the knowledge that with each passing moment, Nigel suffered more from the simple but effective punishment the tropical forest wreaked on those foolish enough to tempt her power.

His pleas for food and water were ignored, as were his moans of horror as insects attracted by the blood of his wound began to crawl over him. Bound to the tree, he could not prevent the stinging bites that quickly turned the entire surface of his skin to a throbbing inferno. Not until unconsciousness claimed him did his cries of pain and revulsion taper off, leaving the insects to work in peace.

Most of the warriors retired shortly thereafter as the

first watch was posted. Jordan exchanged a few quiet words with Osei, who showed no surprise at learning of Elizabeth's innocence, before returning to the grass hut that had been erected around her. Slipping out of his boots, he lowered himself onto the mat beside her and gathered her into his arms.

Despite the heat that did not ease with the setting of the sun, he needed the closeness of her flesh against his to reassure himself that he had truly found her again and that she would be all right.

Elizabeth did not seem to mind. She curled against him as naturally as though she had lain thusly every night of her life. Smiling faintly, Jordan closed his eyes. Sleep claimed him before the thick sun-tipped lashes had settled over the high curve of his cheeks.

Shortly before dawn, Elizabeth awoke. In the first gray light of day, she propped herself up on her uninjured hand and studied the man beside her. Asleep, he looked younger and unexpectedly vulnerable. The harsh lines of his face were relaxed, allowing her to catch a glimpse of the boy he must have been.

Tentatively, she reached out a finger to lightly touch the sensual curve of his mouth. His breath was warm against her skin, sending little shivers of pleasure through her.

It came to her that she loved him.

There was no great clap of thunder, no caroling of angel voices heralding this discovery. Only the simple, absolute assurance that she had at last found the missing part of herself.

Her heart's choice frankly took her aback. Never in her wildest dreams could she have imagined herself in love with a man such as Jordan Nash. But then never could she have conjured up the man himself, let alone the feelings he set off in her.

Briefly she debated trying to fight the strange, inexplicable emotion that had seized hold of her. That possibility was quickly rejected. She might as well consider cutting off a limb as attempting to exorcise Jordan from her heart.

Her mouth curved upward at the corners as she let the sheer pleasure of being in love wash over her. Later there might be doubts and recriminations, but just then she was content to enjoy the irresistible happiness he had, all unknowingly, given her.

No wonder the poets spoke so incessantly of love. No wonder people did such outlandish things because of it, and thought any risk worth taking. It was a heady elixir that transformed the world from a cold, often cruel arena to a place of astounding beauty and joy.

All the fear and pain she had experienced the day before faded into unreality. It might never have been. She felt thrillingly alive and eager for whatever the next moment might bring.

A slight, very faint snore stirred the air next to her. Elizabeth's smile widened into a broad grin. He was such a wonderful man. He even snored delightfully.

Shaking her head at her own besottedness, she slipped away from him and stood up slowly. Only a few of the warriors were awake. The rest were taking advantage of the chance to rest after the arduous chase.

She guessed Nigel's escape must have been discovered around daybreak, hours after they had left the camp. To catch up with them so quickly, Jordan and the Ashantes must have maintained a nearly inhuman pace. Their determination impressed her even more than their stamina.

Catching sight of Kwesi, she went over to say good morning. The headman no longer seemed an enemy to her. On the contrary, after her close brush with true violence, she understood that he had treated her very gently.

The concern she saw in his eyes as he took in the bruises and other injuries banished whatever remaining hesitation she might have had about him. Smiling, she took the cooking pot from him.

"I'll fix breakfast, Kwesi. I'm sure you and the other men have better things to do."

He nodded gravely, accepting the gesture of friendship. "Thank you, but you should not hurry to resume your duties. Tomorrow or the next day would be soon enough."

"I know," she said softly, "but I'd prefer to be busy. It keeps me from . . ." Unwillingly, her gaze wandered to Nigel, slumped unconscious against the tree. A shiver ran through her as she hastily looked away.

Kwesi moved very slightly, just enough to interpose his bulk between her and the man whose mere presence still evoked fear. Gently, he said, "Of course, I should have realized that. Go right ahead then and fix breakfast, but do not tire yourself." White teeth flashed against his black skin as he added, "Jordan would not forgive me if I allowed that to happen."

Her confidence in the headman was now so great that she felt able to tease him a bit. Glancing up through the thick fringe of her lashes, she inquired, "Don't you mean my master?"

She watched in fascination as a dark stain spread over Kwesi's features. It took her a moment to realize he was blushing. Hesitantly, he said, "I doubt Jordan truly considers himself as such . . ."

"But he did buy me from you."

"Not exactly . . ." Her silence encouraged him to continue. "You see, Jordan knows that many of the younger Ashantes like myself are opposed to slave trading. We see it as an unfortunate remnant from our past, which is now being used by the British as an excuse to call us savages and perpetuate all sorts of injustices against us. Feeling as I do, I would never sell a human being. However, when I captured you I became responsible for both your behavior and your welfare, much as though you were a sister or cousin. Jordan simply arranged to transfer that responsibility to himself."

Though nothing he had said so far really surprised her, Elizabeth was still puzzled by the exact nature of the arrangement he described. Looking up at the headman, she asked, "How did he do that?"

Kwesi hesitated. Loyalty to one who shared the bond of warrior brotherhood made him wonder exactly how much he should say. But he couldn't deny the wry amusement that led him to admit the truth. "Very simply. He paid a bride price for you."

Elizabeth's reaction did not disappoint him. Her mouth dropped open and the eyes that were the color of a deep lagoon widened in astonishment. "B-bride price . . . ?"

Kwesi nodded benignly. "Quite a large one. You should be very flattered."

"You mean . . . ?"

Not one to mince words, the headman said, "I mean that in the eyes of the Ashantes and our god, Nyame, you and Jordan are married."

Putting the pot down carefully, Elizabeth lowered herself to the ground. She sat crosslegged with both hands stretched out as though to maintain her balance. Numbly, she tried to assimilate this stunning bit of news. Not for a moment did she think Kwesi was teasing her. Despite his wide smile, it was clear he was quite serious and that moreover he thoroughly approved of the arrangement.

Dazedly, she murmured, "But isn't there some sort of ceremony? I mean, some way of . . . becoming married . . . ?"

Crouching down beside her, he nodded gently. "Ordinarily there would be, but with the search for the idol it had to be postponed. Later, if you would permit it, I'm sure Jordan would appreciate the opportunity to celebrate with those he regards as his brothers."

"Then he really is an Ashante warrior?"

"Absolutely. He passed through the manhood trials and proved himself worthy of the markings he bears. He is sworn to defend us, even as we are him."

As Kwesi spoke, he watched her carefully for some sign of outrage or disapproval at the idea of a white man binding himself to those whom so many of his race considered inferior. But there was none. Instead, Elizabeth simply nodded thoughtfully.

"It's good that he has become so close to you, since he is so far from his first home and family."

"A man needs both. But without a wife, he cannot have either."

"And now Jordan has a wife . . ."

"Exactly." Rising, Kwesi smiled down at her. "We of the Ashante believe Nyame wishes to make life a joy for all beings. But that effort requires human cooperation. Only the most foolish throw away the gift of the creator before realizing its worth."

Elizabeth looked up at him steadily. Her voice was quiet but firm as she said, "I am not a fool, Kwesi."

He laughed softly before taking himself off to relieve the night watch and begin what he already suspected might be a very entertaining day.

When he was gone, she began automatically to prepare breakfast while thinking over what he had said. She was married, at least in the eyes of a people she had rapidly come to respect and a god who wanted life to be a joy for his creatures.

But was she also married in Jordan's eyes? Did he truly regard her as his wife? That seemed doubtful. How could he when they had never . . . A warm blush stained her cheeks. The ardent interlude they had shared by the pool had done much to banish her ignorance about marital intimacy.

While she was certain a great deal remained to be learned, she had a fair idea of exactly what she wanted to share with Jordan. Perhaps she should be shocked by the brazenness of her thoughts, but instead she yearned to transform them into reality.

With her attention so thoroughly occupied, she was conscious of very little else, until a quiver of awareness suddenly darted through her. Elizabeth lifted her head, knowing without having to turn around who had come up behind her.

Jordan's warm hand touched her shoulder gently. "I was startled to find you gone from the hut. For a moment, I didn't know where you were."

The relief she heard in his voice touched her deeply. It banished the self-consciousness that might otherwise have left her tongue-tied in his presence.

Facing him, she smiled so warmly that Jordan's breath caught in his throat. His eyes ran over her hungrily, like a man long starved of what he needs most. What he saw reassured him, and made him admire her all the more.

Despite the ordeal of the day before, she looked entrancingly beautiful and vibrant. The feathery curls clinging to her head glistened in the sun. Her skin glowed with health and her sea-green eyes sparkled like twin gems. Her soft, full mouth curved enticingly . . .

He looked away hastily. Another moment and he would have had no choice but to draw her into his arms and kiss her as thoroughly as he had on too few occasions in the past. There was no doubt where that would lead. The warriors would be highly amused, Elizabeth might well be enraged, and he would be left with an ache he could not banish.

Sighing, he glanced round for some safe distraction. His eyes fell on the breakfast simmering in the pot. "Did you cook that?"

Elizabeth was far too taken up in simply looking at him to be aware of what he had said, but she nodded anyway. She would have agreed to anything he asked without a second thought.

Jordan, however, did not know that. He saw only that she was incalculably beautiful, yet vulnerable. The thought that he might add in even the smallest way to the pain she had already endured was intolerable. But if he stayed so close to her in his present state he was likely to do just that. He had to get away long enough to rein in his unruly emotions, but how?

Elizabeth herself provided the solution. As breakfast was eaten, she said, "That's the last of the food supplies except for some rice and dried yams."

"Then we can no longer put off hunting," Osei said. With the decisiveness of a man raised to rule, he continued, "Kwesi, you and three of the men will take Chandler to my father at Kumasi. Jordan, you mentioned seeing fresh traces of impala as we came this way yesterday. Any chance of tracking it down?"

"Certainly. I'll take half-a-dozen men with me and spend the day on it. By nightfall we should have a fair catch."

"Good. In the meantime, the rest of us will return to the river and make camp. Tomorrow, we can set out again with full stomachs and packs."

Elizabeth heard all this with relief. Much as she hated to be parted from Jordan even a short time, she needed a few hours to herself to sort out what Kwesi had told her and to try to decide where she would go from there.

The discovery of her love for him made it impossible to simply allow the present situation to continue, nor did she think he wanted that. Some resolution had to be achieved if they were to have any chance of truly receiving Nyame's gift of joy.

She was sorry to say goodbye to Kwesi, but delighted to see the last of Nigel. He had revived enough to glare at everyone venomously. Without the preconceptions his class and background had imposed on her, she could see him for the truly hate-filled man he was. What the Asantehene would make of him she could not guess, but neither could she truly claim to care.

Jordan and the other men left shortly thereafter as the camp was being dismantled. Elizabeth was wondering what she could take out of her pack to make it light enough for her battered body to carry when Anoyke surprised her by hoisting it over his shoulder. As she protested, he merely grinned and went off to join the others forming up for the march to the river.

"It will be enough for you to walk today, Lady Elizabeth," Osei said quietly. "There is no need to prove your valor to us." His gaze touched on the marks still clearly visible around her neck and on her burned hand as he added, "You fought Chandler as bravely as one of our own women would, so you are deserving of the same consideration."

Though her throat thickened at the knowledge of his approval, she managed to smile. "Jordan told me once that you are very forebearing of women."

Osei shot her a surprised glance before laughing abashedly. "It is true. When a man loves one woman, he tends to look upon all of you with favor."

Keeping pace with him as they left the clearing, Elizabeth asked, "If I'm not being too personal, will you tell me about this woman you love?"

The fierce warrior was silent for a moment, his hard features softening as private images flowed through him. At length, he said, "Her name is Tema. She is the daughter of the chieftain of one of the other tribes owing allegiance to my father."

With gentle teasing, Elizabeth said, "And I suppose she is very beautiful?"

Osei answered her in perfect seriousness. "She is as lovely as a young gazelle, and as gentle. But she also has great spirit. She will make me a good wife and give me strong sons."

Beneath his matter-of-fact words, Elizabeth sensed his yearning for the woman who held his proud warrior's heart in her hands. With her new awareness of love's terrible power, she hoped the two of them would not be long separated.

"Will you be married soon?"

"When I return with the golden idol of the Mande, Tema will be my reward."

Elizabeth did not have to ask what would happen if he did not find the statue. Osei was far too proud a man to claim the fruits of victory without the right to do so. For the first time, she understood the full significance of their search.

The idol was no longer merely a remote, legendary symbol of greatness. It held the key to the personal happiness of two people not very different from herself and Jordan.

During the long trek back to the river, she had plenty of time to think about the consequences should they fail to find the idol. Not only would Osei lose the woman he loved, but the Ashantes would lose a vital symbol of their heritage just when they might need it most.

For decades, the fierce warrior tribe had battled the colonial invaders. Several all-out wars had been fought with inconclusive results. In between were uneasy periods of peace that could end at any moment.

Throughout the last several years, a standoff of sorts

had existed. The British had not felt confident enough to instigate another bloody confrontation, and the Ashantes were too smart to willingly test themselves against the weaponry of an industrial giant.

But if the idol fell into the wrong hands, unscrupulous men would use it as a symbol of tribal weakness and an invitation to take once and for all the rich lands of the interior. No wonder Nigel had been so determined to find the statue. She did not doubt he was being well paid to do so by greedy colonists who understood its potential value.

When they paused briefly at midday to rest, she began to wonder exactly how far Nigel would have been willing to go to steal the idol. A man so utterly lacking in morals might have stooped to anything, even murder.

Her hands trembled as she remembered wondering if Jordan might have known more about Davies' death than he should. How misplaced her suspicions had been. It was Nigel who was capable of the most brutal violence and who let nothing stand between him and what he wanted. If he had murdered Davies, the crime had afforded him nothing. He must have been incredibly frustrated until he discovered who had the map.

Elizabeth shook her head in self-disgust when she considered how willing she had been to trust him. Were it not for her doubts about Jordan, she would never have even thought to separate the map. Nigel would have had it all, and she undoubtedly would have shared Davies' fate.

As it was, she still had the gift of her life, and she did not intend to waste another moment of it.

When they at last reached the river where the warriors had left their canoes and began to set up camp, Elizabeth worked swiftly and silently. She had seen the grass huts constructed often enough by now to understand how it was done, and had little difficulty putting up such a shelter a short distance away from the others. It was sufficiently within the perimeter fence to provide for safety, but far enough apart to offer more than the usual privacy.

With that done, she filled a bucket at the river's edge, took it into the hut, and removed her clothes. Having scrubbed herself thoroughly, she washed her hair and toweled the glistening curls dry. A soothing ointment rubbed into her skin helped ease the pain of cuts and bruises inflicted the day before. Fresh clothes completed her transformation.

She emerged clean, cool, and unknowingly beautiful. Even Osei, deeply in love though he was, could not help but be fascinated by how different she was from the woman he had dragged so unwillingly into Jordan's cabin not so many weeks ago. He chuckled appreciatively as he took note of the hut's position and rightly concluded that his friend had a surprise in store.

Well before nightfall, the hunting party returned loaded down not only with the carcass of an impala but also with the remains of a lion that had foolishly attempted to preempt their kill. Jordan had taken him cleanly with a single shot through the heart, for which he received great praise.

Though he was pleased by their success, the exhilaration that should have accompanied a successful hunt was missing. Instead he was simply glad that they had fulfilled their requirements quickly so that he did not have to be separated any longer from Elizabeth.

Just a few hours without her had been enough to make him realize how much she had come to mean to him. It was all he could do to keep his mind on the hunt when the tantalizing image of silken curls, perfect skin, eyes he could drown in, and a mouth ripe for plundering kept floating through his thoughts.

For a man who had found little need of women

beyond the satisfaction of his carnal desires, he was remarkably in thrall to a slip of a girl who both infuriated and delighted him with equal ease.

Thinking of how greatly his experience with Elizabeth differed from all his prior relationships with women brought him to the consideration of his recent celibacy. Many months had passed since he had last given vent to the demands of his virile nature.

No conscious decision to abstain had ever been made; he had simply found himself increasingly disheartened by casual matings that offered nothing but the briefest relief. Though he had no difficulty finding willing women, he had reached the point where he wanted far more than a warm, supple body and skillful technique.

He wanted . . . what? Commitment? Caring? Love? All those things were too intangible for his grasp. He was a man who dealt in the substance of the world, in reality. He understood what he could see and touch.

Like Elizabeth. She was eminently touchable. Beautiful, beguiling Elizabeth. Standing a little apart from the others, looking at him with those immense eyes, and . . . smiling.

Jordan's breath caught in his throat. Her expression was so tender he could scarcely credit it. The weariness of his body fell away, replaced by exhilaration so profound that it shook him to the core of his being. In the midst of the African savannah, surrounded by incalculable dangers and bound on a quest that could end in death, he was struck by an uncanny sense of . . . homecoming.

Though he managed to respond appropriately to the questions and comments of the warriors, Jordan's mind was on far different matters. Bemusedly, he wondered how she had managed to become even more breathtakingly beautiful in just the few hours they were apart.

A proud smile lit his clear blue eyes as he considered what a remarkable woman she was. Despite the untamed wilderness all around her, she somehow contrived to be utterly serene and enchanting. Was there another woman like her anywhere?

He doubted it. Elizabeth was unique. She had triumphed over a selfish, callous father and a life of immense repression to transform herself into a warm, caring person whose inner beauty was justly reflected in her appearance. She was intelligent, courageous, giving, responsive.

Oh, yes, she was that. He had no difficulty remembering how she had felt in his arms when they lay together beside the pool. There had been no mistaking the arousal of her body or her frustration when he drew away.

Why had he done that? At the time, it had seemed absolutely necessary. But now . . .

Pensively, he rubbed a hand over his stubble-roughened jaw. After days of sloughing through the bush, he was not fit company for a lady. Leaving the other men to finish cutting up the meat, he went off toward the river intent on getting himself a decent bath, and hell take any crocodile stupid enough to get in his way.

His sudden departure caught Elizabeth off guard. While she had not expected him to share her intense pleasure at simply being once again within sight of each other, she had thought he would at least speak to her. Instead he had gone off without a word, leaving her caught between dismay and worry.

Did he really feel so little for her that he was oblivious to her very existence? Surely that could not be. After all, he had cared for her so tenderly the day before and seemed so genuinely outraged by her injuries.

But had his concern really been at all different from what he would show anyone under such circumstances? Or had she simply read more into it in an effort to realize her most cherished dreams?

Biting her lip, Elizabeth struggled against the sudden upsurge of tears that threatened to disgrace her. Fortunately, all the men were so busy cutting the carcasses into smaller portions for transporting that no one noticed her. By the time they had finished and she was able to begin preparing a proper meal, her unruly emotions were once again under control.

It would do no good to get upset by Jordan's seeming lack of interest in her for the simple reason that nothing he said or did could change her feelings for him. Love, she was just coming to understand, was remarkably intransigent. Once firmly in place, it could not be uprooted by any amount of effort.

Turning the skewers of impala steak, she mused over the irony of finding herself in such a position. During all the barren years with her father, she had managed to keep an iron-firm rein on her emotions. Not once had she admitted, even to herself, that she found her life with him intolerable.

Now it seemed that she was paying for that excess of self-control by having none at all. While she could, with great effort, manage to present a serene facade to the world, inside she was a seething tumult of emotion.

Visions of herself with Jordan, each more brazen than the last, brought a vivid flush to her cheeks. She could only hope anyone noticing would attribute it to the heat of the cooking fire. To encourage that misapprehension, she leaned closer, nearly singeing her eyebrows in the process.

"Watch it! You could hurt yourself doing that."

With a sigh of resignation, she looked up, straight into the eyes of the man who so dominated her thoughts. He had shaved and changed into clean clothes. The sight of his face, free of whiskers for the first time in days, startled her. On one level, he looked just as he had when she first saw him in the cemetery. But in another, far deeper way he looked completely different.

There was no mystery as to how that could be; she saw him now through the eyes of love. He was no longer simply a man, but the catalyst for an explosion of forces within her so intense as to be frightening. Because of him, the entire world looked different.

So caught up was she in studying him that Elizabeth did not realize she was undergoing the same kind of intense scrutiny. Jordan could not look at her long or hard enough. Everything about her fascinated him. He wanted to discover the exact number of freckles splattered across her nose, to map the delicate curve of her cheek, to claim as his own the tiny dimple in the cleft of her chin.

Ruefully, he admitted that he wanted to do a damn sight more than that. He wanted to know every inch of her, to absorb the very essence of her into his own being, and to tune her so utterly to his possession that the mere thought of yielding to another would be intolerable to her.

There were just a couple of problems with that. First, he wanted her wholehearted cooperation. It wasn't enough for her to merely be swept away by his amatory prowess. She had to make a reasoned decision to enter into intimacy with him.

Then there was the matter of her virginity. He had never been with a virgin before, had in fact avoided such creatures like the proverbial plague. The mere thought of introducing a woman to sexual pleasure was enough to give him pause. It was quite a responsibility. Done right, it would be glorious. But if she was frightened and repulsed, the results would be quite different.

Fortunately, what he lacked in actual experience he made up by the fortuitous combination of a father who

165

refused to leave his sons in ignorance on such an essential matter and the manhood training of the Ashantes, which covered one or two things besides hunting and fighting.

Aware that she was staring at him curiously, he put an abrupt brake on his unruly thoughts and smiled down at her. "I didn't mean to startle you, but you really have to be more careful. That fire almost burned you."

What fire was he referring to, Elizabeth wondered blankly. The flames over which the impala steaks turned were as nothing compared to those raging within her. With immense effort, she managed to drag her eyes from him and give some slight attention to the dinner she was supposedly preparing.

"Uh . . . thank you. I guess I was distracted . . . "

"By anything in particular?" Jordan asked, sitting down beside her close enough to savor the delicate perfume of her skin.

Yes, you infuriating man, by you. I can't take a breath without thinking of you. You've crept inside my very skin. I'm not myself any more. Part of me belongs to you now. Can't you see that?

"N-no. It's just been an . . . eventful few days."

Jordan laughed shortly, caught up in studying the way the setting sun turned her hair to spun gold. How had he ever imagined her plain? She was gloriously, incandescently beautiful and he ached to make her his.

His body shifted restlessly. It was sweet torture to be so close to her without touching. For a few more hours he could endure it. But when night came and the heavy blanket of darkness hid them from the world, the time of reckoning would come for them both.

Chapter Ten

THE HIGH, FLOATING SOUND OF A WOOD FLUTE drifted on the night air. It flowed through Elizabeth, soothing the jagged edges of her thoughts and gentling her disordered emotions. She sighed softly and leaned back against the stump of a tree, gazing up at the star-splattered sky.

After the first decent meal any of them had had in days, everyone was feeling relaxed and cheerful. The men spoke quietly among themselves, while Jordan and Osei conferred together.

The rains that heralded the end of the dry season were due soon. Already, faint wisps of clouds could be seen between the constellations. When they came, travel on the river would be impossible. It would become a raging torrent of white water rushing to the sea, carrying everything with it.

They would be forced to trek overland through the dense forest. It would be slow going and fraught with danger, but there was no alternative. Not if they were to have any hope of finding the idol before anyone else.

Elizabeth listened to their discussion absently, doing little more than marking time until she could properly retire. The fatigue she had felt earlier in the day was gone. A heady sense of excitement coursed through her. The night ahead might hold everything— or nothing.

When at last several of the warriors stretched wearily and went off to their mats, she seized the opportunity to do the same. Jordan glanced up as she left, but made no attempt to follow her.

Refusing to be disheartened by that, she pulled the cowhide flap closed and undressed. Standing in her camisole and pantaloons, she hesitated just a moment before stripping them off along with everything else and wrapping herself in a thin cotton sheet. It covered her sarong-style from the curve of her breasts to just below her knees.

Looking down at herself, she smiled faintly. Not very long ago, the mere thought of wearing such a garment would have horrified her. Now she felt pleased by her daring and hopeful that it would lead to a great deal more.

The voices around the campfire were dying away. She guessed the other men were retiring for the night. Within minutes, the only sound she could make out was the now familiar music of the African night.

Sitting down on the rush mat, she stared at the closed flap as though willing Jordan to open it and appear before her. Nothing happened. Shifting uneasily, she chewed on her lower lip.

Perhaps Jordan intended to continue sleeping apart from her. If that was so, she had a problem. Instinct warned that such an intensely virile and proud man reserved the privilege of pursuit to himself. The worst thing she could do would be to throw herself at him again, as she feared she had already done.

Doubt gnawed at her. Except for their brief conversation when he found her too close to the fire, they had hardly exchanged a word. But a great deal had still been said with silence. Or so it seemed to her. Lacking experience in such matters, she might well be wrong.

Had she misinterpreted the look she had seen in his eyes throughout the evening? Each time she glanced up, it was to find him watching her. The mingled longing and determination of his gaze emboldened her to hope. Surely no man could look at a woman like that and be oblivious to her.

Her shoulders straightened proudly as her spine stiffened and her soft, full mouth assumed an almost mutinous pout. If Jordan did not understand by now how much she cared for him, he was a fool and the devil take him.

Even as that defiant thought flashed through her mind, a small voice mocked her. If he was a fool, so was she. Sitting there like a forgotten puppet waiting for the right strings to be pulled.

That was hardly a pleasant way to think of herself, but grudgingly she had to admit there was some truth to it. For in the next instant a sound just outside the hut made her head jerk up. Startled, her eyes focused on the cowhide flap.

"Elizabeth . . . are you still awake?"

The low, faintly husky voice reverberated through her. She swallowed hard and tried in vain to slow the frantic beating of her heart. "Y-yes."

"Good. I want to speak with you." The flap was pushed aside as Jordan stepped into the small enclosure. His sheer size made it seem to shrink around them. She raised a nervous hand to her tangled curls, unconsciously smoothing them.

"What about?"

He didn't answer at once. Instead, he seemed absorbed in looking at her. The hard male glitter she had seen in his eyes earlier was suddenly magnified tenfold. So heated was his gaze as it swept over her that Elizabeth could not help but blush. She looked down hastily, her eyes fastened on the small hands twisting in her lap.

Jordan took a deep, shaky breath. He was not off to a good start. Having decided that he had to win her trust and confidence before he could hope for anything more, he had so far managed only to make her nervous and self-conscious.

Not, of course, that she didn't do exactly the same to him. His palms were damp with perspiration and his stomach fluttered just as though he was a young boy on the verge of experiencing his first woman.

A wry smile curved his mouth as he considered that he had been far less apprehensive about losing his own virginity than he now was about taking hers. With a start he realized that in addition to his quite understandable concern about hurting her, he was even more worried that she might think badly of him afterward.

Unless he was very much mistaken, she had begun to offer him the first tentative overtures of friendship. He could not bear to think of them being suddenly withdrawn in shock and horror.

The novelty of wanting a woman not merely for her physical beauty but for all the qualities of her character shook him to the core. Far more was at stake than he had cared to admit. If he simply made her his mistress, he would be left profoundly dissastisfied.

But then she could never be only that, for she was already his wife.

The blood drained from his face, only to come rushing back an instant later as he realized the full implications of what he had just remembered. When he paid the bride price to Kwesi, he did so only out of some half-formed awareness that he could not leave her fate in the hands of another man, even one he had every reason to respect and trust.

Vexed by the aching desire she unleashed in him, he had found a certain relief in hiding the truth from her and insisting that she was merely a slave. That gave him some faint sense of control in a situation where he effectively had none.

But the fact remained that she was his wife, according to the tenets of a culture he understood and accepted every bit as much as that of his native land.

Going down on his haunches beside her, he studied her with new perception. She was not simply Elizabeth, the woman he desired. She was part of himself, joined to him in ways he had never before imagined.

As husband and wife, they were meant to be friends as well as lovers, companions and helpmates, perhaps even parents of the children who would be a living symbol of their commitment to each other.

Tentatively, with something very close to reverence, he reached out to stroke the curve of her cheek. Elizabeth started at his touch but did not move away. Drawing on all her courage, she managed to look up, meeting his gaze bravely.

What she saw in his eyes took her breath away. Where was the tough, determined adventurer she thought she knew? He seemed to have vanished, to be replaced by a gentle, vulnerable man who appeared as uncertain as she.

Emboldened by the realization that she was not alone in her confusion, Elizabeth reached out to him tremulously. The stubble that had scratched her soft skin when they kissed by the pool was gone. She felt only smooth firmness along his taut jaw.

His lips were cool and slightly parted as she ran the

tip of her finger over them. A pulse leaped to life in the hollow of his cheek when she brushed a feather-light caress over the prominent bones beneath his eyes before reaching up to smooth the contours of his brow.

"E-Elizabeth . . ."

"Hmmm."

"Do you have any idea what you're doing?"

"Some."

"Oh . . ." Silence for a moment before he asked, "Have you thought of the likely consequences?"

She sat back slightly, surveying him with a shy smile, "I suppose you will either be displeased by my forwardness and leave, or . . . stay."

"Which," he muttered huskily, "do you want me to do?"

A shaky laugh escaped her as she admitted, "I know I've angered you in the past, sometimes purposefully. But I would never deliberately offend you."

It took a moment for that to sink in. When it did, Jordan gently seized her hands and held them between his own. He had to stop the innocent but nonetheless tantalizing caresses that threatened to snap his slim hold on self-control.

His gaze pierced her to the very core as he took in the luminous glow of eyes softly green as the first leaves of spring, the faint quiver of ripe lips, and the rapid rise and fall of full breasts beneath the scant covering of the sheet.

Still holding her hands in one of his, he let the other drift down along the silken line of her throat to her delicate shoulders. Lean, brown fingers grazed the satiny flesh just above the sheet, deliberately seeking her response.

The instant tremor that raced through Elizabeth was impossible to conceal. She felt shaken to the very center of her being. Nothing mattered except to hold on to the incredible sensations spiraling through her and to follow them to some conclusion she could not envision but knew to be inevitable.

Jordan's smile was so piercingly sweet as to almost wring a sob from her. As he drew back, his hand shook and a faint sheen of perspiration shone on his brow.

"You are magical," he murmured thickly. "A spell cast by an enchantress. You can't be real."

Elizabeth swayed toward him, helpless against her overwhelming need for his touch. "But I am completely real," she whispered breathlessly. "There's nothing magical about me. I'm just a woman . . ."

A slashing grin lit his bronzed face. "There's no 'just' about it," he teased. "You're the sum total of everything a woman can be."

Her eyes widened in astonishment. Could he possibly mean that? And if so, what did he intend to do about it?

Jordan looked away hastily. The wide wonder of her gaze tempted him unbearably. He feared he was going too fast, rushing her toward something that in her innocence she was not yet ready to accept.

The sterner part of his mind told him he should leave her before the situation got completely out of hand. But that was impossible. To stand up and walk away required more strength than any mere mortal could ever hope to possess.

But perhaps there was some middle ground, some way to stay close to her without doing anything to hurt or frighten her. When his fingers, lightly grazing her back, caused her to wince, he had the excuse he needed.

"Turn around," he demanded tightly.

Elizabeth hesitated, too bewildered by what was happening between them to really understand what he had just said. Jordan had to repeat himself before she reluctantly obeyed.

The sharp curse that broke from him when he saw

her back made her stiffen. Quickly, she tried to minimize her injuries. "It really doesn't hurt that much. There are just a few scratches."

Staring at the alabaster skin rent by cuts and welts, he swallowed hard. If Nigel had been there at that moment, his life would have been worthless. Not even Jordan's vast respect for the Asantehene could have prevented him from giving vent to the rage he felt.

Much of the damage must have been done when she lay bound in the bottom of the canoe. But more had occurred during the trek inland, when she was torn by thorny branches, and later still when she had fought with her attacker just before the rescue party arrived.

If she had been less dazed by her ordeal, she would have realized the extent of the damage. But as it was, something must have kept her so preoccupied that she didn't understand how badly hurt she really was.

Perhaps that was just as well. She had enough to bear without having to confront anything more. Very gently, so as not to frighten her, Jordan said, "You must let me take care of these, Elizabeth. You can't reach them and no injury can be allowed to go untreated out here."

"All right. What do you want me to do?"

"Just lie down on the mat . . . that's it, on your stomach. Good. Now try to relax. I'll do my best not to hurt you."

True to his word, Jordan's touch was infinitely gentle as he rubbed the ointment into her upper back. The cool relief he brought made her aware for the first time of how uncomfortable she had been. Other painful areas she had not noticed began to throb, making her shift uncomfortably beneath him.

"Easy, you'll feel better in a few minutes." Reaching beneath her, he deftly loosened the sheet enough to lower it beneath her waist.

Elizabeth meant to protest but somehow she could

174

not find the words. His fingers continued to move over her bruised body with such soothing results that any objection she might have made died away unsaid.

A soft sigh escaped her as he began to work the same enchantment on her small feet and the slender calves of her legs. Moving upward, he folded the sheet back to give him access to her thighs. The pressure of his touch increased slightly as he fought against the tremors of desire racing through him.

With each stroke of his fingers, she was becoming more and more exposed. Frightened by feelings she could not control, she gripped the top of the sheet above her breasts, until he gently compelled her to let go.

"Don't be afraid, Elizabeth. Nothing will happen unless you want it to."

Her implicit faith in him made it possible to obey. As she loosened her grip, the sheet fell away to reveal the ripe swell of her breasts pressed against the rush mat. Jordan inhaled sharply. It was all he could do not to give in to the driving urge to plunder the delicate beauty before him and make it completely his own.

But he had sworn to himself that for both their sakes he would go slowly and that was a vow he meant to keep. Again he wondered if she had any idea of the effect she was having on him. It seemed doubtful. If she understood the full extent of his arousal she would hardly lie so calmly before him.

Grateful for the fact that her innocence protected her from such knowledge, he moved to straddle her, his hands stroking the vulnerable line of her bare back clear to the curve of her buttocks. A soft purr of pleasure rippled from her, encouraging him to tempt her even further.

Slipping a hand beneath her, he took hold of a corner of the sheet and pulled gently. It gave easily. Instead of being swathed in a loose cocoon, she was now no more than marginally covered by a single layer of almost sheer fabric.

A blatantly appreciative smile lit Jordan's cobalt gaze as he took in the delectable picture she made. With her head cradled on her folded arms and her eyes closed, she might have been peacefully asleep in her own bed far from any predatory male. Only the flush of her sun-warmed cheeks and the sensual tension radiating from her told him how far from peace she truly was.

He could not deny being gratified that she was susceptible to the desire strumming like a finely drawn cord between them. Her responsiveness encouraged him to do what he had longed for since first entering the hut. Grasping both ends of the sheet, he lifted it away entirely.

Elizabeth's eyes opened wide and she started to sit up, then thought better of it. Why should she feel embarrassed when nothing was happening except the realization of her fondest hopes? Subsiding onto the mat, she forced herself to lie quietly beneath the searing impact of Jordan's gaze.

The impudently rounded curve of her bottom made him grin even as he struggled against the memory of striking her there. Deeply ashamed of that action, he reached out shakily to caress the petal-soft flesh.

Elizabeth quivered at so intimate a touch. She bit her lip hard in an attempt to stop the moan of pleasure that rose in her throat. Despite her best efforts, she did not entirely succeed. A husky purr resonated through her, making her sound for all the world like an exquisite feline being petted by its master.

Remembering that Jordan had claimed to be exactly that, she smiled fondly. How strange to think that she had been frightened by him when now all she wanted was to . . .

Her vocabulary failed her. She could put no name to what she yearned for besides the stilted label of the "marital act." That sounded vaguely like something two marionettes might go through. Since she had ceased to feel like a puppet the moment she stopped fighting the natural urges of her body, she could not imagine herself in such a role.

But she could imagine other things, all of which deepened the blush already staining her cheeks.

"J-Jordan . . ."

"Hmmm?"

"I-really feel much b-better now. Thank you."

"You're welcome."

"What I mean is . . . you could stop . . ."

"Really?"

"If you . . . want to."

Still straddling her, he leaned forward slightly so that his breath stirred the silken curls of her hair. "Do you want me to?"

"I . . . that is . . ."

"Yess?"

His drawling amusement stirred her temper. Without pausing to think, she took advantage of the fact that he was holding almost all his weight off her to turn over suddenly. "Don't you dare make fun of me!"

The sight of her bare breasts, their honeyed nipples full and taut, so startled Jordan that he was oblivious to anything she could have said. For long moments he could only stare at her, drinking in the sight of beauty that stirred him to the depths of his soul.

Following the path of his ardent gaze, Elizabeth paled. She tried to cover herself, only to be stopped when he gently but implacably seized her wrists and stretched her arms out above her head.

"Don't. I want to look at you."

"But . . ." The conflict between modesty and pride

177

shone clearly in her eyes. Seeing it, Jordan's gaze softened. He did not release her hands but he did smile at her so tenderly that her breath caught in her throat.

"You're beautiful, Elizabeth. The most beautiful woman I have ever seen. Would you deny me the pleasure of looking at you?"

It was on the tip of her tongue to tell him she would deny him nothing at all, but she wisely stopped herself. She could feel the tremors of barely checked passion racing through him and sensed that any such declaration would immediately unleash the desire he was struggling to contain.

While she luxuriated in the knowledge that she could so arouse him, she was not yet ready to face the full consequences of her own sensuality. The new, vastly more confident woman she had become in the last few weeks was every bit as much a virgin as her plain, repressed predecessor. Just enough maidenly fear remained to stop her from encouraging him so openly.

Jordan seemed to understand her need for reassurance. Without releasing her hands, he lowered himself beside her and gently brushed away a lock of sun-kissed hair that had fallen across her forehead.

"Trust me, Elizabeth," he murmured huskily. "I won't let anything bad happen to you."

She wanted desperately to believe him, but could not quite shake the feeling that she was teetering on the brink of a precipice. A dark and mysterious abyss lay before her. If she fell into it, she might discover happiness beyond her greatest dreams. Or anguish so profound as to destroy her.

Beyond even her fear for herself, she worried that she would somehow disappoint him. He was an intensely virile, experienced man. How could he fail to find her clumsy or boring?

"J-Jordan, I—don't know . . ."

"What, sweetheart? Tell me what troubles you."

"I'm so . . . ignorant of certain things. I have no idea how to . . . please you . . ."

He broke off nuzzling the silken line of her throat and looked up, his crystal blue eyes wide with surprise. "Please *me*? Why should you be concerned about that?"

"Because I . . ." She stopped. It was too soon to tell him that she loved him. To do so would be to expose the most vulnerable part of herself. "Isn't that what you want?" she hedged. "I thought men expected to be pleased . . ."

Jordan laughed huskily. He was stunned by her concern for him. How could she possibly have any doubts about his response to her? His entire body was on fire with passion beyond any he had ever known.

He wanted so badly to hasten his possession of her that his hands trembled and a fine sheen of perspiration shone against his burnished skin. But he knew he had to go slowly. As uncertain as she was, patience was essential.

When he could draw enough breath to speak, he murmured, "Elizabeth, forget whatever you've heard about men and women. Nothing matters except the two of us. I promise we will please each other greatly."

Her small tongue darted out to nervously moisten her lips. "How can you know that?"

"Because you already enchant me," he said thickly, his eyes fastened on her mouth. "And if you will just relax enough to trust me, I will work the same magic on you."

But she was already under his spell, Elizabeth thought dimly. The sight, sound, scent of him enthralled her. She wanted nothing more than to lie back in his arms and discover whatever he wished to teach her.

179

Jordan waited until he felt some of the tension ease from her body before tenderly brushing his lips across her forehead and down along the delicate line of her cheek. Finding the small, shell-like ear hidden in the silken curls, he traced its outline with his tongue before nibbling gently on the lobe.

The quiver that ran through her delighted him. He guessed that she was as yet unaware of the full power of her sensuality. The knowledge that he would be the man to reveal it to her touched him deeply.

He was overcome by the need to protect and cherish her. She lay so small and trusting beneath him, her eyes as wide and soft as a newborn fawn's. Slipping a hand beneath her breast, he felt the rapid beat of her heart and knew the battle she was waging against her very natural fears. Her courage made him all the more determined that he would allow no one—not even himself—to harm her.

Releasing her hands, he cradled the back of her head as his arm slipped beneath her to urge her closer. Elizabeth nestled against him, dazed by the massive strength of his body. Freed of their restraint, her hands slipped down his broad back. The cotton shirt he wore was soft to her touch. Through it she could feel the power of muscle and sinew rippling beneath her touch.

Jordan groaned deep in his throat. Her touch turned his loins to flame. Never in his life had he experienced the ravenous need she sparked in him. Without some immediate relief, he was in danger of forgetting all his promises and plundering the beauty before him as savagely as a starved wolf.

To prevent that, he had to at least loosen the taut rein he was keeping on his desires. As he found her lips warm and moist and softly parted, he allowed himself to momentarily forget the full extent of her innocence. Steely arms tightened around her as he lifted her into a kiss that was at once as thorough as it was devastating.

Jordan gave no quarter, and Elizabeth asked for none. The hard male lips against her own demanded every bit as much as they gave. His tongue thrust deeply, filling her mouth, making her vividly aware of the hollow ache building within her.

Moaning, she twisted in his arms, striving to come even closer to the source of release from all the pent-up need threatening to spill from her. Her hands slipped beneath his shirt, savoring the rough silk texture of his skin. As though of their own volition, her breasts rubbed against the thick mat of dark hair covering his chest as her hips arched helplessly.

"Elizabeth . . ."

The sound of her name uttered deep in his throat emboldened her. Tearing her mouth from his, she let her lips run over his smooth jaw, down the corded column of his throat. Driven by instincts she had not even known she possessed, her tongue darted out to taste the faint saltiness of his skin.

"Please," she whispered urgently, "let me touch you. I can't stop . . ."

The purely male growl that tore from him was all the permission she needed. Eagerly, she pushed the shirt from his shoulders and let it drop to the floor.

Hardly aware of what she was doing, she rubbed against his naked torso, exhilarated by the tensile strength so different from her own far softer form. Enchanted by sensations tumbling one after the other through her dazzled mind, she barely noticed the effect of her caresses until Jordan suddenly seized her shoulders and pressed her to the mat.

Hoarsely, he demanded, "Can you lie on your back without pain?"

Enflamed by voracious need for him, she could only

nod. All awareness of her injuries had vanished. The anguish spiraling through her was caused only by unbridled passion demanding satisfaction.

Moving some slight distance away from her, he yanked off his boots and unfastened the wide leather belt around his taut waist. Elizabeth watched wide-eyed, unable to look away, as he unbuttoned his trousers and stepped out of them. The single garment he still wore did little to conceal the burgeoning fullness of his manhood.

As he returned to her, he saw the sudden fear in her gaze and moved immediately to banish it. Though his voice shook with the force of his need for her, he managed to murmur, "Easy, sweetheart. I know how new this all is to you. We'll take it nice and slow. There's no rush."

That wasn't quite true. He had to seriously doubt how long he would be able to control his rampant desire. But the exquisite responsiveness of her body assured him an extended delay would not be needed.

The slightest brush of his callused palms over her breasts made her taut nipples harden even further. As his thumbs pressed against them in a slow, circular motion, he let the rest of his fingers close over her, squeezing gently.

She tried to shut her eyes against the blinding sensations exploding within her, but Jordan stopped her. Tersely, he demanded, "Look at yourself, Elizabeth. I want you to see what I'm doing to you."

Torn between embarrassment and fascination, she hesitantly obeyed. Her cheeks burned as she took in the bronzed strength of his hands startlingly dark against her far whiter skin. Her breasts were swollen, her nipples taut. It was impossible to deny that she was a woman in the throes of intense passion.

Reluctantly, she lifted her eyes to meet Jordan's. He was smiling, a triumphant male smile that made it clear he understood the full depth of her need. But his gaze was gentle. It quieted the remnants of her fear and enabled her to offer no resistance when his hands slipped lower to grip her hips and hold her still.

Slowly, he lowered his head to taste the bounty his hands had savored. His tongue teased first one nipple and then the other with tantalizing strokes that made her ache for more. Her fingers tangled in his ebony hair as she silently urged him to meet her passion with his own.

When he complied by drawing a straining nipple into his mouth to suckle her gently, Elizabeth cried out. She was unprepared for the shocking bolt of pleasure that ripped through her.

His erotic caresses reached clear to the core of her being. Liquid heat flared deep within her loins. Perhaps because she sensed that this time there would be no turning back, she was utterly unrestrained in her responses. No remnant of fear dimmed the ardent welcome that radiated through every inch of her body.

Jordan lifted his head and drew a deep, ragged breath. He was stunned by the impact she had on him. All his senses were vividly, painfully alive. He was acutely conscious of the incredible softness of her skin, her delicate scent, the rapid pulsing of the blood through her veins, the shuddering rise and fall of her breasts.

Nothing beyond her penetrated the enchanted circle of his awareness. Even his sense of his own self grew blurred as all his attention focused on the enthralling woman in his arms.

Much later he would wonder if that ability to so completely lose himself in her might not be an indication of caring and commitment beyond any he had ever thought to experience. But just then he was oblivious to anything except the ardent response of her body.

Joy surged through him as he allowed himself to realize that she truly wanted to be joined with him in the most intimate way possible.

The knowledge that all her fear and hesitation were gone snapped the thin hold he had managed to keep on his self-control. A low growl broke from him as he rose slightly and slipped off the last barrier between them.

As he returned to her, Elizabeth's arms closed around his broad back and her hips lifted to savor the surging strength he offered. Deep in her throat she purred. The infinitely feminine sound sent tremors of delight through Jordan. He looked up, meeting her passion-dazed eyes, and smiled warmly.

"Lizzie, you are a marvel. You make me feel more than I ever have in my life."

"M-me too . . . " she gasped as his big hands stroked her slender waist and the gentle curve of her hips. "I've never . . . even dreamed . . . I could feel like this . . . "

"It's only the beginning," he promised huskily. "There's so much more."

Her eyes opened wide, revealing fire-lit pools washed by the dancing shadows of the sea. *"More?"*

Her astonishment made him laugh. A broad grin split his burnished features as he savored the thought of how much pleasure he would give her. His earlier experiences with women, which had come to seem so empty and meaningless, suddenly took on a different quality. Not only had they prepared him to fully appreciate Elizabeth, but they had also given him the skill to express his feelings for her in the most eloquent ways possible.

Continuing his slow, deliberate caresses despite the torment such restraint caused them both, he gazed down at her lovingly. "Oh, yes . . . a rebirth you must experience to understand. Let me show you . . . "

No thought of refusal remained in her mind. She

yielded to him totally, opening her body without restraint or hindrance. Recognizing the completeness of her surrender, Jordan swallowed hard. Her absolute trust in him meant more even than her desire. He was determined she would never regret such faith.

Sliding down her satiny length, he traced the delicate line of her ribs first with his fingers and then with his tongue. Her waist was deeply indented above the flare of her hips. Her abdomen was a flat, velvety plain dotted by the small navel that proved acutely sensitive to his touch.

As his tongue touched her there, the spasms of sensation it provoked were poised midway between pain and pleasure. Small cries rippled deep in her throat, becoming ever more urgent as his ardent exploration continued.

Her hands stroked the broad sweep of his shoulders and back. Her legs intertwined with his and her lower body pressed against the rough silk of his chest.

Jordan hesitated only briefly before his pleasure-dazzled mind decided she would not begrudge him even the most daring satisfaction of his desperate need to know her fully. Gently separating her legs, he touched a tender finger to the downy mass of curls at the cleft of her thighs.

A soft gasp escaped her, but she made no other protest. Reassured that he had not been wrong, he moved his hand very slightly, just enough to separate the moist petals of her womanhood and explore her tenderly.

Elizabeth went very still beneath his careful touch. She could barely cope with the shock of such intimacy, yet could not endure the thought that he might stop. Hardly realizing that she did so, she lifted her hips slightly to give him better access to the mysteries he so lovingly sought to discover.

Beneath her clutching hands, she felt the long, urgent tremors racking his body and sensed he had reached some crucial point of no return. Dimly, she thought he would come to her now, but that was not the case. With the last of his restraint gone, Jordan was driven not to initiate his own release, but rather to assure hers.

Always before he had considered the most intimate tasting of a woman to be no more than an enjoyable prelude to complete possession. But that was no longer so. With Elizabeth, he was discovering that her response meant far more to him than his own.

Caressing the silken softness of her inner thighs, he moved slowly upward to drop feather-light kisses along the sweet, warm folds of her femininity. Opening her gently with his fingers, he traced the moist crevasse with his tongue before nipping tenderly at the center of her desire.

Drawing her carefully into his mouth, he suckled her through long, exquisite moments before at last flicking over her repeatedly with his hot, strong tongue.

Elizabeth believed she was dying. There was no other explanation for what she felt. The world was falling away, plummeting into nothingness while she was rising on a cloud of agonizing delight.

For a timeless instant she hovered just above a burning sun whose heat dissolved the physical barriers of her body and freed her soul to fall unhindered toward its burning core.

She pierced the glowing star even as Jordan pierced her, penetrating the barrier of her virginity with a single thrust that brought not pain but only a long tremor of ecstasy that built and built upon itself until they were both engulfed.

He cried out her name even as she sobbed his. The fulfillment they found together was so complete as to alter for all time their perception of themselves and each other. For a timeless instant, they were a single entity fused so totally that they could never again be complete apart.

When the last resonating cords of ecstasy died away, they drifted slowly to earth tangled in each other's arms. Jordan lay on his back with Elizabeth nestled against him. Their bodies glowed with perspiration and their breathing was labored, but each was utterly content.

So much so that sleep was irresistible. In the last moment before it claimed them, he drew her even closer. His big hand cupped her breast as with infinite satisfaction he murmured, "My wife . . . "

Elizabeth's lips curved against his chest. Despite the absolute fulfillment of her mind and body, she did not miss the elated note of possessiveness in his voice. It followed her into her dreams, where a golden idol lay in wait, cloaked in mystery and haunting hints of peril.

Chapter Eleven

THE LONG, WOEFUL CALL OF A HOOPOE BIRD WOKE Elizabeth shortly after dawn. She came awake willingly, drawn back to consciousness by tantalizing memories that made her blush even as she smiled unabashedly.

Sunlight filtered through the woven roof of the grass hut. Outside she could hear the muted sounds of the camp coming to life, but inside it was very quiet. Only the regular sound of her breathing and Jordan's broke the stillness.

He was lying on his side next to her. Despite the warmth of early morning, they had not moved apart. Her head lay against his shoulder and her hand curled into the dark mat of hair covering his chest. A powerful arm rested on her waist and a sinewy leg was thrown over hers, holding her in gentle bondage.

As though he needed to ensnare her, she thought lovingly. She would fight the world to stay with him.

A slight frown marred the smooth contentment of her features. Why should she be thinking about fighting? Some remnant of her dreams flitted through her mind, only to vanish before she could catch hold of it.

Shrugging, she dismissed the phantasms of the night. They were meaningless against the joys of the day. Never had she looked on the world with such wholehearted enchantment.

The spider spinning a web across a corner of the hut was enthralling. The lizard peering at her from behind a leaf provoked a smile. Each crackle, slither, hoot, and chirp drifting on the air was music to her ears.

But even in paradise, all was not perfect. It was already very hot and perspiration slicked her body. Her hair was tangled and unkempt, and her mouth was dry.

She didn't want Jordan to wake and find her like that. Slipping carefully from beneath him, she stood up and stretched luxuriantly. Never in all her twenty-four years had she felt so utterly relaxed and content.

Not even the full awareness that she had violated the most fundamental laws of her society dimmed her happiness in the slightest. The rigidly repressive world she had escaped from seemed part of another life, just as the plain, dutiful girl she had been belonged only in the past.

Gathering up her clothes, she dressed hurriedly and left the hut, pausing just long enough to cast a lingering glance at the man still deeply asleep on the mat. She was smiling when she stepped outside to confront the new day and the perceptive glance of Osei.

"Good morning," the warrior said gravely, despite the grin that lifted the corners of his mouth. "I trust you slept well?"

Elizabeth laughed unabashedly. "Extremely so, thank you. Jordan is still resting. I'll start breakfast before I wake him." It delighted her to know that she had the right to perform such wifely tasks for him. The explosive joy they had shared the night before was by no means the sum total of love. It colored every aspect of life, even the most mundane.

Osei could no longer suppress his smile, or the urge to tease her a bit. "That's a good idea. He's bound to have worked up quite an appetite."

Meeting her startled gaze ingenuously, he added, "From the hunt, of course."

"Oh . . . yes. Of course." Rejecting the impulse to ask exactly which hunt he was referring to, Elizabeth hastily took herself off. After washing her face and running her fingers through her hair to smooth out the worst of the tangles, she got a small fire going and began preparing a meal of impala meat and guinea eggs.

The repast might not have passed muster in London, but to the men facing another grueling day on the river, it was most welcome. The warriors gathered around eagerly, laughing and joking with easy camaraderie.

She was greeted with friendly nods and smiles, and her tentative attempts at a few words of Oji were generously encouraged, despite what she suspected was an atrocious accent.

The acceptance of Anoyke and the others touched her deeply. For the first time in her life, she began to understand what it meant to be part of a family. But the pleasure it gave her did not prevent her from glancing repeatedly toward the hut from which Jordan had yet to emerge.

If he slept much longer, he would miss breakfast. That was the only reason she put down her ladle and, ignoring the amused looks of the men, started off to wake him. The fact that even just a few minutes without him made her ache inside had nothing to do with it.

She had almost reached the hut when the flap opened and Jordan stepped out. Still half-asleep, he did not see her at once. She was free to observe him unawares as he yawned and rubbed the stubble on his chin before glancing around bleary-eyed.

As his gaze fell on her, his shoulders tensed and a dull flush stained his cheeks. Elizabeth observed his discomfiture with mixed emotions. Was his reaction merely that of any normal man encountering a woman with whom he had just shared hours of unbridled intimacy? Or was he already regretting what had happened between them?

A pulse sprang to life in the hollow of his cheek. His hands dropped to his sides, where they clenched and unclenched nervously. Hesitantly, he took a step toward her. "Elizabeth . . ."

His obvious uncertainty pierced the fog of her blissful contentment, making her abruptly aware that there were ramifications to the night before that she had not considered. The independence she had just attained in the weeks since her father's death was gone.

So fleeting had its presence in her life been that it might never have existed. In its place, she was utterly, frighteningly dependent on a man who suddenly seemed very much a stranger.

Where was the loving light she had seen in his eyes the night before? What had happened to the tender joy and gentle humor they had shared? How had they come to face each other like wary adversaries, each trying to judge the other's intentions?

Each? Elizabeth took a deep breath and forced herself to look more closely at Jordan. What she saw rattled the hasty barriers she had been tossing up between them. He seemed no more confident than she. If anything, he appeared to be bracing himself for some terrible blow.

Concern for herself vanished as she thought only of reassuring him. A shy but unmistakable smile lit her face, revealing the love which, for a foolish instant, she had tried to hide. "Good morning. I was just coming to tell you breakfast is ready."

Jordan's apprehension eased somewhat, but did not vanish entirely. Cautiously, he said, "Thank you. I . . . didn't mean to sleep so late."

The moment the words were said, he clearly regretted them. Elizabeth lowered her eyes demurely, but could not quite restrain a smile. There was a certain feminine satisfaction in knowing that she had worn him out, if only temporarily.

Taking pity on his embarrassment, she murmured, "If you want anything to eat, you'd better hurry."

Jordan seized the excuse to put some distance between them while he tried to gather his shattered wits. She had the most astounding effect on him.

He had awakened half-believing that the night before had been nothing more than a wondrous dream. The utter contentment of his body, coupled with a soaring sense of anticipation, had warned it was not, but he had still stumbled out of the tent not quite certain what had happened. Until he had come face to face with her, and was suddenly forced to acknowledge the enormity of what he had done.

Even as he tried to feel some flicker of shame or remorse, he could not manage it. Elation so profound as to be dizzying surged through him. He had claimed her in the most fundamental way possible and he'd be damned if he'd regret it. Especially since he now had some reason to believe she shared his happiness in their new relationship.

By the time he reached the circle of men around the campfire, Jordan was grinning broadly. There was a lightness to his step and a gleam in his eyes, the source of which was unmistakable.

Osei took one look at him and laughed. "It seems

you survived the night, my friend. We were beginning to wonder."

Jordan laughed unabashedly. Helping himself to what was left in the pot, he sat down and observed to no one in particular, "Looks like a beautiful day."

The men grinned at each other. Even to those accustomed to it, the heat was all but unbearable. The parched air crackled ominously. Far in the distance, the low, incessant rumble of thunder could be heard.

No one had to question what that meant. The rains were coming. Soon sheets of water would pour out of the sky so heavily that it would be impossible to see more than a few feet ahead. The river would become a raging torrent tearing away huge trees, large animals, and men foolish enough to be caught in it. The dusty ground would turn to mud, clinging to everything and everybody.

As essential as the wet season was, it still posed grave dangers, especially to those who had to travel during it. Unless they were able to reach the city of the Mande before the rains began, they might be unable to go on.

"Since the day meets with your approval," Osei observed, "I suggest we make the most of it."

Jordan took the laconic comment good-humoredly. He knew he was acting out of character and frankly did not care. While he fully appreciated the seriousness of the challenge confronting them, it could do nothing to dull his happiness.

He was—for the first and he was quite certain only time in his life—in love. The experience was at once terrifying and miraculous. He meant to make the most of it.

When Elizabeth returned to the campfire, having dismantled the grass hut and packed both her and Jordan's belongings, he stood up and went to her side.

193

She watched his approach with mixed feelings.

Her earlier self-assurance had faded somewhat, replaced by tremulous concern. Did he think her too forward, perhaps even wanton? Was he displeased by his susceptibility to her? For such a proud, strong man, the sense of being in thrall to a woman must be deeply distressing. Would he react badly to it?

Anxiously, she gazed up at him, unaware of the remarkable sensuality of her beauty or the poignant uncertainty of her expression.

Jordan found he had forgotten to breathe and dragged air into his lungs. His heart raced painfully and the palms of his hands were damp with perspiration. Far from feeling more confident with her now that he had possessed her body, he felt even less.

Huskily, he said, "We're about to leave. Are you ready?"

Elizabeth nodded. The effort to speak seemed beyond her. She was as self-conscious as a gawky schoolgirl; perhaps even more so because the hungers of her body belonged to a fully awakened woman.

Seeking to divert herself, she turned away to put out the fire and bundle up the pots, only to find those tasks had already been seen to by a smiling Anoyke and several other young warriors. There was nothing left for her but to go with Jordan.

Settled into her accustomed place in the prow of the first canoe, she tried to concentrate on her surroundings rather than the man directly behind her. The attempt was useless.

She was vividly conscious of his every movement, the warmth of his body, the faintly musky scent of his skin. The very rhythm of his blood coursing through his veins seemed to reverberate through her.

In a vain effort to halt her spiraling senses, she closed her eyes and breathed deeply. That was a mistake. The canoe surged forward, knocking her off balance so that she fell against Jordan.

Their bodies touched for barely a moment before she hastily straightened herself, but the damage was done. Desire ripped through her, making a mockery of her efforts at restraint. Elizabeth bit her lip hard to smother a gasp. Her hands clenched tightly together, the nails digging into her palms.

"Are you all right?" Jordan muttered thickly.

Without turning around, she nodded. If she looked at him, she would be lost. The desperate struggle to keep from touching him absorbed her sufficiently so that she gave little thought to the passage of time or the changes happening to the river.

As they moved further north, the water became shallower and slower-moving. Within a few days, that would change dramatically. But just then they were reaching the point where the canoes could go no further.

At Osei's signal, they grounded the boats and began unloading their supplies. Beyond the thin stretch of savannah bordering the river lay the thick tropical forest. Elizabeth viewed it with trepidation. She had already had one taste of the damage it could wreak, and she was not looking forward to another.

But this time she was with men who understood the forest and respected it. Unlike Nigel, they took care to blaze the best possible path, one that allowed them to pass without being scratched, bruised, or otherwise battered by the dense undergrowth.

Nonetheless, it was difficult going. She couldn't help but be glad of the fact that she had only a very light pack. The men were weighed down with supplies and weapons, which they refused to let her help carry. Her offer to do so was met by a quelling glare from Jordan, who quickly disabused her of any such notion.

"You do your share by taking care of the cooking," he informed her flatly. The spurt of pleasure she felt at his recognition of her efforts was promptly spoiled when he added, "Only a nitwit would try to take on more than she can handle."

Elizabeth did not react well to that. The hours spent so close to him without being able to yield to the overwhelming desire he provoked had strained her temper. Waspishly, she snapped, "I'll have you know I am perfectly capable of looking after myself. If you imagine I need your help, you are sadly mistaken."

"Oh, really?" Jordan shot back. "In the short time I've known you, you've gotten yourself into more trouble than any ten *sensible* people could have managed in a year."

"I have not!"

"What do you call going off into the bush with that bastard Chandler? Further evidence of your excellent character judgment?"

"How could I help but be misled by him? I thought he was a gentleman. Anyone would have made the same mistake."

"Not anyone. I knew he was a slimy crook—and worse—the minute I laid eyes on him. But you were too damn hotheaded to listen to reason. A warthog has more sense!"

"More than you, certainly! You thought I was actually letting him touch me."

Jordan didn't want to be reminded of that. The image of Elizabeth hurt and terrified in Chandler's hands was acutely painful to him. Angrily, he snapped, "It doesn't matter whether you were letting him or not. You set yourself up by going off with him in the first place."

"Are you seriously suggesting it was my fault?"

"No, of course not, but . . ."

"Then what you are saying? That I wanted him

196

to . . ." She broke off. The thought that Jordan believed her capable of inviting such intimacies from another man sickened her. If he could believe such infamy, all her hopes for them were nothing more than torturous delusions.

Turning away, she struggled to hide the sudden rush of tears that threatened to make her humiliation complete. With her head bowed, she was unaware that Jordan had stopped and was motioning the other men to go on.

They passed her silently, with sympathetic glances, but showed no great surprise. It was inevitable that lovers should fight, especially when circumstances prevented them from being alone together.

When the rest of the party was some slight distance ahead, Jordan approached her quietly. When his hand touched her arm, she attempted to wrench away, but he would not allow it. Gently but firmly he drew her to him.

Elizabeth was stiff in his embrace, refusing to yield despite the incessant outcry of her body. Anger was her only effective defense against him.

"Let me go! I don't want you touching me."

"Yes, you do," he insisted matter-of-factly. "We both want that very much. That's why we're snapping at each other." Tilting her head back, he gazed into tear-washed eyes the color of the sea. His throat tightened painfully as he took in the evidence of her hurt. Thickly, he murmured, "I'm sorry."

She didn't want his apology, or the warm passion of his gaze, or the piercing closeness of his body pressed to hers. Or so she tried to tell herself.

A tiny sob of mingled relief and frustration broke from her. Helplessly, she swayed against him as all the resistance flowed from her. "You don't really believe I wanted him to . . . ?"

"No, of course not! I was just being stupid—and

cruel. Why I should want to hurt you, I'll never know. You're the one person in the world I can least bear to see suffer. I want to care for you and protect you forever."

Though that was not precisely the declaration of love she longed for, Elizabeth was deeply touched by it. Hardly aware that she did so, she snuggled closer to him and let her arms twine around his neck.

Jordan wasted no time taking advantage of her acquiescence. His powerful head swooped, closing the distance between them in an instant. Even as he tried to remember to treat her gently and with patience, he could not prevent the soul-wrenching kiss that robbed them both of breath and set the very air around them to shimmering.

Elizabeth met his unbridled urgency with her own. At another time, she would luxuriate in the tenderness of which she knew him to be capable. But just then she wanted only to feel the full power of his desire and be reassured that what had happened between them the night before would indeed occur again.

If Jordan's behavior was anything to go by, night could not come soon enough. His lips parted hers insistently as he sought to assuage some measure of his desperate need.

The urgent thrust of his tongue made her moan raggedly. Trembling, she pressed even closer. The taut male body racked by tremors of desire thrilled her. Dimly, she wondered if she would ever take for granted her ability to stir him so intensely.

Implicit in that question was the presumption that they would have a future together. That remained to be seen, not simply because of the emotional pitfalls that might be strewn through their own relationship, but because of the mortal dangers posed by their quest. While the idol remained undiscovered, thoughts of the future were more than simply presumptuous; they were a needless challenging of fate.

Reluctantly, Jordan raised his head. The men were almost out of sight. They would have to hurry to catch up with them. Battling both her frustration and his own, he murmured, "We can't stay here. You know that."

Elizabeth managed a tremulous smile. "It's a nice thought though, isn't it? All alone here in paradise."

He smiled indulgently. "Paradise had a serpent."

Her nose wrinkled as she stepped back slightly, enough so that they could continue hand-in-hand along the trail. "I should have known you'd say something like that."

"Let me finish, brat," he teased. "The Ashantes believe that the first man and woman were lacking in a certain fundamental common sense; they couldn't quite figure out how to have babies. So they turned for help to an obliging serpent, who explained the process to them. To this day he's thought of most gratefully. After all, without his help, none of us would be here."

"Was there an apple tree anywhere in this tale?"

"No . . . maybe a mangrove."

"Silly."

Jordan pretended to look hurt. "Does that mean you don't believe the story?"

"On the contrary, it makes at least as much sense as the other version." Impulsively, she added, "I don't notice any snakes whispering instructions to you."

Abashed by her own boldness, Elizabeth looked away hastily, only to be drawn back by Jordan's booming laughter. There was a dangerous gleam in his eye as he asked, "Does that mean I pass muster?"

"You know perfectly well it doesn't!"

"Oh? Why not?"

"Because I don't . . . that is, I've never . . . It just doesn't, that's all!"

Lifting her hand in his, he pressed a gentle kiss to her fingers as he said quietly, "Because you were a virgin and therefore have nothing to compare me to?"

Though her cheeks flamed and shivers of pleasure ran down her hand clear to the secret core of her body, she met his gaze unflinchingly. "I suppose."

"There's no 'suppose' about it. You were as innocent as they come."

Despite herself, she could not resist the urge to ask, "Do you mind?"

"No."

The one-word answer told her next to nothing. Determinedly, she persisted, "Why?"

Jordan hesitated. He was uncomfortable with the subject and uncertain what to say. Why was he so pleased to have found her untouched? The fact that men of his upbringing simply expected their brides to be virgins didn't seem to come into it. None of the other rules of society had applied to his relationship with Elizabeth, so why should that?

Yet the fact remained that he was fiercely glad she had never been with another man. The knowledge that he was her only lover struck a primitively male chord deep within him. It made him feel at once possessive and protective. He wanted to be the only man who would ever know her intimately; the only man who would give her children.

But he couldn't tell her that, not when she had only just escaped from her father's domination and would naturally fear any encroachment on her newly won independence. She was like a beautiful, proud bird testing its wings for the first time. Any effort to hinder her would only make her all the more determined to escape.

Doubt clawed at him. In the blinding bliss of passion

he had seized on their Ashante marriage as moral justification for their lovemaking. But how had she rationalized it? A bolt of near-physical pain struck him as he realized that to her it had been no more than a burst of defiance to celebrate her freedom.

"Jordan . . . what's the matter . . . ?" Elizabeth was hesitant to intrude on the thoughts that so obviously absorbed him. But she could not ignore the sudden grayness beneath his burnished tan or the abrupt tightening of his hand on hers.

Pride made it impossible for him to reveal his fear. As calmly as possible, he murmured, "Nothing. I was just . . . preoccupied."

Elizabeth frowned. Apparently, she could not hold his attention. He seemed to have forgotten all about her question and to have his mind very firmly on other things.

Maddening man! If only she could manage to get really angry at him, perhaps she would be less vulnerable to his slightest word and deed. As it was, she could only nurture her hurt in silence and acridly hope that whatever was on his mind proved entertaining.

When they rejoined the other men, she moved away from him further down the line of march. Osei set a brisk pace. She needed all her energy to keep up as the long hours of daylight passed in numbing sameness.

The forest closed in on them on all sides. Even at the end of the dry season, the thick canopy of trees, bushes, and twining creepers blocked out much of the sky. She could see only slivers of cobalt blue dotted by ever increasing clouds.

From time to time she caught sight of forest creatures going about their business. An occasional curious chimpanzee peered at them from behind a veil of leaves high in a tree. A long, feline genet with the spotted yellow coat of a leopard and an impossibly long tail vanished into the underbrush as they passed.

A striped squirrel chattered at them disapprovingly. Gloriously plumed touracos fluttered their purple wings and bobbed their crested emerald heads in consternation at the intrusion.

Ordinarily, she would have been delighted by the opportunity to see such an exotic part of the world close up. But her unhappy thoughts about Jordan severely dampened her enthusiasm.

She was all too conscious of him walking just ahead, his lean, powerful body perfectly at ease in an environment that would have overwhelmed most other men. The heavy machete he used to clear the undergrowth for the others moved in graceful arcs again and again. He seemed utterly tireless, an attribute Elizabeth could not claim to share.

The pack that had seemed so light that morning now felt filled with stones. Straps dug into her shoulders and her arms ached. The muscles of her thighs and calves had begun to throb. She longed to sit down and rest, but knew that was impossible.

With the rains so near, not a moment could be wasted. The little band plodded on, hour after weary hour, following the trail indicated in the map and taking some small measure of comfort from the sighting of landmarks that ensured they were on the right path.

"That looks like the mountain over there," Jordan said at one point, where through a break in the trees they could make out the looming bulk of ancient rock far in the distance. "The Mande's city should lie due west."

"I agree," Osei said, "but how far?"

"It's hard to tell. The map's scale varies. It could be as little as one day's march, or as much as a week."

"We do not have a week. The rains will come before then."

Jordan frowned. Once the deluge began, they would

202

not be able to see more than a few feet ahead. The ruins of the city would be virtually invisible. If they did not find it first, they might as well give up.

He glanced back worriedly, seeking Elizabeth among the line of march. She was pale and grim-faced, but determined. A tender smile curved his mouth. Whatever doubts he harbored could not detract from his pride in her.

She endured hardship as well as any man, better in fact than most. Not once had she complained or asked for the slightest concession. He almost wished that she would, but fought down that thought as unworthy.

Reluctantly, he said, "Then we must keep going. We can camp for a few hours after dark, long enough to eat and rest. But when the moon rises and there is once again enough light to see, we must continue."

Osei agreed. He knew that less driven men would spend the moonlit hours constructing a more substantial shelter to protect them should the rains come early. But he was willing to gamble they would not. In truth, he had no choice.

As the last rays of the setting sun were fading from the sky, the exhausted band came to a halt. Elizabeth wanted nothing more than to sink to the ground and never move again. She was sore from the top of her sweat-drenched head to the bottoms of her aching feet. Her limbs felt leaden and the mere effort of breathing seemed almost beyond her.

Yet she could not rest, not when everyone else was stoically going about the tasks of setting up the camp and securing it for the few hours they would be there. Trying not to think about how soon they would again be on the march, she concentrated on getting a small fire going and sorting through the supplies to decide what she would fix for dinner.

At least all that could be done sitting down. By the time a savory assortment of rice, meat, and vegetables was simmering over the fire, she felt somewhat better. Enough so that she could long for a bath, or even a cool cloth to wipe away the sweat and grime that had accumulated throughout the day.

But this far from the river, with no guarantee of finding streams or ponds that had survived the dry season, every drop of water they carried was precious. Until the rains came, she would have to be content with looking like a dirty urchin.

Sighing, she left the stew to simmer and lay back against her pack. She meant to rest for only a moment, but many more passed before she was gently shaken awake.

"Elizabeth, dinner is ready. You have to eat."

Groggily, she sat up and rubbed her eyes. Jordan was bending over her, his dark eyes suffused with concern. Gently, he asked, "Are you all right?"

"Yes . . . of course. I just dozed off."

"You're sure?"

His persistence strained her already over-taxed nerves. Did he think her some weakling who could not endure the slightest hardship? Irritably, she snapped, "I told you I'm fine."

Jordan laughed softly. He was glad of her temper. It reassured him that she still had the strength to go on. For a moment, as he bent over her, he had doubted she would be able to do so. She looked so fragile and vulnerable that he ached inside.

The longing to protect her from every discomfort was almost irresistible, yet he knew she would never allow it. The most he could hope for was to watch her closely and offer what slight help she was likely to accept.

"I've brought you some food," he said quietly. "You should eat, then rest again. We'll leave in a few hours."

Elizabeth nodded reluctantly. She was too weary to

resent his kindness, no matter what prompted it. As Jordan went off to confer with Osei, she turned her attention to the stew, eating slowly despite her great hunger. When the last drop was gone, she couldn't say whether it had tasted good or not. But it had filled her stomach.

Curling up against the pack, she fell asleep at once, not waking again until a shaft of moonlight pierced her lids and she knew it was time to go on.

At night, the forest came alive in ways she had not seen before. A rustling near the ground drew her attention to a chequered shrew about to take shelter in a tree. Its huge dark eyes blinked balefully as it scampered out of sight.

Elizabeth's stomach tightened with fear. Though they were traveling close together with weapons at the ready, she could not suppress the thought of how swiftly the giant cats could leap from cover and drag off an unwary human before a shot could be fired.

The men clearly shared her concern. Though they did not slacken their pace, they kept a careful eye out for the slightest sign of impending attack.

The few hours of rest had barely dented her weariness. It took all her concentration simply to put one foot in front of the other. Not even the dangers lurking on all sides could penetrate the fog of utter exhaustion that was rapidly closing in on her.

Long before the moon began at last to sink in the sky, Elizabeth was blessedly numb. She could no longer feel the weight on her back or the straps cutting into her shoulders. Her feet might not have been attached to her legs for all her awareness of them. She moved forward automatically, her head drooping with weariness and her eyelids weighed down by stones.

When she stumbled over a thick creeper, she barely realized she was falling. Not until the ground rushed up to meet her did she cry out. Jordan was instantly at her side. Picking her up gently, he cradled her trembling body against his own as he quickly gauged her injuries. The palms of her hands were cut and there was a gash on her forehead, but she seemed otherwise unharmed.

"It's nothing," Elizabeth insisted, trying to twist free of him. But Jordan would not allow it.

"I've already told you that no injury can go untreated here. The risk of infection is too great."

To her chagrin, the entire band was made to wait while he meticulously cleaned and bandaged her wounds. The fact that no one showed the slightest impatience with her only made it worse. When Anoyke beamed her a sympathetic smile, she had to fight an urge to cry.

As they moved off again, Jordan kept her at his side. She tried to drop back and lose herself among the men, but he would not allow it. Instead, he ignored her objections and removed her pack, adding it to the far larger burden he was already carrying.

"Stop being so stubborn, Liz. You're ready to drop and we both know it."

Too tired to deny what was patently obvious, she gave up her protests and continued slogging along beside him. Without the pack, the going was a little easier, but not much.

When she stumbled again, Jordan was there to grab her before she could fall. Straightening her, he murmured gently, "Not much longer, Liz. We'll rest soon."

She could only pray he was telling the truth. Through the numbness of her deadening fatigue, she was aware that even the men were close to exhaustion. The long trek had taxed their stamina to the limit. If they went on much further, they would be unable even to defend the band against attack.

No one was more acutely conscious of that than Osei. Much as he longed to press on, he knew it was impossible. As the first gray light of dawn banished the lingering rays of moonlight, he raised his hand.

The small, bedraggled group staggered to a halt around him. Only Jordan was still alert enough to realize that they had come to a ridge shown on the map. If the route traced by a Portuguese sailor more than four centuries ago could be believed, they were within sight of the lost city of the Mande.

But far from the noble structures he had vaguely envisioned, there was only more of the same endless forest they had just come through. Nothing about the site hinted that anything other than the usual forest creatures had ever lived there. Though the keen edge of disappointment and frustration knifed through him, he was careful to give no sign of it.

Jordan and Osei exchanged a quick look before the Ashante prince said calmly, "We will camp here on the high ground, probably for at least several days. This will allow us to hunt again and prepare shelters before the rains come."

Whatever the men thought of this they did not reveal. Silently, they went about the tasks of setting up the defensive perimeter and clearing enough of the ground so that everyone could stretch out comfortably.

Jordan and Osei took the first watch. With the rest of the band so exhausted, the responsibility for protection fell to the two leaders. It gave them the opportunity to talk quietly after everyone else was asleep.

"We have a problem, my friend," the Ashante prince said, gazing out over the thickly covered ridge. "This is the location shown on the map, yet there is no sign that the Mande, or anyone else, ever lived here."

"We can't be sure that means they were never

here," Jordan pointed out. "The forest grows so quickly that without constant vigilance it soon overcomes any work of man. You see that in your villages."

"True. But our villages are made of wood, mud, and grass. The Mandes supposedly built their city of stone."

"Even so, I believe it is possible that after so many centuries we could stand directly on top of the ruins and not see them until we look very carefully."

Osei badly wanted to believe his friend, but doubts still lingered. Ruefully, he said, "You have always been an optimist."

"But not a fool," Jordan parried. "There is precedent for the belief that cities can be swallowed up by their surroundings. Remember Schliemann, that German who announced he had found Troy? People thought he was crazy, until he uncovered buildings, friezes, caches of gold and bronze, and so on."

"I also remember that it took him decades to excavate the ruins," Osei pointed out. "We have only a few days."

"And only one objective, the idol." Putting his hand on his friend's shoulder, Jordan said quietly, "We will find it. I am certain."

He spoke rather more confidently than he felt. As he and Osei separated to patrol the perimeter, Jordan silently acknowledged that the possibility of there having once been a great city where he now stood seemed increasingly remote.

No matter how hard he tried, he could see only the usual thick growth of the forest. Wearily, he set down his gun long enough to rub his eyes. Leaning back against an exposed ridge of rock covered with tangled vines, he tried not to think about the consequences should they fail to find the idol.

The Ashantes were depending on the golden symbol

of their legendary forebears to reaffirm their rights to their lands and strengthen their determination to resist encroachment by the colonizers.

That was an important enough goal by itself, but added to it was the fate of two people he cared a great deal about. Without the idol, Osei could never marry his beloved Tema.

His own experience with Elizabeth made him realize as never before what a tragedy that would be, and strengthened his determination to prevent it. But how? The forest seemed unwilling to give up its secrets.

Alone on the edge of the camp, Jordan sighed deeply. He was not given to despair, but just then it was nipping at his heels. Plagued by doubts about both the woman he loved and the quest on which the fate of a people might depend, he had to force himself to concentrate on his surroundings.

Straightening, he walked some little distance alongside the rocky projection, noting absently that it seemed to run in a straight line more or less at the height of his waist. While he was mulling this over, a sound caught his attention.

Leaning forward, he listened intently. Drawing closer to the source, he carefully pushed aside a mass of creeper vines and leaned down to peer within a small cavity.

A sparkling flow of pure water rippled past his startled eyes. Grinning he cupped his hands and drank deeply. The liquid was delightfully cool and wet. With the worst of his thirst quenched, he considered how it had survived the ravages of the dry season.

The stream must be fed by some underground source that broke through to the surface at this point. It was likely that there were other outlets in the same immediate area.

Sitting back on his heels, he considered the immense advantages of a constant source of water in a land where so many streams and ponds were dry half the year. Had the underground river been running centuries before when the Mande swept down from the north? If so, it was reasonable that they would have founded their city nearby.

Thoughtfully, he reached a hand back into the cavity through which the water ran and felt the smooth, cool stone. Contrary to his original belief, it was not a single rock eroded over time by the constant rush of water. Instead, there were many parts to it, all neatly joined together. Laid down with the precision only men could achieve.

His hand shook slightly as he stood up, still staring at the water. Long moments passed before he realized that it lay at an opening in the low ridge he had walked alongside, which then cotinued on out of sight.

Slowly, fighting the excitement that threatened to overwhelm him, he pulled out the machete fastened to his belt and began to chop away at the thick tangle covering the ridge. Before he had gotten very far he stopped. There was no need to continue. He knew what he had found.

The ridge was a stone wall, as carefully put together as the channel that guided the water to the surface. Long ago, in some vanished time, the channel had been shattered and the flow diverted back into the ground. Only enough remained to show that it had once been an aqueduct wide enough to bring water into a great city.

The presence of the vanished Mande hung in the air around him and echoed the joyous shout which brought Osei and the others on the run.

Chapter Twelve

Elizabeth glanced down at herself ruefully. Thick red soil clung to her khaki slacks and shirt. Her hands and arms were covered with the stuff. Even the inside of her mouth felt gritty.

Yet she couldn't say she minded. The elation that had carried them all through the last several days overrode every other consideration. Since Jordan's stunning discovery, they had worked almost nonstop to survey and begin clearing the ruins.

The task was immense, yet they were slowly making progress. By relying on the map in which they now had absolute faith, they were able to identify the main temple where the idol was believed to have been kept. Most of the thick vines obscuring the entrance had already been chopped away.

For the first time in centuries, the magnificent edifice of white stone stood revealed to the sunlight. Elizabeth stared at it in fascination, forgetting for the moment that she has supposed to be helping to cut a path through the dense growth that clogged the interior of the temple.

The intricately carved figures of legendary deities enthralled her. She felt as though she could stare at them for hours. Already she could see a resemblance to the fabulous gold masks and statues worked by the Ashantes. Their belief that they were direct descendants of the Mande seemed more likely than ever.

Wiping the sweat from her forehead, she glanced up worriedly. Massive storm clouds obscured a good portion of the eastern sky. Their looming presence, complete with the incessant rumble of thunder and the crackle of electricity in the air, made everyone acutely conscious of the need for haste.

Yet they could not go too fast without taking the risk that they would overlook some essential clue. As it was, they were cutting every possible corner in an effort to find the idol before time ran out.

Both the map and the quick survey they had made before beginning confirmed that the remains of the city spread over some ten acres of thickly overgrown hillside. To excavate it properly would take decades, but the rewards might well be tremendous.

More even than the gold and precious gems that were likely to be found was the invaluable opportunity to resurrect a lost civilization and discover how men had lived in the dim reaches of the past. If it accomplished nothing else, the city of the Mande would put the lie to claims that Africans could not reach the same cultural achievements as Europeans. The principal excuse for colonization would be exposed for the fraud it was.

But before any of that could happen, the idol had to be found. Elizabeth stifled a sigh as she returned to cutting away the undergrowth. She was hot, tired, and aching in every bone and muscle. Yet she refused to give up, not so long as Jordan worked tirelessly beside her.

Since discovering the city, she doubted he had slept more than a few hours. Long after exhaustion drove her each night to seek her mat, the work continued. She had grown accustomed to the constant thonk of the machetes and the low murmur of voices excited by each new find.

Even when the rest of the men slept, he and Osei steadfastly persevered. Each foot of ground they regained from the forest was a victory, yet the ultimate prize continued to elude them.

They were well within the temple sanctuary now. Elizabeth had only to raise her head to see the huge walls towering above them, the remnants of the roof that had collapsed uncounted ages ago, and the statues of idols, some still in place, that had once been worshipped there.

One in particular caught her eye and she called Jordan's attention to it. "Look over there. Whoever carved that was greatly skilled. It's magnificent."

"Yes, it is," he agreed, pausing a moment to rest his arm and glance at the fallen idol. It was more lifelike than many others they had found, depicting the figure of a young and graceful woman carved out of obsidian. The goddess's full breasts and rounded belly indicated she was with child.

Jordan guessed it was a symbol of the female life force that primitive people would naturally have worshipped. He thought it both beautiful and oddly touching. It made him even more conscious of the woman at his side, and of the deep contentment he felt at simply being near her.

The grueling work of the last few days had left them little time to be together and no opportunity at all to make love. There was a gnawing ache deep inside him which increased every time he so much as thought of her. Yet he would not have had it otherwise.

He smiled faintly as he wondered what she would say if he told her that she was the source of all his strength and determination. It was likely she would not believe him, yet he knew it to be the truth.

Each time he was tempted to give up, he had only to look at her to gain courage. Her slightest glance or touch, the mere sound of her voice or the scent of her skin were enough to vitalize him.

For once, Elizabeth was unaware of his scrutiny. Kneeling down, she examined the statue more closely, shifting it slightly so that she could get a better look. As she did so, a worry that had flitted through her mind several times came again.

"Jordan . . . do you think it's possible that the legend of the golden idol was exaggerated?"

He rubbed the stubble-roughened line of his jaw pensively. "Why do you ask?"

"Because we've found more than a dozen idols here already, but they are all made of stone." Gesturing around her, she said, "Perhaps one of these we've already discovered is the idol of the legend and we just don't realize it because it isn't what we were expecting."

Jordan listened to her gravely but then shook his head. "I don't think so. The map makes it very clear there was one idol different from all the rest. It is shown as being in the center of the temple on the high altar."

Turning, she looked toward the huge slab of stone toward which all their efforts were now concentrated. Even covered with forest growth it was still an immensely impressive sight. Taller than any man, it easily dominated the vast inner reaches of the temple. There was no doubt that if there had ever been a great golden idol, that was where it would have rested.

But a few hours later when several men were at last able to climb to its top, the altar turned out to be empty. A thorough search all around its base revealed nothing that might have fallen from it. By the time the complete circumference of the altar had been gone over, night was falling. Reluctantly, Jordan and the rest withdrew to discuss what they had so far found, or—more correctly—failed to find.

Over broiled chunks of peafowl and roasted yams, theories were offered as to the possible fate of the idol.

"The Portuguese explorer who drew the original map claimed to have seen the statue with his own eyes," Jordan said. "He left a notation to the effect that it was being guarded by the last surviving remnants of the Mande, the rest of the tribe having been destroyed by subject people who rose up in rebellion."

"Since this anonymous mapmaker seems to have been right about everything else," Osei pointed out, "I think we can safely believe his claim that the idol was here some four centuries ago. However, we have to realize that in the intervening time anything might have happened to it. Arabs, Euorpeans, and other Africans have all come through this land. If any of them found the idol, they would have taken it away with them."

"If that had happened," Elizabeth ventured, "wouldn't there at least have been some rumor of the statue's whereabouts? I don't think anyone who discovered such a prize would have kept it a secret."

"Perhaps not," Jordan agreed, "but the fact remains that we are right where the idol is supposed to be and there's no sign of it."

No one could dispute that. The little group fell silent. Off in the distance, thunder continued to rumble. The sound was closer than it had been even a few hours before. Already the air was becoming muggy and a few slivers of lightning could be seen.

With the gathering darkness, an ominous force seemed to descend on them. Even the most stalwart of the warriors glanced around nervously. They were treading on ancient ground where once powerful gods had walked. It was impossible to know what supernatural powers might have been awakened by their presence.

Elizabeth instinctively moved closer to Jordan. He smiled down at her gently and took her hand in his. The comfort of his touch gave her the courage to voice the strange thoughts flitting through her mind.

"What do you think it was like for the Mande during their last days here?" she asked softly.

Startled by the question, Jordan looked out into the night. Shadows cloaked the brooding ruins, but could not lessen their impact. Tragedy hung in the air, and hopelessness.

Hesitantly, he said, "I don't think it's possible for any of us to imagine how it was here in those final days. We've never experienced anything remotely like it. The Mande had been a great people for centuries, believing that the strength and favor of their gods enabled them to rule the world. When the tide turned against them, they must have felt abandoned and betrayed."

"Then you think they were angry?" Osei asked.

Jordan glanced back at the ruins. Pensively, he murmured, "All the power, glory, honor of the past was gone. The few who were left alive could look forward only to captivity and death. Under such terrible conditions, they might very well have blamed their gods."

Osei frowned as he heard that. "Are you suggesting they might have destroyed the idol?"

Reluctantly, Jordan nodded. "I think we have to face the possibility that the statue may not have been found because it no longer exists."

Silence stretched out among them. No one wanted to believe that their quest was in vain, but just then there was very little evidence to the contrary. With the grueling labor of the last several days sapping the strength of even the strongest, it was all too easy to give in to despair.

But before that could happen, Elizabeth intervened. The gloom she saw stamped on Jordan's face made her ache inside. Driven by the most fundamental need to protect him, she said, "Everything we see around us suggests that the Mande were a highly practical people, skilled in understanding the world and shaping it to their requirements. Even when fate turned against them, I think they would still have realized the futility of being angry at the gods. But they might well have felt grief."

Her eyes were dark as she stared out over the spectral shapes. "Perhaps when so many of them were killed by their enemies, they concluded that the same fate had befallen their gods."

Jordan and Osei glanced at each other. What she was suggesting made a certain amount of sense, especially when weighed against what they knew of the Mande's religious beliefs.

"But what would they do with a dead god?" Osei murmured thoughtfully.

"Bury it?" Jordan suggested.

"Perhaps. We know that the Mande customarily interred their dead. But I don't see how that helps us. If Elizabeth is right, the god could have been hidden away anywhere in this area. It might never be found."

"Maybe not," she admitted. "But I keep coming back to the idea that people really aren't all that different, no matter what place or time they happen to live in. We all share common characteristics, including the need to set certain things apart as special. Surely even a slain god would be accorded respect and buried somewhere in keeping with its sanctity."

The men considered that carefully. No one disagreed, but neither could anyone, including Elizabeth, come up with a suggestion as to where the god might rest.

The most obvious place was beneath the altar where it had once stood, but that had already been checked and found to be a solid block of stone that could not have been shifted to conceal a burial. If a holy tomb did lie within the precincts of the temple, it was so well hidden that it was unlikely ever be found.

Baffled and at a loss as to what to try next, there seemed nothing to do but grab a few hours' rest and hope for better luck tomorrow. Even Osei and Jordan saw no point in continuing to work until they digested what they had already learned and came up with a plan.

Having made her way to the small stone enclosure where she was sleeping, Elizabeth was sorting through her clean clothes and contemplating the possibility of a bath when Jordan joined her. He stooped low to clear the doorway, then straightened with a weary smile.

"This is the first time I've come in here and found you awake."

Feeling unaccountably shy, she looked down at the shirt crumpled in her hands. Just then she couldn't remember why she had picked it up or what she had intended to do. Nothing registered on her mind except Jordan. Even as dirty, worn-out, and worried as he was, he was the epitome of everything she wanted in a man.

She yearned to go to him and express her love in the most fundamental way possible, but something held her back. It wasn't that she didn't trust him; she gladly placed her life in his hands. But she had no confidence about what he really felt for her.

That he desired her she could not doubt. Nor had his admiration and affection escaped her notice. But she wanted far more. She wanted him to be as helplessly in love as she herself, as subject to the moment-to-moment vicissitudes of uncertainty and longing.

A self-deprecating smile curved her mouth. So much for the vaunted selflessness of love. She who would be willing to lay down her life for him would be only too happy to see him suffer a bit on Venus's behalf.

"Elizabeth . . . ?"

Snatched from her thoughts, she looked up warily. "What?"

"You were very far away."

Tempted to correct him, she stopped herself. Let him think there was something on her mind besides himself. At least her pride would be salved. Evasively, she said, "I was just going to bathe. If you're asleep when I get back, I'll be careful not to wake you."

"Thank you," Jordan muttered drily, "but I have no intention of letting you wander off by yourself."

"You said just the other day that the stone pool is safe. I've been using it ever since."

The large reservoir unearthed during their work around the temple had proved a welcome and highly useful discovery. After clearing away the lily pads, lichen, and algae clogging the surface, the water turned out to be blessedly fresh and cool.

Osei believed it was fed by the same underground stream Jordan had discovered. He and the other men made twice-daily use of it, but kept scrupulously away the rest of the time. Elizabeth had quickly fallen into the habit of swimming each morning and evening. It was the only comfort her surroundings offered and she had no intention of relinquishing it.

But then why should she consider doing so just because Jordan had suddenly decided she couldn't be trusted there alone? Despite the nervousness that twisted her stomach she said, "You're perfectly welcome to come along."

His startled look made her swallow a laugh. On a resurgence of confidence, she added, "It's certainly big enough for two."

Without waiting for his response, she swept out of the hut. Behind her Jordan stood frozen in place, but only for a moment. Whatever prompted her startling invitation, it was far too good to miss. Pinning a deliberately casual expression on his face, he followed her quickly.

"Hold on. I want to tell Osei where we're going."

She hardly had any choice, since he had gotten a firm grip on her arm. Though she carefully avoided meeting Osei's eyes, she sensed the warrior was amused but not surprised. Fortunately, he was too much a gentleman to take advantage of the situation. Reminding them not to linger too long lest the moon set and leave them stranded in the dark, he returned to cleaning his rifle without another look.

The light of the huge silver globe hanging low in the sky clearly illuminated the path to the reservoir. They walked along in silence. From the corner of her eye, Elizabeth could see the tense set of Jordan's shoulders and the firm, determined line of his mouth. Guessing that he was waging some inner battle against uncertainty, she unbent enough to try to ease it.

"You and Osei are more than just friends, aren't you? Two brothers couldn't show more care for each other."

Relaxing a bit, he acknowledged, "We have been through a lot together."

"How did you come to meet?"

"Ten years ago when I first arrived in the Gold Coast, Osei was attending a mission school here. His father had the sensible idea that a knowledge of English and the ways of the white man would prove helpful in the struggle against them. Osei was such an excellent student that he quickly outstripped his teachers. So he and I struck a deal; I tutored him in return for his promise that when he went back to his people he would take me with him."

Jordan grinned, remembering those early days of their friendship. "Osei was true to his word. Before the next rains came, I found myself in Kumasi receiving the education of an Ashante warrior." Laughing ruefully, he admitted, "It damn near killed me. I've never worked so hard in my life before or since. But the training took. When it was over, I was welcomed into the tribe and adopted by the Asantehene himself."

"How long did you stay with them?"

"That first time about a year. Then Osei and I went off together to see a bit more of the world. We sailed down the coast to the horn of Africa, then back up the other side, stopping in Madagascar, Somalia, the lands of the Ethiopians, all the way to Egypt and the Nile delta. From there we struck out across the desert, following the ancient caravan route to Timbuktu, and eventually made our way back to the Gold Coast."

"What a fabulous adventure! You must have seen so many marvelous things."

"And a few not so marvelous. We saved each other's lives so many times that we both lost count."

"So you got in the habit of protecting each other . . . Is that why Osei was standing guard on the *Tara* the night I went there?"

Jordan nodded reluctantly. He didn't like to be reminded of how he had treated her when she first turned to him for help. Ever since, he had been trying to make up for it, but thought he had only partially succeeded.

"Your father's death disrupted the British authorities' plans to find the idol. They couldn't take the risk that I would go off looking for it before they could regroup. So it was reasonable to assume they would try to stop me."

Despite the warmth of the night air, Elizabeth shivered. She knew the colonists bitterly condemned Jordan's closeness to the Ashantes and even went so far as to suggest he had betrayed his race. But to actually try to kill him . . . .

"They must be very much afraid of you."

Without warning, he turned to her, his face inscrutable in the moonlight, and asked, "Do you think they have reason?".

Recovering quickly from her surprise at such an unexpected question, she correctly gauged his concern and answered with deliberate lightness. "Let's just say I no longer make the mistake of underestimating you."

"When did you do that?"

"When I came to see you on board the *Tara*. I had the idea that you would agree to search for the idol because of the glory and prestige its discovery would confer."

"And now you know differently?"

Quietly, Elizabeth said, "I know you are far too honorable a man to try to steal what rightly belongs to someone else. And you're too intelligent and fair to claim racial or cultural superiority as the excuse for actions that are nothing short of loathsome."

Jordan was silent for a moment before he murmured, "Your views would not make you popular in Accra or, for that matter, in London."

"I don't care about that. For twenty-four years, I lived according to other people's rules. From now on, I intend to be guided by my own instincts."

Though he badly wanted to believe her, Jordan was still hesitant. It was unlikely that she fully appreciated the power of social disapproval. In the seclusion of the primeval forest far from any other whites, she might well mean what she said.

But later, when she faced the choice of returning to the comfort and security of her old life, would she still be so certain? Or would what had happened away from the eyes of the world seem no more than a dreamlike interlude to be hidden in the far reaches of her memories?

Whatever lay ahead, one thing was certain; he would not waste another moment of their time together. Already too many days had passed since their lovemaking. His body ached for her, as did his heart. He wanted nothing so much as to claim her utterly, even as he gave himself without restraint.

As they reached the pool, he hesitated, wondering how to broach the subject. The irony of his predicament did not escape him. Without conceit, he knew that his skill, gentleness, and genuine affection had enthralled a host of beautiful women, to their mutual enjoyment.

But before one unworldly girl he was awkward and tongue-tied. All his experience and assurance deserted him. Once again he was struck by the fact that his nervousness was more appropriate to a young boy about to experience his first woman.

In possessing Elizabeth, he had discovered that to know her once was to yearn for her again and again. If he made love to her each day for a century, he would not have enough. And if he did not touch her again soon, he would be in the direst straits imaginable.

To distract himself, he made a half-hearted effort to shake the strange calm he sensed in her. Unfastening the top buttons of his shirt, he glanced at the smooth expanse of water glistening in the silver light. "You did say that's big enough for two?"

Instead of the blush he was counting on, Elizabeth

regarded him serenely. "It's big enough for a dozen."

Not quite able to believe what she seemed to be saying, he persisted. "Does that mean you're willing to share?"

She hesitated barely an instant before beginning matter-of-factly to remove her boots. "Of course."

"Oh . . ."

"After all, there's no reason for you to stand guard, is there?"

"I guess not . . ."

"Good." Straightening, she dropped the boots on the ground and unfastened her shirt. Jordan could not hide his fascination, as with artless grace she proceeded to remove it and her slacks, adding them to the growing pile without the slightest hint of self-consciousness. She might have been completely alone for all the concern she felt.

In fact, Elizabeth was anything but calm. Clad only in her camisole and abbreviated pantaloons that came only a few inches down her thighs, she shivered slightly.

What must he be thinking of her? She was behaving with incredible immodesty, and yet she could not help herself. The long days of being near him without experiencing his lovemaking had built up intolerable pressures that demanded release. Later she might regret her boldness, but just now she was not about to retreat.

Instead she took a step toward him, her hands resting lightly against the hard wall of his chest. Fingering one of buttons he had not yet unfastened, she said softly, "May I help you with that?"

Jordan nodded dumbly. Not for the world could he have moved or spoken. The blood pounded through his veins and his body felt on fire. Her audacity thrilled him, even as he could not help but wonder just how far she meant to go.

He got his answer quickly enough. With great care, Elizabeth undid each button until at last his shirt fell open, baring the broad width of his chest to her appreciative eyes. The sharp intake of her breath delighted him. He watched in fascination as her small, pink tongue darted out to moisten lips that had gone suddenly dry.

Her hands trembled as she gently pushed the garment from his shoulders. Crystal blue eyes glittered as he shrugged it off and smiled down at her. "You make an excellent valet."

Without shifting her gaze from his chest, she murmured absently, "Thank you."

Jordan's smile widened. A reckless sense of pleasure surged through him. He was suddenly feeling very good about things. "Shall we see how competent I am as a lady's maid?"

Elizabeth's eyes flew to his face. When she saw he was serious, she exhaled shakily. "Why not . . . ?"

Why not indeed, Jordan thought a moment later as he gently lifted the camisole and drew it over her head. The beauty thereby revealed to him taxed his self-control to the limit. He had to clench his hands to keep from seizing her at once and slaking the desire she so effortlessly provoked.

But that would be a mistake. He sensed she needed to be assured of her own ability to set the pace between them. Summoning all his patience, he managed to murmur, "Your turn."

She hesitated, but only infinitesimally. Small hands reached for the clasp of his belt and adroitly undid it. As he watched with tender amusement, she concentrated all her attention on unbuttoning his fly.

The task was almost beyond her. Her cheeks were bright red and her breath came in little pants before it was at last completed. As she sagged slightly in relief, Jordan laughed tenderly.

"My God, Liz, you enchant me. I've never encountered such a mixture of seductress and innocent."

"I'm not innocent," she reminded him a bit tartly. Just then she was feeling very woman-of-the-worldish and she wasn't about to let him forget it.

"Oh no . . . ?"

The hint of challenge in his voice puzzled her. It seemed to suggest that even after their earlier lovemaking, there were mysteries she had yet to discover. The mere thought of that was enough to increase her nervousness tenfold, but not to drive her from him.

Bravely, she met the ardent male gaze that swept hotly over her still-concealed hips, small waist, and bare breasts before settling at last on her face. When his big hands reached for her, she did not flinch but stood quietly under his touch.

"You'll never be anything but innocent, Liz," he murmured gently, "because you have the rare capacity to always believe the best of the world. That's a precious gift, but it can also lead to danger."

"Are you saying," she murmured breathlessly as his callused palms cupped her breasts and squeezed lightly, "that I need to be protected?"

No. If I said that, I'd be denying myself. What you need—deserve—is to be cherished. As only a lovely, warm, passionate woman can be."

As he spoke, his thumbs rubbed over her straining nipples, quickly bringing the hardened peaks to aching sensitivity. Lowering his head, he gently trailed his lips along the delicate curve of her jaw and down her throat to the hollow where a pulse beat throbbingly.

"You want me, Liz," he muttered raggedly. "I can feel it."

So could she. Desperate hunger beyond anything she had ever known made her writhe deep inside. Modesty, caution, restraint had all become meaningless. Nothing mattered except to free the ravenous forces that could no longer be denied.

Boldly, she slid her hands down his sculpted back to the waistband of his trousers. There they lingered for just a moment before easing gently within to tease and caress the hard curve of his buttocks.

Jordan growled deep in his throat. He was visibly shaken by her touch. Long, powerful tremors ran through him. His chest tightened spasmodically even as his manhood rose hard and urgent to press against the silken curve of her belly. "I hope you know what you're doing," he muttered thickly.

"Actually, I'm making it up as I go along."

An appreciative chuckle broke from him. "You've got an excellent imagination."

"Hmmm . . ." Elizabeth was too distracted for conversation. The response of his huge, virile body thrilled her. When he suddenly drew back, she tried to stop him, only to yield instantly as he muttered, "I've got to take my boots off."

As he dropped onto a nearby rock she knelt before him and smiled with unconscious provocation. "Let me."

Jordan was about to protest when the sight of her high, full breasts bobbing gently as she moved stopped him. He swallowed hard as she turned her back, presenting him with an unobstructed view of her delectable bottom hidden by only the thinnest barrier of silk.

Gripping first one boot and then the other, Elizabeth managed to get them both off before straightening to face him again. The look in his eyes drew her up short.

Never had she seen such unbridled passion. So intense was his regard that despite everything they had already shared she knew a moment of fear. It vanished instantly when Jordan brushed a gentle kiss across her lips.

Teasingly, he murmured, "I think you show great potential as a valet, but with very limited prospects for employment."

"Oh, really? Why's that?"

"Because," he informed her coolly as he slipped out of his trousers and tossed them away, "I've discovered recently that I'm a very possessive man and . . ."—his sole remaining garment followed, leaving him as nature had intended—". . . I will never share you with anyone else."

Elizabeth swallowed hard. She could not tear her eyes from him. He was so gloriously, blatantly male as to scarcely appear real. From the top of his tousled head to the bottom of his long, strong feet—including what lay between—he fascinated her.

"P-possessive . . . ?" she muttered absently, hardly aware that she was speaking.

"Very." Jordan was having trouble breathing. Her scrutiny left him nonplussed. It had not occurred to him that he would feel shy with her, but that was turning out to be exactly the case.

The first time they made love, she had had little opportunity to see him. In the darkness of their hut, he had relied on his skill and gentleness to enchant her and felt he had succeeded admirably. But now that every inch of his body was revealed to her, he had to wonder if she found him wanting.

Perhaps she would have preferred him not to be so large and heavily muscled. The prevailing fashion for male beauty celebrated soulfulness over brawn. Where any concession was made, it was toward the smooth perfection of classic Greek sculpture that even at its most explicit seemed free of earthy concerns.

But he was no brooding poet, far less a marble statue. He was a man, complete with scars and imperfections. If she found him less than she had imagined, he could not help it.

Elizabeth had no hint of what was going through his mind. She was far too caught up in the magnificence of his body to suspect for even an instant that he harbored the slightest doubt about her response.

Never would she have thought anything could be so beautiful. To her, he was the highest form of perfection brought to vivid, triumphant life. She adored everything about him.

The proud head resting on the strong column of his neck and the wide sweep of his shoulders delighted her. She loved the rough silk mat of ebony curls covering his chest, narrowing down across his flat, muscled abdomen to thicken again at his groin.

That part of him that most proclaimed him man held its own special fascination. For years she had heard the secrets of the male form whispered about with mingled ignorance and fear. At last she was free for herself to see what all the mystery was about.

She frowned slightly as she considered that he really didn't look all that practically made. How was it possible to move about in comfort when such a very large projection was . . .

A memory from their first night together surfaced in her mind. After they had made love and were drifting to sleep in each other's arms, she had noticed that the hard length which such a short time before had been pressed deep inside her was now small and limp. It appeared to have undergone some remarkable transformation which had since worn off.

Puzzled though she was, she did not yet feel bold enough to question him on such an intimate matter. Her unbridled study of his body had sapped her boldness. She was suddenly acutely aware of her own near-nudity and its likely consequences.

Murmuring, "I thought we came here to bathe," she turned her back, stripped off her scanty pantaloons, and pausing just long enough to draw a breath, dove into the cool, clear water.

Jordan hesitated barely an instant before following her. He cut cleanly through the surface of the pond and swam underwater almost to its edge before emerging again. Silvered moonlight glistened off his hair as he tossed it back, sending a shower of diamond droplets in all directions.

Treading water a short distance away, Elizabeth tried not to watch him. But her gaze was drawn back irresistibly. Separated by the space of several yards, their eyes met.

"Where did you learn to swim?" he demanded teasingly. "It's not generally considered a ladylike pursuit."

"By the time I found that out it was too late," she countered. "I was already quite adept."

"I'm not surprised. You're a quick study."

He got his wish at last as she blushed fiercely. There was no doubt in her mind as to what he meant. Pleased though she was to know he found her a capable lover, she was beginning to feel out of her depth. Flirtatious repartee was still beyond the bounds of her experience.

Without replying, she swam back to the edge of the pool where she had left her soap and turned her attention to scrubbing away the red dirt that clung to every inch of her. Or at least she tried. Jordan continued to intrude on her awareness. She was vividly conscious of his every movement.

A dozen times he swam the width of the pool with swift, easy strokes that gave her a new appreciation of his strength. When at length he stopped and floated over on his back, staring up at the star-splattered sky, she looked away hastily.

He drifted in silence for some time as she worked up a lather in her hair, then ducked under the water to rinse it all away. When she straightened, she found him standing in the shallow end of the reservoir, close enough to touch her.

Her instinctive move to cover her breasts ceased as he murmured, "Don't." Taking a step toward her, he gently seized both her hands in one of his and drew her into the circle of his arms.

So softly that she had to hold her breath to be sure of hearing him, he whispered, "I want to look at you . . . and touch you . . . all over. But I'll stop if you tell me to. All you have to do is say so."

Elizabeth swallowed painfully. Not for the world could she have done what he was suggesting. The very ability to speak was gone from her, as was any thought that what was happening between them was wrong.

While some remnant of the apprehension she had felt the first time still lingered, it served only to heighten her excitement. When he correctly took her silence for assent and drew her even closer, she went gladly.

Since her hands were held captive, she could only touch him with the rest of her body. Floating in the water, secure in her confidence that he would not allow her to go under, she let her slim, white legs brush teasingly against his.

The contrast between his hard, sinewy limbs and her own smooth softness enchanted her. Repeating the caress, she savored the stroke of rough silk hairs that sent little shivers of pleasure down her spine.

When he pressed against her, making her vividly aware of his arousal, she smiled with unconscious seductiveness. Buoyed by the cool water, her thighs parted instinctively as her womanhood sought the thrusting urgency of his maleness.

Jordan groaned deep in his throat. He couldn't bear

to wait any longer, yet the thought that he might inadvertently hurt her held him back. It was left to Elizabeth to take matters into her own hands.

Gently twisting free of his grip, she reached down to stroke and caress his phallus with innocent fascination. The swift rush of blood to his cheeks and the fierce glitter of his eyes were eloquent testament to her skill. A small, utterly feminine laugh escaped her as she drew him to her.

Grasping her hips, he positioned her swiftly. On the verge of claiming what he so desperately desired, he paused just long enough to give her a last chance to draw back. When she did not he brought his mouth down on hers at the same instant that he plunged deep within her moist haven. Sheathed in hot, undulating velvet, he moved hard and fast. Her cry of ecstasy matched his deep growl of pleasure as together they found completion in blinding release.

When the world at last ceased to quake about them, he cradled her tenderly in his arms and lifted her from the pool, setting her upon the low, moss-covered ledge. Blissfully satiated, they rested side by side, gazing up at the benevolent face of the watching moon and marveling at the sheer joy of love.

Chapter Thirteen

"I WANT TO RINSE OFF AGAIN BEFORE WE GO BACK," Elizabeth murmured a long while later, when she had at last recovered sufficiently to speak.

Jordan nodded lazily. Rising, he held out a hand to help her up. Together they slipped back into the pool, floating close to each other, their arms and legs entwined as they talked and laughed softly.

"You are so beautiful," Jordan murmured, brushing a finger down the petal-smooth curve of her cheek.

"Even with all my freckles?" Elizabeth teased. In the aftermath of complete satisfaction, she felt supremely confident and able for the first time to believe that perhaps he really did find her at least pretty.

A wicked grin curved his mouth as he raised his eyebrows suggestively. "Come over here and we'll find out if you've got them anywhere besides your nose."

Evading his hand, she swam some little distance away and glared at him in mock dismay. "Egad, sir, what sort of woman do you think I am?"

"An extraordinary one. Now come here." Again he

reached for her, only to miss by inches as she moved nimbly away.

Falling in with her game, he chased her across the pool, allowing her to elude him again and again until at last he grew tired of the sport and lunged. Elizabeth yelped as a steely hand closed around her ankle. Despite her halfhearted efforts to escape, she was drawn close to him.

Turned onto her back, she floated languidly with her legs outstretched on either side of him. Releasing her ankle, he trailed both his hands up her slender calves, pausing at the sensitive back of her knees, before gently caressing her thighs.

"Elizabeth . . ."

"Hmmm . . ."

"I meant what I said about your being beautiful."

Her half-closed eyes opened wide. Through the crystal-clear water she could see her body fully exposed to his gaze. Instead of the embarrassment she would have expected, she felt only a tremulous sense of pride and wonder.

So softly that her words were little more than a whisper on the night air, she murmured, "You make me feel beautiful."

Jordan's gaze was infinitely tender. Even as he marveled at the fierce resurgence of desire following so swiftly on utter satiation, he was aware that a great deal more lay behind his appreciation of her. She stirred him in ways he had never experienced before, and made him think far beyond that single moment to a future he was just beginning to envision.

Drawing her closer, he slid his hands along the silken curve of her buttocks. Her breasts brushed the thick pelt of hair covering his chest as her arms twined round his neck. With boldness she could not have imagined only a few days before, she drew his head down and gently touched her lips to his.

Jordan's response was instantaneous. He claimed her mouth as urgently as he had possessed her body. His tongue traced the ridge of her small white teeth before stroking gently inward, meeting hers in a languorous duel that left her weak with longing.

The water lapped softly about them, cooling the heat of their bodies but not lessening the force of their desire. So intense was it that both were deeply shaken. There had been no time to recover from their earlier lovemaking, yet already renewed passion tempted them almost beyond endurance.

Only the knowledge that the moon was sinking inexorably toward the top of the trees and that soon the forest would be plunged into darkness kept them from yielding to the force of their desire.

Reluctantly, Jordan lifted his head. He touched a light kiss to her upturned nose as he murmured huskily, "Let's finish up here and go back to the hut."

The glow of his eyes coupled with the throaty timbre of his voice were enough to tell her what would happen then. Content to wait some brief time, she slipped from his hands and dove beneath the water.

Moonlight filtering beneath the surface revealed the interior of the pool. She could easily make out the large blocks of white stone fitted so perfectly together that no mortar was needed. The air was almost gone from her lungs when a shadow along the wall caught her attention.

Surfacing briefly to draw breath, she dove again to take a closer look. As she got nearer, the shadow turned into an alcove cut into the rock and extending so far back that she could not see the end of it. Puzzled though she was as to why anyone would construct such a recess she knew better than to try to explore it alone.

Swift kicks took her back to the top. Again filling her straining lungs, she called, "Jordan."

He had just finished soaping the last of the dirt from himself and grinned challengingly. "So anxious to get back?"

Tartly, she said, "Not any more. There's something over here I want you to see."

Startled by her sudden shift of interest, he swam toward her slowly. "What is it?"

"I don't know. That's why I want you to look."

Together they dove beneath the surface and swam in the direction of the recess. Jordan examined the entrance carefully before gesturing to Elizabeth to stay where she was while he took a closer look.

He missed the adamant shake of her head as she determinedly followed. Together they entered a narrow underground channel cut below the waterline and extending as far ahead as they could see.

With their air almost exhausted, they had no choice but to head back. No sooner had they broken through to the surface than Jordan snapped, "I told you to stay where you were."

Despite the efforts of her starving lungs to draw breath as quickly as they could, she managed to shrug dismissively. "You can't—boss me—around. I found—the recess—and I want to see—what's in it."

Jordan muttered something she guessed was uncomplimentary. Without waiting for her, he dove again and vanished beneath the water. She followed swiftly, more determined than ever not to be left behind. A half-formed sense of excitement drew her on as together they entered the channel and swam toward its end.

The light grew steadily dimmer until it almost vanished entirely. Through the gloom enshrouding the far end of the channel an eerie green glow began to emerge. Its origin was a mystery they could not resist at least attempting to solve.

The stone walls on either side of them began to

widen, forming an inner chamber where the light became strong enough to see clearly. Once the water might have reached all the way to its ceiling, but over time it had dropped enough to provide a pocket of air where they surfaced.

When she had again caught her breath, Elizabeth glanced around curiously. "What is this place?" Her voice bounced hollowly off the stone walls, as did Jordan's.

"I have no idea, but at least I can see now where the light comes from. Look up there."

As she followed the direction of his hand, she could make out an opening cut into the chamber's ceiling. It was thickly overgrown with veins, but through them she could see the silver face of the moon, perfectly positioned to illuminate the interior.

A shiver of awe ran through her. Bemusedly, she said. "There must be very few times each year when this chamber is lit. It's incredible that we should have stumbled across it at just the perfect moment."

"Actually, it makes a certain kind of sense. I've thought all along that the pool was part of the temple enclosure. It was probably the only source of water during the dry season. See those ledges over there?"

Elizabeth nodded. "They look like miniatures of the big altar we found."

"I'll bet they were used to make offerings to whatever god was responsible for bringing rain. The Mande priests must have cut this opening for the moon to signal when their prayers were about to be answered."

Thoughtfully, she studied one of the small ledges where the remnants of withered flowers could still be seen twined around tiny gold effigies that despite the passage of time still glowed brilliantly. Absently fingering one of the little statues, she asked, "Couldn't they have found an easier place from which to track the changing seasons?"

"Undoubtedly, but the priests probably wanted to keep their knowledge secret, so they created a sanctuary hidden from everyone else."

"And it worked, didn't it? No one's found this place until now."

"I guess not, judging by what's still here . . ." His voice trailed off. They stared at each other silently as the same thought roared through both their minds.

Barely an instant passed before Jordan said, "I'll take the other side. You look here."

Elizabeth paused only long enough to nod before drawing a deep breath and diving again beneath the water. She swam close to the wall, searching for an alcove, a niche, any sign that their sudden hope was more than just a wishful dream.

Her breath was almost gone and she was reluctantly about to surface before trying again when a cloud drifted across the moon and momentarily obscured her vision. When it passed she peered forward, trying to make out the elusive hint of something lying on the bottom of the pool.

A bolt of electrifying shock ripped through her. Heedless of her empty lungs, she pushed downward and reached out a trembling hand to confirm what her mind told her could not possibly be.

A sheet of beaten gold at least a foot in either direction lay before her. That was astounding enough, but the single sheet was joined to another and another and another, stretching clear out of sight.

Trailing her hand across the glowing metal, she traced its path in desperation. Her empty lungs were screaming for air and her head whirled dizzily, but still she persisted until at last she could make out the shape of a carved head resting on broad shoulders.

Hardly daring to believe what she had found, she moved forward a few inches, only to abruptly freeze in place. A soundless scream escaped her as she found herself staring into glittering eyes set with diamonds larger than her fists.

Before her terrified features swam the face of an ancient god whom long-ago worshippers might have believed dead but which just then seemed vividly, horrifyingly alive.

Elizabeth had no memory of how she reached the surface of the pool. One moment she was staring dumbstruck into the face of the god and the next she was gasping for air and crying out for Jordan.

He was beside her instantly, strong hands grasping her shoulders as he drew her to him. "Liz! What is it? What's the matter?"

She couldn't answer him at once. All her energy was focused on replenishing her famished lungs. Finally she was able to gasp, "The god!—I found it—down there."

She thought he would leave her immediately to see the discovery for himself but instead he only pulled her closer, stroking her back and murmuring soothingly. "That's good, sweetheart. Now just take it easy. Everything's okay."

Misinterpreting his seeming lack of interest, she blurted, "But I found it, I tell you! Lying on its side under the water. It's huge and its eyes . . ."

"What about them?" he asked gently, continuing the tender caresses that were slowly easing the tension from her.

"They're made of diamonds, huge ones! Just as the legend said."

Not even this astounding news was able to distract him. He continued to hold her until the worst of her painful shock was passed. Tilting her head back, he gazed down at her gently. "Are you all right now?"

"Yes! Jordan, I'm telling you the truth. I really did find the idol."

"I know that. You'd hardly say it if it weren't so."

"Then why aren't you more excited?"

Confusion gave way to amusement. "Now that you're all right, I will be. Wait here while I take a look."

For once she did as he said. It wasn't precisely that the idol frightened her; she just didn't see any reason to confront it again within its watery grave. Once had been enough.

When Jordan resurfaced he was grinning broadly. "Fantastic! It's everything the legend claimed and more."

"How big do you think it is?"

"Ten feet easily." His smile faded as he added, "It's going to be a hell of a job to get it out of here."

That proved to be an understatement. After hours of backbreaking effort by the light of torches, the men managed to rig long lengths of twisted hemp to primitive pulleys driven into the stonework around the pool. Dawn had barely cast its first pale shadows into the cavern when Jordan and Osei began securing the other ends of the ropes around the idol.

They quickly discovered that its size and weight made it impossible to move more than a few inches at a time. Relay teams of men had to be organized, some returning to the surface to breathe, others on their way to the subterranean caverns, and still others lifting and tugging at the idol.

It was midafternoon before the huge golden statue at last reached the bottom of the reservoir. As sunlight shone off it for the first time in centuries, Osei grinned exuberantly.

Although he had already done more than his part to help move the statue, it was he who took the lead position on the pulley ropes and shouted out the powerful cadence by which the men hauled the dripping statue inch by laborious inch out of the water.

When at last it lay on the ground staring up at the cloud-draped sky, the men cheered. Astonished at its size and beauty, they exclaimed over the magnificent workmanship.

The most highly skilled artists of the Mande must have labored together to create so magnificent an image of their greatest god. For centuries it had looked out over their temple and their city, the focal point of their belief in the almighty and their confidence in themselves.

Only a long string of savage defeats could have convinced them the god was dead and their own fate sealed. Even then they treated it with loving awe and laid it to rest in their holiest sanctuary.

Elizabeth could not help but be glad that the idol had been found by people who would truly understand its significance and accord to it the respect due its creators.

But before it could truly be considered safe, it had to be gotten to Kumasi where the armed legions of the Asantehene would be able to protect it against even the most determined looters. Barely had the golden idol begun to dry off than Jordan and Osei were planning ways to accomplish that.

The difficulties were staggering. Throughout the search for the idol, the presumption had been that it would be no more than a few feet high and weigh less than a hundred pounds. The task of transporting such a find all the way to the capital high in the northern mountains would have been difficult enough. But with a statue more than ten times the expected size, the trip took on an entirely new meaning. Achieving it would be a greater feat even than finding the idol.

"We'll have to build a platform," Jordan said, drawing a quick diagram in the dirt. "And use large tree trunks as rollers. That should help us at least over level ground."

Osei nodded, considering in his mind the miles they would have to cover. "Half the men will go in front to clear the underbrush, the others will stay behind to push. We can haul ropes through pulleys on the upward slopes and use them in reverse as brakes when we're going downhill."

Jordan's face was somber as he quietly asked the question that was on everyone's mind. "How long do you think it will take us?"

Osei hesitated. He wished desperately to be able to give an optimistic answer, but regard for the truth overrode every other consideration. Reluctantly, he said, "Several weeks, at least."

Elizabeth struggled to hide her dismay. Although she had been expecting something to that effect, it was still hard to take. Long before they could hope to reach Kumasi the rains would come. The ground would turn to mud, the rollers would bog down and become useless, and the hemp ropes would lose all flexibility and snap under their load.

"Perhaps," she ventured, "the rains will hold off."

The men clearly did not believe that was likely, but they had no alternative but to take the chance. To stay where they were would accomplish nothing.

Accordingly, a group was quickly set to work under Anoyke's direction to chop down a dozen trees and strip the branches from them. Osei led the search for sufficient hemp to make ropes while Jordan and the rest of the men set to work building the platform.

By the following day all was in readiness. Camp was broken and the band prepared to move out. Elizabeth settled her belongings on her back and took her place alongside the idol near the front of the march.

As the rollers began to move beneath it and the first

steps were taken on what was certain to be a long and exhausting journey, she took a last look at the lost city. With all her heart she hoped that other people of goodwill would someday come to clear away the rest of the rubble and discover the glory that had been the Mande.

But she sensed she would not be among them. Her fate lay not with the shadowy secrets of the past but with the far more dangerous mysteries of the future.

She could only hope that it also lay with the man who had captured her heart as surely as he had enthralled her body.

Jordan's presence alone would give her the strength and courage she needed to face the task ahead. Resolutely, she did not think of the sheer enormity of their undertaking but concentrated instead on getting through it moment by moment and hour by hour.

The first day went well. Allowing for the interminable stops to clear the ground and rig the pulleys, they made excellent progress. Buoyed by the excitement of their discovery, the men threw off their weariness and worked with a will.

Not even the first pelting drops of rain that presaged the torrent to come dampened their enthusiasm. They did not stop until the last glimmers of light were gone.

With clouds obscuring the moon and torches too damp to light, it was impossible to see well enough to construct the usual grass huts. But they were able to find a rocky overhang that afforded protection. Gathered together beneath it, they chewed on dried strips of beef and talked eagerly of the idol.

Elizabeth sat beside Jordan, his arm around her shoulders and her head nestled against his chest. She no longer felt any shyness at being so close to him in public. Their time together was too precious to allow for any such concern.

The men were still talking when she drifted off to

sleep, unaware of the poignantly tender look that lit Jordan's eyes as he carried her some slight distance away and set her gently on a mat.

A few gusts of rainy wind found their way beneath the overhang, but for the most part they were dry and snug. Lying down beside her, he drew her into his arms. Resolutely ignoring the urgent demands of his body, which seemed to neither know nor care that they were not alone, he closed his eyes and sought the release of sleep.

Elizabeth woke shortly before dawn and turned over cautiously, anxious not to disturb the man who rested so soundly beside her. Sitting up, she could make out the shape of Osei standing at the edge of the overhang, looking out at the forest.

When she went over to wish him good morning and ask if there was time for her to cook breakfast, he smiled and shook his head regretfully. "I can hardly believe our luck that the rains have not yet come in full force. While we have the chance to move, we must not waste a moment."

She nodded, then surprised herself by suggesting, "Perhaps the god is responsible for our good fortune."

Osei raised an eyebrow quizzically. "Do you really believe that is possible?"

"I don't know," Elizabeth admitted. "A few weeks ago I would have scoffed at the idea that an idol could be anything more than an empty symbol. But now I'm not so sure—about that or a lot of other things."

"The other English people who come here have no such doubts."

"No, I suppose they don't. But I'm different from them." Even as she said the words, she was struck by their accuracy. She *was* different, in ways she was only just beginning to understand.

Her extremely insulated, circumscribed life had nurtured a hidden benefit. By keeping her from more than the most superficial contact with others, it had left her free to follow the dictates of her own intelligence and conscience.

That could only be considered fortunate, yet there were dangers inherent in such freedom. Without the preordained values, beliefs, and prejudices of her society to guide her, she had to make her own way through the rocky shoals of life and hope to find a safe harbor.

Perhaps she had, but if so she was not yet convinced of it. As tender and giving a lover as Jordan was, he had never said anything to suggest he envisioned a future with her beyond the limits of their quest for the idol. Once it was safely in Kumasi, he might consider the whole affair, including its more intimate aspects, at an end.

Osei was watching her closely. He had little difficulty interpreting the flow of emotion across her face. Like his beloved Tema, she was a passionate, feeling woman who would never be able to hide her thoughts. But unlike Tema, she did not know she was loved and that was clearly tearing at her.

Gently he said, "There is always much mystery in the forest, but there is also certainty. Sometimes it is difficult to tell the difference. The worst mistake you can make is to see only the dangers instead of the great beauty and joy to be found here."

Elizabeth had no doubt what he was trying to tell her. Meeting his gaze, she asked softly, "You've known Jordan for a long time. Do you think he's capable of really . . ." She broke off, embarrassed by what she had been about to reveal of her own feelings.

"Really loving?" Osei prompted gently. At her silent nod, he went on, "No man can speak for another, but I do know that Jordan is a true friend who does not fail to give trust where it is deserved."

Her absolute certainty that she would never do

anything to disappoint him did not quite banish her lingering doubts. Trusting was only a part of love, as was desire. He could give her both without giving his heart. What she wanted, indeed desperately needed, was some reassurance that he envisioned her as part of his future.

But that was not forthcoming. Throughout the rest of that day all personal considerations had to be put aside as everyone concentrated on the single goal of moving the idol.

Slowly, the ground began to slope uphill. Elizabeth barely noticed it at first, so intent was she on doing her part to clear the underbrush and keep the ropes tight. But eventually the ache in her calves and her slight shortness of breath made her realize what was happening.

A brief halt was called while the pulleys were attached. Half-a-dozen men tugging on either side were able to keep the idol moving, but only at the cost of enormous effort. Progress slowed to precious yards, gained over agonizing minutes that stretched into hours.

As they topped the crest of a hill and prepared for the downward slope, Elizabeth glanced apprehensively at the idol lying on its platform. It looked stable enough but she had begun to notice a worrisome tremor that not even the tightest ropes seemed able to prevent.

Telling herself that if there were a problem the others would have noticed, she kept silent. Moments later she had cause to regret that.

The platform moved forward jerkily, restrained from catapulting down the hill by the men who threw all their weight and strength into holding it back. Their effort was almost, but not quite, enough.

Elizabeth was busy yanking tree branches and vines

out of the way when one of the ropes suddenly snapped. She looked up just in time to see the platform break loose and come hurtling down the hillside straight at her.

What happened then was a blur. She screamed and tried frantically to move out of the way, but terror held her in a remorseless grip. Deadly tons of gold hurtled toward her through long paralyzing moments. Scant feet separated her from death when she was abruptly tackled around the waist and thrown to the ground just beyond the idol's reach.

She landed in a tangle of arms and legs and needed a moment to realize that they weren't all hers. Jordan lay beneath her, having instinctively twisted his body to take the worst of the blow when they landed. Beneath his tan, his face was gray and his mouth twisted in pain.

Elizabeth scrambled to her knees, staring down at him in mingled shock and horror. "J-Jordan . . . you're hurt!"

"No," he gritted between clenched teeth, "it's all right."

"It's not! I heard something snap . . ." Her hands reached out to him, only to hover uncertainly. If he was as badly hurt as she suspected, to touch him would be to risk worsening the injury.

Despite what she was certain was great pain, he managed to grin crookedly. "That was my nerve you heard go. When I saw you standing there with that thing barreling down on you . . ." He stopped, clearly unable to continue.

Swallowing hastily, she blinked back her tears and forced herself to think rationally. "You have to be moved, but very carefully. I'll get Osei . . ."

About to get up, she found that was unnecessary. The prince was already at her side, staring down at his friend with great consternation. Quietly but with an underlying tremor of concern, he asked, "What have you done to yourself?"

Jordan laughed tightly, then winced as he immediately regretted it. "That damn shoulder is out of line again."

Osei shook his head ruefully. "You were supposed to be careful of it, my friend. But under the circumstances . . ."—he glanced from Elizabeth to the fallen idol with darkened eyes that expressed his own dismay at what had almost happened—". . . I can understand how you forgot."

As he spoke, he ran capable hands along Jordan's left shoulder, quickly finding the point where the bones were out of alignment. His manner was calm and clearly experienced. A little sigh of relief escaped Elizabeth as she realized that Osei was as well prepared to heal as he was to fight.

But not even his careful touch could prevent the white-hot spasm of pain that tore through Jordan as his shoulder was maneuvered back into place. He gritted his teeth to keep from crying out, as Elizabeth held his hand tightly and fought to contain her own anguish.

A thin film of perspiration shone against Osei's ebony skin by the time he was finished. He sat back shakily, relieved to note that Jordan's breathing was already returning to normal and the ashen pallor of his skin was quickly disappearing.

Wryly, the prince asked, "I suppose now you will insist on getting up?"

Elizabeth started to protest but was cut off as Jordan said, "You know as well as I do that we have no time to waste." Determinedly, he hoisted himself to his feet, being careful to keep his left arm close against his side. A wave of dizziness seized him and he swayed slightly.

With a muttered exclamation of disgust at the vaunting braggadocio of men, she moved quickly to support his weight. Jordan allowed that much, but no more. He stubbornly remained standing as Osei fashioned strips of cloth to hold the injured shoulder in place.

When that was done and his shirt slipped back on, he said, "I'm not going to be much use on the ropes, so I'll move up front and help clear the underbrush."

That was too much for Elizabeth. Heedless of the consequences, she turned on both men, her face flushed and her hands clenched at her sides. "Of all the idiotic ideas! A chimpanzee would have more sense! Just what are you trying to prove? You haven't been hurt badly enough?"

As she paused for breath, she glared up at the men who were both eyeing her tolerantly.

"Quite the little spitfire, isn't she?" Jordan said pleasantly.

Osei nodded. "A woman of spirit is always more desirable than one without. You are most fortunate, my friend."

"Oh, I agree, but she could still do with a bit of taming."

Her infuriated snarl only made them laugh. Grinning broadly, Jordan drew her close and despite her angry wiggles planted a gentle kiss on her mouth. Before releasing her, he murmured, "If you want to make yourself useful, go find my rifle and carry it for me. I'll have all I can handle with the machete."

Much as she tried to deny it, his lightest touch so disarmed her that she could not argue further. With a final glare at both men, she went off to find the rifle that lay further up the slope of the hill, at the spot where Jordan was standing when he realized her danger.

To cross such distance in so short a time he must have hurled himself directly in front of the falling idol. She shook her head dazedly as she considered how close they had both come to death.

Life, which was already so precious to her, took on an even greater sense of urgency. Whereas a short time before she had been reluctant to look beyond the end of the quest, because of the uncertainty clouding the future, now she was determined to face it bravely. She would regret nothing so long as she knew she had shared every possible moment with him.

Returning to his side, she met his gaze demurely and was rewarded by a flash of puzzlement in his crystal blue eyes. Clearly, he had expected her to continue trying to convince him to rest. But instead she put all her energies into helping him as unobtrusively as possible.

By midafternoon, she knew her efforts were not enough. Jordan's face was coated with sweat and his color had a grayish tinge. Though he swung the machete with his right hand, the repeated movement could not help but jar his injured shoulder.

She had to grit her teeth to keep from begging him to stop. When they at last paused for a brief rest, she knelt beside him and studied him carefully. His eyes were closed and he was breathing raggedly. A light touch of her hand against his forehead confirmed the fact that he had begun to run a high fever.

On the pretext of finding out when she could prepare dinner, she went to talk with Osei. "Jordan can't go on like this," she told him urgently. "He's exhausted and in pain. I'm afraid an infection may be starting."

The prince heard her out grimly. He glanced over toward the man slumped against the tree. Much as he understood and shared Jordan's pride, he could see that Elizabeth was right.

Quietly, he said, "We are only a short distance from a village where we can spend the night. The obeah doctor should be able to help him."

Relieved, she went back to Jordan as the troupe started moving again. As Osei had promised, barely an hour later they came within sight of a good-sized village nestled against a hillside.

At first glance, it appeared to be everything she had hoped. The compound was large and well-kept, dotted by numerous grass huts and ceremonial lodges. A few goats and chickens moved about, but no people were in sight.

Even as she told herself they must be staying inside out of the misty rain that had once again begun to fall, she began to doubt that was true. Surely they would have heard the approaching band and come out to greet them?

Osei raised a hand, drawing the party to a halt. He and Jordan conferred quietly between themselves as the men glanced at each other with growing concern.

Elizabeth shifted uneasily. The rifle was heavy on her shoulder, she was hot, tired, and sweaty, and she wanted only to get down into the village and find care for Jordan.

What did it matter that they couldn't see anyone? They were just staying out of the rain, like any sensible people. Why were Osei and Jordan wasting time? They could have been down there by now, safe and dry and . . .

A shot rang out. A man screamed. Elizabeth whirled in time to see Anoyke fall, part of his chest ripped away and blood streaming down his side.

Another shot cut through the air, followed by a volley as weapons hidden in every hut suddenly opened fire. Instinctively, she threw herself flat on the ground and reached for the rifle.

Jordan was struggling toward her and Osei was already firing as she got the weapon to her shoulder and took careful aim. A numbing calmness had settled over her in the instant after she saw Anoyke fall.

When the attackers suddenly broke from the shelter of the huts and began advancing toward them, she felt no surprise at the discovery that they were fully armed white mercenaries. Nor did she hesitate as she methodically squeezed the trigger.

In the back of her mind, she understood that they were gravely outnumbered and underarmed. There was no chance that they could win. Bravely, she met Jordan's tormented gaze.

Amid the bursts of gunfire and the screams of wounded men, they could not exchange even a word. But at least she had the comfort of his nearness in the moments before their position was overrun and all her dreams for the future shattered against the immediacy of death.

Chapter Fourteen

"HOW NICE TO SEE YOU AGAIN, YOUR LADYSHIP," Nigel drawled. "I can't tell you how I've been looking forward to it."

Elizabeth didn't answer. She kept her eyes averted from the strutting, grinning man before her and concentrated on her surroundings.

Jordan, Osei, and the other men had been taken off to a barricaded compound near the center of the village. Anoyke lay unconscious on the ground near her. He seemed to have stopped bleeding but his color was sickly and his breathing irregular. She needed no great medical training to know that if he did not receive help soon he would die.

Help was the furthest thing from Nigel's mind. He was wallowing in his victory, basking in the knowledge that the people he hated most were at his mercy.

His hand shot out to yank painfully on Elizabeth's hair as he jerked her head up. "Look at me when I speak to you," he snarled, his eyes glittering with a half-mad light that made her shiver inwardly.

Though he frightened her badly, she was determined

to show no sign of it. He would get nothing from her but the derision and contempt he so richly deserved.

Her defiant stare wrung a harsh laugh from him. "Still so proud, bitch? After lying with Nash and those black savages you can hardly claim to be picky."

Elizabeth refused to dignify that with an answer. Her eyes remained blank, her expression impassive. Despite the bruises inflicted on her body when she was pulled from Jordan's valiantly protective embrace, she stood straight and resolute.

Whatever Nigel intended to do, she would not give him the satisfaction of seeing her grovel. He would learn how a true member of the British nobility died—with dignity and honor intact.

His grip on her hair tightened, wrenching her neck back. She could feel his hot breath on her face as he leaned toward her, his narrowed eyes seeming to stare straight into her soul.

"I can see what's going through your mind," he muttered hoarsely. "You think you'll win in the end because you won't plead with me. But you're wrong, bitch. You'll beg and crawl and do anything else I want. And I'll enjoy every moment of it."

Ignoring the anguished twisting of her stomach, Elizabeth met his gaze unflinchingly. As coolly as though she sat in a London drawing room discussing the weather, she said, "You are a disgrace to your class, Mr. Chandler. You shame the very name you bear and debase the sovereign you claim to serve. I cannot prevent you from doing anything you choose, but I can promise that you will never break me. That satisfaction, at least, I will deny you."

The color seeped from his taut features, only to come rushing back in an angry flush. Elizabeth watched in reluctant fascination as the battle waging within him showed clearly on his face.

It was as though there were two men inside him: one

who admired her courage and another who was enraged by her contempt. She had no illusion as to which would triumph in the end, but an appeal to some lingering remnant of the virtues he had once been taught might win her a little time.

Quietly, she said, "You want to believe that I am a loose, immoral woman in order to justify what you intend. But if you do so, you will be in error. The plain truth is that I am a lady thrown into desperate circumstances and in need of protection."

Nigel's mouth twisted derisively. "Are you trying to appeal to my better nature?"

That could hardly be the case since she was well aware that he had none. But something might be gained by pretending otherwise.

Softening her tone, she said, "I am trying to prevent you from making a terrible mistake. You may wish to appear utterly without conscience or scruples, but I cannot believe that is the case. If you were so insensitive, you would not have been affected by your wealthy relatives' unfeeling treatment of you. Nor would you ever have been able to face the challenges of a dangerous world so stalwartly."

Though the flattering words threatened to stick in her throat, she managed to utter them with a calmness that could easily be mistaken for sincerity. At least, she hoped it would be. A swift glance at Nigel through the thick fringe of her lashes showed that he was surprised, if nothing else.

Slowly, he said, "If you believe that, why did you denounce me just now?"

"Because of what I think you intend to do, not what you have already done." That was as blatant a falsehood as she had ever uttered, but she prayed he would accept it. Meeting his eyes steadfastly, she added, "There is still time to remember who and what you are."

The grip on her hair relaxed ever so slightly. "And what is that?"

"An English gentleman and the discoverer of the golden idol of the Mande."

"But it was Nash who found it."

"No one need know that. If we went back to England together, I would say that it was you who located the lost city and the statue. Who would disbelieve me? After all, I am the orphaned daughter of a renowned scholar. The story of how you befriended and helped me would quickly seize the public's imagination. You would be lionized as the epitome of everything an English gentleman should be."

Though the picture she painted was undeniably attractive, Nigel was still suspicious. Without warning, he demanded, "Doesn't it bother you that I killed that bastard Kwesi?"

Elizabeth flinched inwardly. Though she had been prepared for that, it still hurt. Since being attacked by the white mercenaries led by Nigel, she had assumed he had been rescued from the warriors taking him to Kumasi.

The Ashantes would have fought valiantly, and most if not all would have died before relinquishing him. But knowing all that did not prevent her from grieving for the death of a gentle, brave man she had come to think of as a friend.

Worse yet, she had to acknowledge the fact that Kwesi's death was only one of many. Along with the other warriors, there was the fate of the villagers to consider. Some might have managed to flee into the hills when the mercenaries arrived, but she suspected many had been killed.

Later there might be time to mourn properly, but only if she found the courage to continue her desperate masquerade. There was much blood on Nigel's hands.

If there were not to be more, she had to muster all her cleverness and determination.

Quietly, she said, "I imagine you did what you had to."

"That's right," Nigel snapped, abruptly letting go of her hair and taking a step back. "I saw to it that he died slowly, just as Nash and the rest of them will."

Elizabeth's stomach heaved sickeningly, but she managed to transform her revulsion into a ladylike shiver. As she swayed delicately, she held up a slender hand and murmured, "Forgive me, but I am only a woman with a woman's sensibilities."

So convincing was her pallor that Nigel felt a twinge of regret. Her reminder of a few moments before that he was an English gentleman and the bait she had dangled that he might yet be able to redeem himself in the eyes of his class were beginning to have some effect. Somewhat pompously, he told himself there were certain things one simply did not say to ladies, no matter what the circumstances.

Gruffly, he muttered, "Perhaps you'd better sit down."

Leaning on his arm, Elizabeth managed a weak smile. "I would appreciate that."

Hope surged through her that her ploy was working, only to be dashed a moment later when Nigel said, "Don't think this means I'll go easy on you. It's just that you're in the way right now and I have better things to worry about. So you'll stay in here . . ." He shoved her toward a small hut that had been hastily rigged with a barrier across the door.

Glancing back at the unconscious Anoyke, he called to one of the mercenaries, "Bring him in here, too. It won't do her ladyship any harm to be reminded of what happens to those who anger me."

Elizabeth needed no reminder, but she welcomed

the opportunity to care for the young warrior. "So long as he is going to be in here anyway," she said quietly, "may I have water and bandages to care for him?"

"Why should you want to do that?" Nigel demanded.

"Because I feel a sense of obligation to him. If I had not been so foolish as to try to stop you from escaping, you would have gotten safely away and none of this would have happened. Therefore, I am at least in part responsible for his injury."

Not for a moment did she believe any of that was true. If Nigel had managed to escape that night without her discovering him, she was certain he would have headed straight back to Accra or wherever else he thought he could meet up with the mercenaries.

Driven by their lust for the idol, they would have pursued Jordan and the Ashantes remorselessly, with the end result likely to have been the same. But she was determined to convince him otherwise, if only for Anoyke's sake.

Nigel stared at her for a long moment, mulling over her words. What she said was consistent with the values and duties of the nobility, and with his image of what a lady should be. Reluctantly, he nodded. "All right, but don't read more into this than you should. I'm still not convinced you weren't in league with Nash and the rest, or that you are at all deserving of the privileges reserved to a lady."

Demurely, Elizabeth murmured, "I can understand your suspicion of me, for I have behaved shamefully toward you. I shall just have to do everything possible to win your trust.

Praying that God would excuse her lies as being in the service of a good cause, she stepped into the hut. Anoyke's unconscious form was dumped on the ground near her before the door was closed and the bolt rammed into place.

Swiftly, she knelt at his side and examined the wound. It was every bit as bad as she had feared. The bullet had entered between the third and fourth rib and was lodged somewhere in the body.

Had it been an inch or two higher, it would have gone directly into his heart. Even as it was, death was inevitable unless she could get the bullet out.

Swallowing hard, Elizabeth glanced round the hut. It was neatly furnished with the belongings of the family that up until a short time before had lived there.

She was quickly able to find lengths of material that could be used to clean the wound, but without water she was prevented from doing so. Going over to the tiny window, she peered out and was rewarded by the sight of one of the mercenaries' bearers bringing a bucket of water and a wad of bandages.

The man's dress and lack of shoulder tattoos told her he was not Ashante, but she nonetheless tried out her few words of Oji on him. Despite his obvious surprise and distrust, he unbent enough to return her greeting.

Building on that, she grappled with her extremely limited vocabulary and managed to ask him how many mercenaries were in the camp. He glanced round warily before counting off on his fingers to show that there were a dozen. Immediately regretting his loquaciousness, he left hurriedly.

Satisfied that she had gotten all possible information, Elizabeth set to work on Anoyke. She studied the wound carefully as she debated whether or not to risk leaving the bullet in place or take what might be the even greater risk of trying to remove it.

The slow seepage of blood that had started up again

made the decision for her. The bullet had to come out, or Anoyke would die within a matter of hours.

Looking around the hut again, she reluctantly concluded that the only tools she could use were her own fingers. After scrubbing them as thoroughly as possible and bathing the wound, she gingerly began to feel her way along the bullet's path.

Anoyke moaned fitfully beneath her. His head tossed from side to side in protest against the pain she inflicted. Blinking back the tears that threatened to blind her, Elizabeth persevered.

For once, luck was with her. Not only had the bullet remained intact but it was lodged only a couple of inches inside the wound. Despite the tremors that coursed through her, she was able to get a firm grip and remove it smoothly.

A gush of blood splattered her. Dropping the bullet, she pressed cloths against the wound and waited through long, agonizing moments until the flow eased off.

The possibility of infection following such primitive surgery was immense, but there was nothing she could do to prevent it. Unless Anoyke received help soon from the obeah doctor, her efforts would likely be in vain.

Leaving him still unconscious but breathing more regularly, she cleaned her hands again and went to stand by the window. Nigel and the mercenaries were gathered around a cookfire where black servants were preparing dinner. Near them lay the idol, which they were busy admiring and exclaiming over.

Their rough, boastful voices coupled with their complete disregard for the well-being of their prisoners sickened her. She turned away, trying to block out the effects of her mounting exhaustion. With the shock of being captured rapidly wearing off, she was prey to all sorts of dismal thoughts.

Sitting down on the hard-packed floor, she stared at Anoyke and tried hard not to cry.

What was going to happen to them? She did not doubt for a moment that Nigel was capable of immense cruelty. Would he carry out his threat to kill them all? If so, would she be able to bear the sight of Jordan's suffering without losing her grip on sanity?

For that matter, was Jordan still alive? She knew only that he had been taken to the compound. What had happened since then was a mystery.

A sob rose in her throat as she considered the possibility that he might already be dead, but hardly had the thought occurred to her than she forced it down. If he were gone, she would know. So vital a part of her life could not have been ripped away without her sensing the loss.

But that didn't mean he hadn't been hurt. His injured shoulder made him a far easier target than would otherwise have been the case. She could only hope that Nigel had not realized his incapacity or, if he had, had not yet taken advantage of it.

That hope proved unfounded. As she sat slumped on the ground, the door to the hut was suddenly slammed open and two of the mercenaries entered. Before she had a chance to ask what they wanted, they seized her by the arms and yanked her outside.

Dangling between the two big men, she was half-carried, half-dragged toward the center of the compound and deposited in front of Nigel.

When she got her breath back sufficiently to speak, she swallowed her first angry outburst and schooled herself to inquire calmly, "What is the meaning of this?"

Nigel smiled coldly. "I thought you might be in the mood for some company, your ladyship. Perhaps even some food."

Though she had not eaten since early morning and

her stomach was painfully empty, she would cheerfully have died before accepting food from him. Not while the others went without. Wisely, she refrained from telling him so and instead sat down gracefully at his side.

Despite her bedraggled clothes splattered with dirt and blood, she somehow contrived to look remarkably feminine and appealing. A fact which did not escape her captor's notice.

He could scarcely credit the transformation in her from their first meeting in the graveyard. Then he had thought her homely and sexless, the absolute opposite of everything that attracted him to a woman. Now he had to admit his impression had been wrong.

Remembering the feel of her body beneath his hands during the moments they had struggled in the clearing, he smiled grimly. He intended to touch her like that again and in fact to do a great deal more. But he was no longer sure that was all he wanted of her.

What if she was telling the truth and really did not feel any great loyalty or attraction to Nash? What if she really would return to England with him and proclaim him both her rescuer and the discoverer of the idol? The rewards to them both could be immense.

For him, it would mean the wealth and respect he had craved all his life. For her, the wholehearted approval of society and a position any woman might envy.

So attractive a picture did it appear to Nigel that he went so far as to consider the ultimate reversal of his original plans; instead of raping and killing her, why not make her his wife?

The idea was not as outlandish as it first appeared. Her pedigree was beyond reproach; she came from one of the oldest and most respected families in England. Added to that was the fact that she was an heiress. While he could not put a precise figure on Sir

Alfred's wealth, he knew it was more than sufficient to make her a matrimonial prize in and of itself.

But there was also her indisputable beauty. She stirred him carnally to a degree no other woman had ever managed. As a man of wealth and position, he would naturally want children. Why shouldn't he enjoy the getting of them?

So pleasant had his thoughts become that Nigel began to relax, sending Elizabeth a look that was so unexpectedly warm as to make her heart lurch. She vastly preferred him cold and calculating. Any hint that he was returning to the aroused state she had glimpsed in him briefly was enough to horrify her.

Taking a deep breath, she sought to turn his attention to other matters. "Thank you for sending the water and bandages for the native. He is still unconscious, but I believe he will live."

"Long enough to be executed," Nigel said, dismissing her gratitude. He leaned forward, taking her hands in his and holding them so tightly that she could not pull back without hurting herself.

Slowly, he said, "I don't like the idea of your touching any other man. From now on, you will save all your caresses for me."

Elizabeth managed a shaky smile. "Please, you embarrass me. I cared for Anoyke as a nurse."

Tightening his hold just enough to inflict the beginnings of pain, he demanded, "And was that your relationship with Nash?"

She hesitated. Whatever else he was, Nigel was not stupid. He was well aware that her dealings with Jordan were not platonic. If she attempted to lie to him, he would know at once. But on the other hand, she could not afford to admit too much of the truth lest he use it as justification to treat her vilely.

Cautiously, she said, "You must realize that I led a very sheltered life prior to my father's death. I was in

no way prepared to deal with a man like Nash."
Blushing, she lowered her eyes. "He . . . attempted
to seduce me."

"Attempted?" Nigel demanded harshly.

Mutely, she nodded.

"Then you feel nothing for him but revulsion?"

Steeling her heart against the lie, Elizabeth said,
"Believe me, I loathe Mr. Nash and everything he
stands for. Not only is he a rake and reprobate, but he
is also a traitor to his race."

Nigel delighted in her words and wanted badly to
believe them. But he still needed a bit more convincing. Drawing her closer so that she was forced to let
his arm brush against her breasts, he said, "Good,
then you won't mind watching while I question him."

Elizabeth could think of nothing she would mind
more, but she had no choice except to agree. The hard
glitter in Nigel's eyes told her what he was up to. This
was a test. If she passed it, there might come a chance
to help Jordan and the others. If she failed, there
would be no hope for any of them.

Though she had no idea how she was going to get
through the next few minutes, she forced herself to
smile sweetly. "I trust you to do only what is right.
Therefore, why should I wish to withdraw?"

Nigel did not respond directly, but he did continue
to watch her closely as he summoned a mercenary and
gave his orders. Moments later, Elizabeth had to
watch impassively as Jordan was pulled from the
compound and dragged toward them.

She could see at a glance that he was in bad shape.
His shirt had been torn from him along with the
bandage holding his shoulder in place. Livid bruises
covered his face and chest. One eye was almost closed
and blood caked a corner of his mouth.

Stifling the almost irresistible urge to go to him, she

turned to Nigel and inquired mildly, "It doesn't look as though he put up much of a fight, does it?"

"His kind is always full of bluff. Put him up against a real man and he caves in instantly."

Fighting the urge to ask what kind of man it was who needed the help of a dozen others to vanquish a single enemy, Elizabeth said, "While you question him, would you mind if I help with dinner? As I'm sure you know, these native cooks are abominable."

Nigel waved a hand magnanimously. "By all means. But I still expect you to take note of what happens to Nash. He may say something you know is not truthful."

"Then I will of course correct him."

Satisfied that he had thwarted her attempts to distract herself, Nigel turned his attention to the prisoner. He stared at him for a long moment, enjoying the glare of hatred that poured from Jordan's single good eye.

At length, he said, "Her ladyship is quite right, you do look rather the worse for wear."

"Not as bad as you'll look when I get my hands on you," Jordan snarled. "If you've hurt her . . ."

"Such gallantry! And to think I was just hearing all about how you attempted to seduce her and how she loathes you for it."

Startled, Jordan glanced at Elizabeth. She met his gaze for just a moment before turning away. Her sudden withdrawal and the wall he sensed between them bewildered him.

What reason did she have to tell Nigel such a lie? What did she hope to gain by it? Safety for herself was certainly a vital consideration, but he could not believe she would stoop to such infamy to assure it. Yet no other explanation immediately occurred to him.

He was forced to watch grim-faced as Elizabeth calmly filled a gourd with the rather disreputable-looking stew and brought it to Nigel along with a mug of palm wine. He accepted both before drawing her back down beside him.

When she attempted to shift slightly away, Nigel's grip tightened. "Oh, no, my dear, I want you close by. After all, we have been apart for days. Surely you would not begrudge me the pleasure of your nearness?"

Elizabeth would have gladly begrudged him life itself, but she did not say so. Instead she blushed prettily and murmured, "But it isn't proper for us to sit so close together."

His mocking smile faded, replaced by a dangerous sneer. "Perhaps not, but you must remember that I have cause to be very angry with you. To win your way back into my good graces, you will have to unbend and forget the social proprieties."

"I am not sure I can . . ."

"You have to. Starting right now."

Without giving her a chance to reply, he put one arm over her shoulder and the other around her waist. Glancing at Jordan, he smiled mockingly.

"You see how agreeable she is. Before very long, I'll have her obeying my slightest whim."

"You bastard!" Jordan snarled. Straining against the two men holding him, he managed to take a step forward before another of the mercenaries slammed his fist into his stomach, driving the air from him and making the world spin sickeningly.

A blow to the back of his head sent him reeling. With his hands tightly bound, he was powerless to protect himself. Nigel and the mercenaries laughed as he fell to the ground, landing face down in the dirt.

He was just about to be kicked in the side when Elizabeth intervened. Pale and trembling, she fought to control her rage as she said, "Is this really necessary? It's hardly sporting to strike a man in his condition."

Nigel took a contrary view, finding it most amusing to see his hated enemy in such abject shape. But her seeming lack of any but the most superficial concern made the exercise seem pointless. Reluctantly, he agreed.

After grudgingly helping Jordan to his feet, the mercenaries were waved away. The two men eyed each other coldly. His adversary's failure to look properly chastised piqued Nigel's temper. Tightening his hold on Elizabeth, he insolently allowed his hand to drop onto her breast.

She sucked in her breath but resisted the impulse to pull away. To do so would only be to thwart herself. Resolutely, she endured his touch and tried hard not to imagine what Jordan must be thinking.

It was just as well she did not know what was passing through his mind. At the first sight of Nigel touching her so intimately, he had come close to erupting in blind rage. As seconds passed and he realized she was not resisting, his anger changed to something very close to despair.

How could she allow such a violation of her body? Did she hold herself in such low esteem that the caress of a man like Chandler was not revolting to her? And if that were the case, then what did it say about her response to his own lovemaking? Perhaps what had meant the world to him was nothing to her.

His face was gray and a jagged pulse beat in his jaw. The possibility that all the hopes and dreams he had nurtured about her were nothing more than illusions threatened him with blackest despair.

He fought against it for long, pain-filled moments until through the haze of his self-inflicted agony the sweet light of reason began to shine.

Shaking his head as though to clear it, he allowed himself to remember all the beauty and tenderness that had passed between them. Only a madman could believe that her innocent passion was a sham. She had trusted him utterly when he most needed it; how could he fail to do the same for her?

Beneath tangled ebony locks, his brow knit thoughtfully. What possible motivation could she have for accepting Chandler's touch so docilely? Or was she?

A closer look made his mouth tighten ominously. To one who did not know her well, Elizabeth appeared completely unaffected by the violation of her person. But to the man who had held her in his arms and shared the joy of her first sweet surrender, her embarrassment and anger were clear. Far from being a willing partner, she was struggling against revulsion and outrage.

Desperate to help her, he cast round for some way to use the only weapons still at his disposal, his wits and his tongue.

Pinning a sneer on his bloodied mouth, he said, "You're welcome to her, Chandler. She's more trouble than she's worth."

Nigel frowned. He had expected Jordan to be incensed and tormented. Instead, he looked as though he truly didn't give a damn about Elizabeth or anything that happened to her.

Chagrined, he dropped his hand and stood up. From a safe distance, he scoffed, "Do you really expect me to believe she doesn't mean anything to you?"

"No," Jordan said matter-of-factly, "she did mean something once, back when she was my easiest route to the idol. The fact that she turned out to be a good-looking woman was a bonus."

"Is that why you attempted to seduce her?"

Glancing swiftly at Elizabeth, Jordan took in her pale features and the slight tremor of her slender shoulders before he answered. "That's right, but she fought me off." He grinned humorlessly. "You know how uncooperative she is."

"Correction," Nigel taunted, "how uncooperative she *was*. She's changed her mind about me."

Returning to Elizabeth, he yanked her to her feet and smiled coldly as he ran his hands over her curves before pulling her taut against him so that she could feel his unmistakable arousal.

Loudly enough for Jordan to hear, he said, "Go wait for me in my hut. Soon enough I'll give you a chance to prove what you've been telling me is true."

It was on the tip of her tongue to refuse his loathsome order, but she stopped herself just in time. Jordan's words had lashed her. For just a moment she had come close to believing she had been nothing more than the victim of a brutal joke.

Then her more sensible self had spoken up, sternly telling her not to make a bad situation worse by being a ninny. Whether Jordan loved her or not, he was far too honorable a man to have taken advantage of her in the way he now claimed. He was lying to protect her, and the lie had worked.

Alone in Nigel's hut she would have time to think and plan. At the moment, that was the best she could hope for. But even knowing that she should welcome such an opportunity, she could not find it in her heart to do so. Not when it meant leaving Jordan tied up and helpless.

In a desperate bid to win some slight protection for him, she managed a weak smile at Nigel as she said, "You won't be long, will you? I hate being by myself out here."

Her stomach tightened as he looked her up and down lewdly. "Don't worry. I have no intention of waiting much longer for you."

A shiver of revulsion ran through her as she turned

her back and walked steadfastly toward the hut. Once inside, away from Nigel's vile stare and Jordan's tormented gaze, she collapsed. Burying her face in her hands, she gave way to the racking sobs that would no longer be denied.

Much as she despised crying, she had to admit it afforded a certain degree of release. When her tears at last slackened off, she was feeling calm enough to give some rational consideration to her predicament.

The position seemed hopeless. They were without arms and surrounded by enemies far from any hope of rescue. Even if she were able to escape from the hut and free the men, they would still have to find weapons and take the mercenary force by surprise. It was highly unlikely that they would be able to do so, since as venal as Nigel's men undoubtedly were, they were not in the least lax.

Through the small window of the hut, she could make out guards being posted around the village perimeter. As night began to fall and the moment when Nigel would walk through the door came ever closer, she had to give serious thought to the possibility that there would be no escape.

If that turned out to be the case, she was resolved to risk everything on a final, desperate gamble. No matter what the cost to herself, she would contrive to distract Nigel sufficiently to get his weapon away from him.

That might well mean submitting to his possession, the mere thought of which filled her with loathing. But she would do it if there was no other way to help Jordan and the others.

Immersed in desperate planning, she did not at first notice the faint sound coming from just outside the hut. When it finally penetrated her consciousness, she looked up puzzled.

Someone was scratching on the wall opposite the

door. Going over to it, she knelt down and pressed her face close to the interwoven palm fronds. Through them, she could make out slivers of the night.

An indistinct shape moved in front of her eyes, blocking out her view. Elizabeth gasped, only to be instantly silenced as a soft but firm voice said, "Shh."

Without knowing why, she obeyed. Moments later a neat opening had been cut in the wall and her mysterious visitor stepped into view.

She had to swallow an exclamation of surprise as she found herself staring into the velvet brown eyes of a young black woman, whose remarkable beauty was equaled only by her proud carriage and obvious intelligence.

Shakily, Elizabeth whispered, "Who are you?"

The woman smiled. Stepping closer, she hesitated barely an instant before saying, "I am Tema, Osei's woman. Or I will be if he hasn't been so foolish as to get himself killed. Now come, it is time to leave here."

Chapter Fifteen

FOREVER AFTER, ELIZABETH WAS TO REMEMBER that mad dash across the village with Tema at her side. The Ashante war party—alerted by the sole survivor of the attack on Kwesi and his men—had already overcome the perimeter guards and was heading toward the locked compound.

Some of the mercenaries, overconfident after their victory, had drunk heavily of palm wine. When their throats were deftly sliced, they slipped from sodden stupor into the embrace of death.

Of those who did wake in time to realize what was happening and reach for their weapons, many were mowed down by a barrage of deadly spears and arrows launched from the cover of darkness.

Emerging from his hut to a nearly incomprehensible scene of upheaval and destruction, Nigel panicked. Ignoring the ever-present risk of fire, he ordered lighted brands shot into the air to illuminate the night in the futile hope that his few remaining men would be able to turn the tide of battle.

No sooner were the torches ablaze than they caught on the tinder-dry roofs of the huts. Lashed by a sudden wind, the flames swiftly turned the village into a raging inferno.

Choking on smoke and ash, Elizabeth stumbled. She went down hard on her knees, but was helped up instantly by Tema. "Come on," the black girl urged, "we have to keep moving."

They ran on, past burning huts and screaming men, in the direction of the compound. Looking up suddenly, Elizabeth caught sight of a smoking beam about to crash down in their path. She pushed Tema aside, rolling with her as they both hit the ground, the breath knocked out of them.

There was no time to recover before they were on their feet and running again. Singed by fierce heat and almost overcome by smoke, they could take some comfort in the sight of the prisoner compound standing empty.

The warriors had succeeded in forcing the door and freeing all those inside. Without guns and in the close quarters of the village, they had to rely on hand-to-hand combat against the remaining mercenaries.

A strangled scream broke from Elizabeth as through the billowing clouds of smoke she saw Nigel raise his rifle to fire. The demonic hatred stamped on his face and the direction of his gaze told her his intended target was Jordan.

Desperately, she tried to get close enough to stop him, but before she could do so, Osei acted. A whirling length of hemp with small stones attached to its end lashed out and wrapped around the rifle, jerking it from Nigel's hands.

Taken by surprise, he nonetheless recovered quickly enough to pull out a long, gleaming knife just as Jordan hurled himself at him. The two men struggled through seemingly endless moments.

Jordan was armed only with a machete he had found outside the compound. That coupled with his injuries gave Nigel the advantage, but not the victory. Even as Osei and several other warriors rushed to his aid, he broke loose of Nigel and, lifting the machete high, brought it down in a deadly arc straight for the Englishman's chest.

Elizabeth judiciously looked away as her nemesis died, only to find her gaze focused on the hut she had occupied earlier and which was about to go up in flames.

"Anoyke!"

Her frantic shout brought the attention of Tema and the men, who joined her in a desperate effort to save the young warrior. To reach the hut, they had to cross the width of the village. In the center of their path lay the golden idol surrounded by a funeral pyre of fallen wood and flaming tinder.

There was an instant when a decision had to be made. Jordan and Osei glanced at each other, then at Elizabeth and Tema. In four pairs of eyes, not the slightest doubt showed. Without hesitation, they raced past the idol and concentrated all their energies on reaching Anoyke in time.

As it was, they barely made it. Jordan and Osei lifted the young man's limp form while Elizabeth and Tema kicked burning brands out of their way. They had only just broken from the hut and were running for the shelter of the forest when the roof caved in behind them.

Behind them, the fire was reaching its peak. Smoke and darkness obscured their vision, but they could see enough to watch in awe as the golden idol, created centuries before by a race that believed it too would last forever, began to vanish before their eyes.

Drops of liquid gold flowed together little by little, until they formed rivulets seeping into the earth from which the precious metal had once come. Within the space of hours, nothing would be left of the god but its diamond eyes, buried beneath the ruins of the village.

Though the worst of the danger was passed, there was still no time to rest. Heedless of smoke-ridden lungs and singed skin, Elizabeth knelt beside Anoyke. With Tema's help, she was able to confirm that he yet lived and had suffered no additional injuries.

Greatly relieved, she leaned back against the trunk of a tree and closed her eyes. The lids felt gritty but she barely noticed them, so great was her weariness.

The thought of clear, cool water trickled through her mind, but she was too exhausted to pursue it. Looking up once to confirm that Jordan was truly all right and nearby, she yielded to the irresistible need for sleep.

When she awoke, she was lying under a rude shelter. It was still dark, but a campfire cast a warm circle of light that reached just beyond her. Of the village, there was no sight. Only the acrid smell of charred wood and soil remained to mark where it had stood.

Shifting gingerly, she discovered that she was sore in every muscle and limb but otherwise apparently unhurt. As she started to rise, a shape suddenly appeared in front of her.

"You're awake," Jordan murmured, going down on his haunches at the edge of her mat. His face was still streaked with grime and sweat, giving him a rather menacing appearance, but his eyes were infinitely gentle. "We were beginning to get worried."

Not yet fully alert, Elizabeth shook her head dazedly. Grotesque images crowded before her, making her doubt the evidence of her own memory. "What happened? I can't seem to remember too clearly . . ."

Concerned, Jordan moved closer and studied her carefully. Since finding her asleep under the tree, he had not left her side for even a moment.

Though Osei and Tema tried to urge him to rest, he

could not. The knowledge that she was safe and unharmed was too precious to be readily believed. He needed the moment-to-moment reassurance that could only come from keeping watch over her.

"Do you remember the fire?" he asked gently.

Elizabeth's eyes widened as recollection rushed in. She sat up suddenly, her throat tight with fear. "Anoyke, is he all right?"

Jordan grinned and nodded. "Right enough to be awake and complaining about having missed all the action."

"And the other men? Were many killed?"

"No," he said softly, his voice full of profound relief and gratitude. "And the only injuries are minor." Hesitating a moment, he added, "Nigel and the mercenaries are dead. The few that survived our attack perished in the fire."

Though Elizabeth could not help but feel regret for the loss of any life, she did not waste herself on senseless sorrow. The mercenaries had depended on superior arms and treachery to protect them. If they had not been stopped, they would have gone on killing helpless men, women, and children indefinitely.

As for Nigel, she shuddered at the thought of him. For all his claims of having been mistreated by his family, the fact remained that he had received far more than most people ever had. Instead of benefiting from those advantages, he had wallowed in greed and envy. The saddest epitaph he could receive was that his death was a blessing for all he left behind.

Resolutely putting the ordeal of the last few hours out of her mind, Elizabeth reached for Jordan's hand. She needed the comfort of physical contact, however tenuous. Turning it over in her own, she stared down at the burnished skin lightly dusted with dark, curling hairs.

There was so much strength in him, and so much

gentleness. He was everything she wanted in a man. To spend her life with him was more than she could ever dream.

Stricken by an unexpected bolt of shyness, she lowered her eyes, but not before she saw the all-encompassing glance Jordan sent her. He seemed uncertain about something, yet hopeful.

Anxious that he not worry unnecessarily about her, she said softly, "I'm really fine now. Besides, it's you who should be resting. Your shoulder . . ."

Jordan started to shake his head, then abruptly surprised her by agreeing. "You're right, it is very uncomfortable. If you don't mind, I'll just lie down here next to you . . ."

Suiting his action to his words, he stretched out beside her and casually dropped an arm around her in a light but firm embrace.

Much as she longed to nestle against him and lose herself in his nearness, Elizabeth hesitated. A bit of restraint, however belated, might help undo at least some of her shocking boldness toward him and convince him that she could actually make a good wife.

Reluctantly, she said, "I should go help Tema."

"She doesn't need your help," Jordan said bluntly. "She's busy impressing Osei with how good a cook she is."

Despite herself, Elizabeth laughed softly. "I think she's already impressed him on a rather more important score."

"Oh?" Jordan drawled. "What's that?"

"You know perfectly well. Tema is very beautiful and she loves Osei dearly. He would be a fool not to marry her as quickly as possible." A sudden thought caused her to straighten, looking down at him anxiously. "They still will be able to marry, won't they, even though the idol is lost?"

Jordan cast a tolerant eye toward the two figures

seated so close together near the fire. Already he sensed a deep happiness in his friend that matched what he felt within himself. It was unthinkable for such love to be denied.

Quietly, he said, "The Asantehene is a very wise man. He knows that the paramount importance of this mission was to deny the colonists the idol. Since we've achieved that, I don't believe he will begrudge Osei his reward."

That was just as well, Elizabeth thought, since by the look of it the prince and his beloved would not be able to restrain themselves much longer.

A short time later, when she and Jordan joined them by the campfire, they had to hide their grins at the sight of the indomitable warrior and the proud woman almost overcome by the strength of their love.

Osei was all ardent gazes and lingering looks while Tema alternated between radiant smiles and unconsciously languorous sighs. By the flickering light of the flames, Elizabeth could see that in addition to being remarkably courageous, the prince's betrothed was also breathtakingly lovely.

Her skin was as dark as Osei's and gleamed with a satiny sheen. Short black curls clung to her well-shaped head. Above a broad forehead, her soft brown eyes were large and fringed by thick lashes. Her nose was long and straight, her mouth soft and full. Dressed in a single length of kente cloth dyed with vivid reds, blues, and greens, she moved with artless grace.

When the two women had at last been properly introduced, Elizabeth felt free to ask how her rescuer had happened to come along on a raiding party of warriors.

"Not that I wasn't delighted to find you outside the hut," she hastened to add, "but the last thing I would have expected to see was another woman. Are your customs so different from those of my country that you are allowed to fight with the men?"

"No," Osei answered bluntly before Tema had a chance to respond. "She is outrageously spoiled and impulsive. Once we are wed, I intend to reform her."

Shooting him a glance that made it clear what she thought of that idea, Tema asked teasingly, "Are white men as overbearing?"

Elizabeth hid a smile and nodded gravely. "Absolutely. It's no wonder Jordan fits in so well here."

"I like that!" the object of her attention complained. "Here I was beginning to hope you might think I had a few redeeming qualities."

Pretending to look him over slowly and carefully, Elizabeth at length nodded. "I suppose you aren't so bad." Taking a deep breath and gathering all her courage about her, she added, "For a husband, that is."

Jordan's mouth dropped open. Nothing, not even Osei's booming laughter penetrated his shock.

She *knew*. All these days—not to mention the nights!—while he agonized over how to tell her he considered her to be his wife, she had known.

A memory flickered through his mind of Elizabeth and Kwesi in close conversation. Grief for his dead friend tightened his throat even as he realized Kwesi must have been the one to tell her of the bride price.

It meant that when they made love the first time, she was already fully aware of the commitment he had made to her.

"I think," Osei murmured a moment later, when he had managed to get control of himself, "that we should leave these two alone. They have quite a lot to discuss."

Tema had no idea what was going on, except that it was clearly important. Though she had known Elizabeth only a few hours, she already liked and respected her immensely. If leaving her alone with Osei's white Ashante brother would facilitate that, so be it.

Besides, she thought, as she and the prince walked a short distance away, there was the added benefit of having Osei to herself. On the outskirts of the small encampment, away from the discreetly averted eyes of the guards, two figures blended into one as the promise of a lifetime's love was sealed with a tender kiss that presaged far greater delights to come.

Back at the campfire, Jordan stared at Elizabeth narrowly. He was at a loss to understand her actions. Or more correctly, he was afraid to believe what his heart told him must be true.

Hesitantly, he asked, "You knew about our being considered husband and wife according to Ashante law?"

She nodded. Now that the words were said she felt immensely relieved. Whatever happened, she would keep nothing from him.

"Does that mean," he went on slowly, "that you regard us as married?"

"More or less."

Jordan raised an eyebrow. "How can we be *more or less* married?"

Undismayed by his tartness, which with new insight she understood came from his touching concern, she said, "Because there is more than just ourselves to consider. It is all very well and good to say that we are married, and for our Ashante friends to agree, but what would your family back in Boston think of this situation?"

A faint flush stained his high-boned cheeks. "I see your point. As broad-minded as they are, I'm sure they would like us to have a Christian ceremony."

Elizabeth took a deep breath. What she was about to

do was incredibly brazen, but she could not help herself. It was now or never. So softly that he had to lean forward to hear her, she asked, "Is that a proposal?"

A light flared deep in his crystal blue eyes. The corners of his mouth lifted. Very firmly, he said, "It most certainly is. Nothing would make me happier than to be able to call you my wife in all ways."

Her heartfelt sigh and the ardent warmth of her gaze were all the answer he felt he needed. Catching hold of her hand, he stood up quickly and drew her with him.

Before she could utter so much as a word, he had lifted her into his arms and was striding toward the shelter on the edge of the camp. There, setting her down gently, he gave silent thanks for the moonless night and the discretion of the guards, who left them completely to themselves.

"Do you mind," he murmured as he began undoing the buttons of her blouse, "that our wedding won't be as elaborate as Osei and Tema's?"

"Don't count on that. From what you've told me about your family, they're liable to turn out all of Boston to see you married." Seemingly of their own volition, her fingers combed through the thick mat of hair covering his chest, distracting her sufficiently so that her blouse was completely undone before she thought to add, "However, you're overlooking something. I haven't agreed to marry you yet."

"You haven't?" His mouth tenderly traced the curve of her cheek, lingering over the soft roundness of her chin before his tongue licked at the corner of her lips.

"No . . ."

Jordan raised his head. The multitude of stars splattered across the sky provided just enough light for her to see his features clearly. All the pain and rage that had stamped him earlier were gone. In its place was unbridled joy and a devilishly male confidence that made her heart beat faster.

Gently drawing her down beside him on the mat, he made swift work of the rest of their clothes before propping himself up on an elbow and gazing at her.

Elizabeth could not suppress a blush as his heated stare traveled leisurely over the full length of her naked form, but neither could she deny her pride and delight in the knowledge of his love.

Reaching for him, she murmured, "Perhaps if you'd ask me again—very nicely—I might agree to our being married in Boston with all the proper accoutrements."

"My darling," he whispered as his body covered hers, "there will never be anything the least proper about our love, for which I give heartfelt thanks to any and all gods! Still, if you require convincing, I'm happy to oblige . . ."

And so he did, several times before the night ended. With the predictable results.

Proper is as proper does, Elizabeth was to say on occasion over the years to her loving husband and their brood of beautiful children.

But there was no denying that their wedding set old Boston on its ear. The bride and groom had the most outrageous stories to tell about a lost city, a golden idol, and the marriage of a prince.

Incredible tales that could not possibly be true. Or could they?